HOW TO
TRAIN YOUR
Highlander

CHRISTY
ENGLISH

sourcebooks
casablanca

Published by Sourcebooks Casablanca, an imprint of Sourcebooks, Inc.
P.O. Box 4410, Naperville, Illinois 60567-4410
(630) 961-3900
Fax: (630) 961-2168
www.sourcebooks.com

Printed and bound in the United States of America.
LSC 10 9 8 7 6 5 4 3

For Maizie and Emma
Beauty and Grace combined, with just a little Fierceness

One

MARY ELIZABETH'S SOJOURN IN ENGLAND COULD NOT
end soon enough.

She and her brother Robbie had borrowed the
duchess's carriage on their journey from London to
Northumberland, and arrived in sartorial splendor on
the white-graveled drive of the pristine estate. The lines
of topiaries were as clean and well matched as any in
England. The flowers that flanked the front of the grand
mansion made her want to rifle them and plant some
decent heather, but as she climbed from the traveling
chaise she could hear the distant sound of the sea.

Mary Elizabeth took comfort in the sound, though
she could not see the sea itself. She would hare off and
find it as soon as she might.

As she raised her eyes from the graveled ground, she
thought to find her mother's tiresome friend among
those who greeted them. Instead her gaze fell on a boy
from the stables, a boy with ice-blue eyes and large,
competent hands.

He was not a boy, of course, though for some reason the English called their stable hands boys long into their dotage. This fair-haired stable boy was tall—taller than all her brothers save for Ian—and his shoulders were wide, as if he might carry the burden of the world on them and not notice the weight.

Atlas did not shrug as he greeted her. Indeed, he did not greet her at all. Nor did he start to unhitch the horses from their traces. Instead, he simply stared at her, as she stared at him.

"Hello," she said at last, remembering that he was English and, as such, had no manners to speak of.

"Hello." He answered her in the posh tones of the English gentry, and she wondered why the duchess would allow such a man to work with her horses. The English were usually mad about class distinction and would not even allow their stable hands to read, if the boys were ever so inclined. But this stable hand seemed not to care a fig for any of his so-called betters, including her, and that made her smile.

"Here," she said, handing him her favorite bag in all the world.

He accepted the soft leather satchel that held her tartan and fishing lures, as well as her throwing knives. Her best-used knives were on her person, but these were the pearl-handled knives her father had given her before she was sent away. The bag held all that was dear to her in the world, save her home and family.

"If it's not too much trouble," she said, "would you see to it that this bag goes into whatever room I'm bound for? If I know the duchess—and I do know her, as I know my own mother—I'll be shuttled off to tea without time to turn around twice. She'll want to chat about London and look me over as she might a bit of good horseflesh, and there'll be no time for me to put this bag away."

Atlas's blue eyes lit up, as if he somehow understood her trust in him and honored her for it. He bowed almost like a gentleman and would have spoken had Mrs. Prudence, Mary Elizabeth's companion and almost-governess, not intervened.

"Now, Mary, this fine man must see to the horses." Mrs. Prudence plucked the leather satchel from Atlas's hands and passed it to a waiting footman, who kept a poker face like any true Englishman and did not even blink.

Mary Elizabeth loved Mrs. Prudence as she loved her brothers, but she wondered if the lot of them would ever cease to bother her about her own life, and mind their own.

"My friend here looks sensible enough to see to my favorite bag," she said, certain that she sounded like a petulant child but not sure how else to deal with high-handed interference.

Mrs. Prudence was the soul of courtesy, but as always, she was implacable, a woman to be reckoned with, which was why Mary Elizabeth's brother Robbie loved her. "Mary, each person here has his role in the household, and that hierarchy must be respected."

"But why?" Mary Elizabeth asked. She could feel herself digging in, even though she knew she was wasting valuable breath. The English had their system, and they would not change it for the likes of her.

"Why should the groom not handle my favorite bag? I like the look of him. Isn't that reason enough?"

"No," Mrs. Prudence answered. "This is the duchess's household, and we must respect her wishes."

Mary Elizabeth met the eyes of Atlas, feeling her embarrassment rise from the ground as if to strangle her. She wished for the hundredth time that day that her family would mind their own affairs and leave her in peace. She felt humiliation threaten, but then she saw the gleam of humor in Atlas's eyes and knew, the way she understood the minds of horses and kittens, that he was not laughing at her.

She caught sight of a great fat man dressed in formal wear peering out from the curtains of a third-story window. She let all thoughts for her bag and of her humiliation go as she stared into the man's cold, blue eyes. In the next moment, the curtain fell over his face, blocking him from view.

The man had looked down on her and hers as if they were dirt beneath his feet, as if they might have come from the midden heap and not out of the ducal carriage after a long ride North. The man in formal blacks, disgusted with all he surveyed, could only be the duke himself.

Mary Elizabeth wondered for half a moment if her mother and the duchess had lured her to Northumberland to foist her off on the older, balding man, both to amuse themselves and to settle the question of her future and the succession of the dukedom all in one clean sweep. She dismissed the dismal thought at once. Even if her mother were to stoop so low, which she doubted, Mary Elizabeth would not fall to a duke for any reason. To make her stay more pleasant, perhaps if she were quick, and quick-witted, she could avoid meeting the Recluse Duke altogether.

She listened with half an ear as Mrs. Prudence clucked like a broody hen, maneuvering her to the front steps. She watched as some English footman whisked her favorite bag away in a trice. She vowed to let all thoughts of the duke and his bald pate go, and reminded herself that knives and fishing lures—or even her bit of family tartan—were only things, and that things could be replaced.

This logic was not what comforted her as she went to meet her mother's friend in the splendid mansion before her. It was the blue eyes of Atlas and his last surreptitious wink.

❧

Harry—Harold Charles Percy, Duke of Northumberland—was not a man to listen to gossip, especially gossip that found its way so far North, but he knew as he watched his mother's guests climb out of his own carriage from Town that barbarians were upon them.

He wondered to himself which of the girls was the famous Hellion of Hyde Park, the young lady who had wrestled with the Earl of Grathton in the grass and who had almost cut the man in two with a great steel blade. Neither of the women in view looked capable of such violence, and Harry was about to remove himself and hide among the horses in the stable until it was safe to go back to his work in the garden again when he caught the eye of the slight blonde girl with a voice like a siren's call.

The girl was a mere slip of a thing, but she was well-rounded, which suited his taste. Harry knew he was a cad for noticing that, but he dismissed his own scruples for the moment; he would take himself to task later for his irreverence toward a lady. As it was, he simply stared at her, taking in the maple brown of her eyes—staring so long that he soon found that her pupils were rimmed with a bit of green.

He had seen many women in his thirty years, but there was something about this one that fair took his breath away.

He stood, staring still, trying to discern what it was about her that held him, as her governess—a lady doing a terrible job of hiding her good looks behind an ugly gown, oversized spectacles, and a lace cap— shuffled his prize off into the house.

Harry made it his life's mission to avoid all women of good birth save for the occasional merry widow. All women born in the British Isles, some in the Americas, and more than a few in farthest India wanted to marry a duke. And he, God help him, had held that title for the last five years.

But as he watched the little blonde go, he knew that he would make certain to see her again. Surely he might prevail upon her to speak with him without revealing who he was. He did not like the thought of her knowing his title and curbing her intriguing tongue. He wanted to enjoy frank speech with her for just a while longer.

Being a duke must hold some privileges, after all, or what was an august title for?

The large barbarian man who had left the carriage behind the women stepped forward then, placing a gold sovereign in his hand. The Highland Scot handed one to the footman standing by as well, and Harry watched as Charlie slipped the barbarian's coin into his pocket without a blink.

Harry fingered his own sovereign, trying to remember the last time he had actually held money in his hand. He had an army of stewards and lawyers who dealt with his funds. If he needed something, he asked for it, and it was brought to him forthwith. Money was not something that figured heavily in the daily life of a duke. He raised the coin to the light and watched it gleam in the slanting sun. There was something about the gleam that pleased him. Harry suddenly wished he had earned it.

Before the Highlander could speak to tell him what the coin was for, the lovely woman dressed as a dowd came to his side. She spoke not to Harry, as anyone sane might have done, but addressed herself to the Scot. The two continued their conversation as if Harry were a deaf and blind mule who had simply wandered into the yard.

"Robbie, you can't tip the duchess's household," the pretty woman said.

"Why not?" the Scot asked.

"It simply isn't done."

"Yes, it is," the barbarian insisted. "I just did it."

Harry stood in silence, listening to their conversation, staring beyond them to the house, where the little blonde had gone. He felt a bizarre and almost overwhelming desire to present himself at tea, and to eat scones among these people who clearly had no idea who he was.

The Scot and his lady bantered on, as if Harry was not even there.

"The duchess pays her own people. It is not for us to pay them twice," the lovely woman said.

"Northumberland is close enough to the border for these people to know the value of a pound," the Scot answered her. "If a man, even a Lowlander, is given a piece of gold, he takes it and says thank you."

The barbarian turned to Harry expectantly. Harry swallowed a smile, for dukes did not smile in company, even among those who did not realize that they were addressing a duke. He pocketed the sovereign.

"Thank you," Harry said at last, fingering the coin in his waistcoat pocket. He remembered the semblance of his manners and bowed once to the lady before he walked away.

He did not bother with the stables, but went straight to the garden, hoping that some time with his roses might chase the sight of the little blonde from his mind, but it only reminded him of the scent of flowers on her skin. He had taken in a bit of it when she had stood close and handed him her bag.

He pushed the girl from his mind, but her scent would not leave him. His mother had gathered a house party to marry him off. He might, God help him, have to marry one of the ladies on offer. But the party did not start for three more days. He had three more days to live his life in peace and bucolic harmony. He was not going to let even one moment of those three days of peace go to waste, for they might be the only peace he ever had again.

Harry took up the shovel Martin had left for him and went at the bush that needed transplanting along the eastern wall. He got his hands in good solid earth, but still he could smell blooms warmed not by sun but by skin, and he could see the little blonde standing before him, her leather satchel in her hand.

Two

MARY ELIZABETH WAS RIGHT, AS SHE ALWAYS WAS. She barely had time to smooth her curls and wash her hands in the retiring room before she was ushered in to see the Duchess of Northumberland by the great ducal butler.

She winked at the man, just to see what he might do. Billings did not blink in response, nor did he smile, but she thought she saw a gleam of amusement in his dark-brown eyes, which was more than she had bargained for. Pleased with this small inroad, she presented herself to her mother's closest living friend and made her curtsy as gracefully as if her mother were in the room watching her. For all Mary knew, she might well be hiding behind the screen in the corner.

Mary Elizabeth did take the time to make certain that the fat duke was not lurking about. As soon as she saw that he, too, was absent, she relaxed.

The soft light filtered in from the closed French doors, and Mary found herself thinking that with fewer pillows, and a great deal less gilt, the room might even be pleasant. She did not have long to muse to herself, however, for Mrs. Prudence was on her heels, and the duchess had raised her quizzing glass to get a better view.

"You have finally arrived, I see. And none the worse for wear for the abysmal North Road," the old lady said, still peering at Mary as if she might find the family's lost jewels somewhere about her person.

If she had learned one thing in the last three months, it was how to be polite even when faced with the impoliteness of Southerners. Mary Elizabeth managed to smile, wishing for her own granny, who was no doubt sewing a new shawl of hunting plaid for her even as they spoke. Her granny was the one among the family who knew that, one day, Mary Elizabeth would be coming home.

"And good day to you as well, Your Worship," Mary Elizabeth said at last. "I see that you've an eye for a fine-looking woman. I suspect you were a good-looking girl yourself, once upon a time."

The blue-haired duchess dropped her quizzing glass at that bit of impertinence, and it swung down on its gold chain, only to rest against her large bosom. She stared down Mary Elizabeth in the lengthening silence, and Mary knew that it fell to her as the guest to put the moment to rights.

She heard the sound of birdsong, faint from beyond the window, and longed with a depth of feeling that surprised her to be anywhere but there. She breathed once and took herself to task. She was where she was, and she had best face it, until she could manage to be somewhere else.

Mary Elizabeth offered an olive branch. "I must

thank you for opening your home to us, both here and in London. You are very kind."

"Hardly."

Mary Elizabeth wondered why Robbie—for it seemed that he had finally wandered indoors—didn't speak up from his stance beside the parlor door. Robbie was a good soul, but not always willing to step up and speak with a lady when it was needed. That had always been her brother David's job, and he was home, in the Highlands.

Mrs. Prudence, for her part, was quiet as a mouse, as she sometimes was when intimidated. Mary Elizabeth was not sure why anyone would be afraid of this old besom. No doubt, sitting alone in the midst of all that gilt, the Duchess of Northumberland was lonely, too.

When neither Mrs. Prudence nor Robbie said anything, the duchess continued. "And how did you find the town house, girl?"

"Large, Your Worship. And a bit drafty."

Robbie had the good grace to shift on his feet, while Pru cringed and twisted her gloves between her hands. Mary Elizabeth was about to apologize for her blunt speech, in case she might have hurt the old lady's feelings, but before she could offer another olive branch, the duchess laughed—a keen sound, like the honking of a goose.

The duchess's voice warmed, and she patted the cushion beside her. "You remind me more and more of your mother by the minute. Sit down, girl, and tell your brother and your friend to join us."

Once Mary Elizabeth had settled close to her, she felt the tension in her body run out like water over the burn back home. The duchess smelled of lavender, as Mary Elizabeth's own granny did, and a bit of cinnamon.

Mary Elizabeth met Mrs. Prudence's eyes from across the overly fancy room, and Pru managed to take a seat on the settee across from them. The ducal butler rolled the tea tray in and settled it at the duchess's elbow. Mary watched as the duchess played mother, doling out tea and scones as if she were Christ and they all sat at the Last Supper.

Mary Elizabeth found herself liking the old woman more and more the longer they sat with her. Perhaps it was the blue sheen of her hair, which made the faded-blonde locks look more interesting than merely gray. Perhaps it was the way the lady faced the world head-on and stared it down, as Mary herself did. That was most likely a trait that the lady had possessed long before she had married to become the most powerful duchess in the North.

"Your mother was a bit of a scamp, as you are, miss. She was a lady of the house of Blythe, a noble family that traces its antecedents back to William the Conqueror."

Try as she might, Mary could not let that bit of preening pass. "Aye," she said. "And we are kin of the Bruce on my father's side. But go on, Your Worship."

The old lady did not take her to task for interrupting, but smiled at her and patted her hand. "You are a fine specimen of womanhood, young Mary Elizabeth. The House of Blythe and the scions of old Scotland have crossed well, no doubt about it. We need fresh blood in the nobility from time to time. God knows, the days of besieging a castle and carrying off the women to wed are gone."

"More's the pity," Mary Elizabeth said.

Mrs. Prudence choked on her tea, but the duchess continued on her merry way. "Indeed. I often think that I could use a good Highlander threatening the property and carrying me away."

Mary blinked, and the old lady sighed.

"But those days are behind me."

"They are behind us all," Mrs. Prudence offered, by way of civilizing the conversation. Mary Elizabeth watched with faint amusement as her little governess faced down the duchess like a lioness in her den.

"Perhaps not *all* of us," the Duchess of Northumberland said, with a pointed look at Robbie, who was in that instant robbing the tea tray of its last scone and butter.

Mary Elizabeth leaned back against her cushions and smiled as she watched a dark blush rise in Mrs. Prudence's cheeks.

Confident that her last sally had found its mark, the duchess turned back to Mary Elizabeth.

"Your mother, it seems, had a taste for Highlanders. She flirted with every man who crossed her path, as any woman worth her salt did in those days, but it was your father who got her alone on a hunt. He cut her off from the rest of the party, and the two of them did not ride back to the house until well after sundown."

Mary Elizabeth's ears perked up at this. The thought that her parents had ever been remotely wild made her feel less alone in the world, and made her like them more. She tried to imagine her da—her favorite fishing friend and boon companion—keeping a lady out past dark, and she simply could not get her brain to bend that far. The duchess spoke on.

"Well, she was ruined, of course. No other man would have her, save for some nabob they pulled out of the West Indies. But your mother did not give a fig for that, nor for what anyone thought. For she did not just dally with her Highlander, but rode away with him the very next day, only to marry him in the back of beyond three days later."

As taken as she was with the duchess's story, Mary Elizabeth could not let that comment pass. "Beggin' your pardon, Your Worship, but that place at the back of beyond is my home. I won't hear a word against it."

The old lady sniffed, lifting her quizzing glass to take in the contours of Mary's face. "Outspoken, aren't you, girl?"

"That I am, ma'am."

There was a long moment that spun out between them, when Mary Elizabeth thought she saw behind the duchess's facade to the real woman within. There was a softening behind the blue of the lady's eyes and the trace of a smile, as if she looked on Mary Elizabeth, with her fishing, her hunting, and her knives, and liked what she saw. Mary wished to God her own mother might see her as she was and love her for it.

She looked close at her new friend, and the dark blue of the duchess's eyes showed a hint of her soul. It was faint and far away, like the glimmering of a candle in a shuttered room, but Mary was certain that she saw it.

It seemed that the duchess knew she had been

found out, or that her soul at least had been glimpsed from afar, for her spine straightened as if she were on horseback and her tone was acerbic when she spoke. Mary Elizabeth found that she liked her even more for that show of pride. They were more than a little alike, for all this woman's pretensions of grandeur.

"And you have no interest in rank, I see."

Mary Elizabeth did not back down. No matter how the woman beside her fought not to be known, Mary knew how lonely such a life was. Having glimpsed the real woman, she would not now pretend that she had not. If she and the old lady were to be friends—and she had just decided that they were—she could not stand on ceremony, or let the duchess continue to hide. "No, Your Worship. A man is only as good as his two hands and his brain make him."

There was a gleam behind the woman's quizzing glass, a sheen that made Mary Elizabeth think of tears. "And you would say the same of a woman?"

Mary Elizabeth did not flinch. "Yes, ma'am."

The duchess blinked, and the shutter came down over her soul again. But Mary Elizabeth knew it was still there. The lady had shielded her heart, but Mary Elizabeth would take care and not bruise it.

"Well, you've got enough fire and vinegar in you to make two of your mother, and no mistake," the duchess said by way of dismissal of all that had passed between them behind their chatter. "I'm glad I summoned you here. You're just what the place needs to liven it up a bit. The country is deadly dull."

Mary relaxed and bantered with the lady as she knew no one else was brave or foolish enough to do.

"I disagree, Your Worship. You've got the sea right by you, which makes for good fishing if you've the nerve to sail out on it."

"I haven't," the duchess said. "And neither will you. If you drown yourself off my beach, your mother will have my head on a platter."

Mary Elizabeth frowned but knew that she would not let such a stricture deter her. "I am disappointed, ma'am. I had hoped to go sailing."

"My son might take you," the duchess said. "He's a fair sailor, when he'll put his books down long enough."

Mary Elizabeth smelled the trap then and knew better than to spring it. This lady, soul sister though she might be, had plans for Mary—plans that Mary would be quick to botch. Mary Elizabeth would marry a fat, old duke on the day Scotland and all its people fell into the sea. But she feigned ignorance, as if she were a fool.

"Would that be your son the duke, ma'am?"

"None other," the old lady groused, looking peevish. "I've not got another one."

"Well," Mary Elizabeth said, feeling that it was only sporting to let the old besom know her own position, so that there would be no question of confusion and no disappointment later, "your son has nothing to fear from me, Your Worship. He might take me for a sail and come back safe as houses."

The old lady looked shrewd, her eyes narrowing. "Safe, is he? And why might that be?"

"Well, even if he kept me out until dark, he'd still be safe. For I'd never marry him, you see. I'm not the marrying kind."

The duchess stopped pretending and laid her cards on the table. Mary Elizabeth felt a surge of respect for her.

"Your mother wants you married, girl. A duke would be just the thing."

Mary Elizabeth frowned like thunder. She took a breath and tried to sound civil. "My ma and I disagree on this point, Your Worship."

"On marrying a duke?"

"On me marrying at all, ma'am."

The old lady laughed out loud at that, as if Mary Elizabeth might be brought around to her way of thinking. "Well, my son is destined to wed. No doubt he'll be glad that there's one girl at this house party who's not trying to catch him."

Mary Elizabeth smiled at the old lady then, and knew that, just as she had not given an inch on the subject, neither had the duchess. Mary had studied enough of strategy, however, to know the value of a clean retreat. She turned her eyes to the French doors that led out into the garden.

"Might I explore a bit, Your Worship? I've been trapped in a carriage for five days. I'd like to stretch my legs."

"By all means, dismiss the duchess before you and wander away."

"Thank you, ma'am."

Mary Elizabeth smiled, knowing the lady had to keep up the pretense of annoyance but that she understood her. It was refreshing to be understood by someone, after a lifetime of making friends with people who never gleaned a bit of her soul. Catherine loved her, and so did Mrs. Prudence, but they did not understand her, and most likely never would.

Before she fell into a taking and began to droop about the mouth and whine, Mary Elizabeth escaped that room and all its thwarted expectations, leaving the French doors standing open behind her.

When she stepped into the fresh, clean air of that garden, following the birdsong, she also heard the sound of the sea and went off in search of it. She had not gone far when she stumbled across an uprooted rosebush and the man who had dug it up.

Three

HARRY HAD JUST BEGUN TO FIND HIS RHYTHM AS HE dug up the parterre rosebushes so that Simmons might plant them along the east-facing wall when he heard a thump and a curse that belonged on the docks or perhaps on one of his ships at sea.

"Damn and blast it!" the girl said again. "Now I've ruined another gown, and Ma won't give me an allowance for any more."

He looked up then from his work, knowing what he would find, for it seemed he knew the girl's sultry voice already.

His siren from the carriage an hour earlier had wandered back into his domain, and had fallen in one of the holes left by the vacated rosebushes, her pink traveling gown covered in a long streak of ochre. He sighed, the last vestige of his peace falling away like the last bit of an orange peel. He watched it go, then turned to the lady, expecting tears at the very least, followed by sniffling and the need for his filthy handkerchief.

He wondered for one benighted moment if the girl

had heard from the staff that the Recluse Duke was in the garden and, as a result, had come hunting him. His flesh began to cool, both from horror and from the sea wind touching the sweat on his shoulders. He wished for his waistcoat, which he had abandoned somewhere in the stables hours before, just as he wished for his friend Clyde to appear and occupy this woman with charm while Harry made his escape.

Harry reminded himself that he was a gentleman and reluctantly started to help the girl out of her hole, when she straightened her skirt and leaped out of it on her own, apparently unscathed.

"Are you the blighter who left this gaping chasm so close to the path?" she asked.

Harry blinked and nodded. "I am."

She seemed to want to say more, but perhaps she was remembering that she was a lady, for she drew a breath and let it out on one long exhale. "Well," she said. "And this is what comes of letting a stable boy get into the garden. Hand me that shovel there, and be quick about it, before your head gardener sees this mess."

He blinked and obeyed, and then watched as she filled the hole in the space of five minutes, layering the soil loosely so that it might breathe, then packing down the top with a flourish. She found the bag of crushed seashells bleached white sitting close by, and she covered the hole with a liberal amount of those, so that the next person who happened by might not trip as she had done.

Until he stood by and watched a beautiful woman fill a hole in the garden, the skirt of her gown pulled tight over a delightfully rounded behind as she worked, Harry would have said that he was a civilized man. Something was clearly wrong with him, for he had not fled, nor had he offered to assist her.

"I ought to have helped," he said as she finished.

She leaned on her shovel and surveyed her work with what he could only assume was pleasure. His siren tipped her head back and took in the slanting rays of the afternoon sun on her skin. The summer days were long in the North, but the sun was cool. She seemed to drink it in like mead, before she turned her smile on him.

"And ruin a fine job?" she said. "I think not. You're better off with the horses. Has his Royal Grace the Duke too few men to work for him, that a decent man of horses finds himself shifting among the flowers, then?"

Harry had never heard himself referred to in such a blasé yet disrespectful manner. He felt a frisson of irritation. He thought of revealing himself to this girl then and there.

But her curls were falling from their pins in a delightful disarray, catching the light of the sun with hints of honey brown and gold buried in them. She had the coloring his mother once had, when he was still a boy in short pants.

He put aside all thoughts of his mother and her plans for him, as his day had as yet been a pleasant one. He did not want to think of his mother and of all he had promised her.

Instead, he turned to the girl and offered her his arm.

"Might I escort you back to the house?"

"God forbid! I just escaped from there."

"I am told the house is very fine," he said, feeling slightly miffed.

She laughed at him. Her laughter was warm and sultry, as her voice was, but completely free, as if she were a courtesan who had been born into the wrong life. His siren did not seem to notice that he had not spoken again, nor did she seem to care for anything he might have said. She stopped laughing at last and handed the shovel to Simmons, who had appeared out of the bushes at the sound of her mirth.

"I'm off to find the sea, but I thank you." She nodded to Simmons, who bowed to her. She frowned to see him do it, a bit of darkness coming into the maple brown of her eyes. But she rallied at once, so quickly that Harry was not certain he had seen the shadow at all.

"Try not to fall in a ditch on your way back to the stables."

She sauntered off then, her rounded derriere swaying. Harry stood staring after her like a fool, not even offering her a farewell. He felt the eyes of his man heavy on him, and Harry shrugged to Simmons before he took off after her.

She felt a bit sorry for that stable boy and wondered why on God's good green earth he was allowed such liberty. Perhaps His High and Mighty Grace the fat duke had taken him on as a charity case when only a boy and had pledged to look after the simpleton for the rest of his life. The romantic idea pleased her, though it did not fit in with her notion of English dukes. She had never met one, but she had heard that they were as proud as princes and had little thought for those beneath them. And that they considered all the world, except perhaps the king himself, beneath them.

Mary Elizabeth was about to dismiss all thoughts of dukes and their strange stable boys when said stable boy appeared at her elbow, following almost at her heels like a dog on a lead.

"Would you like to see the horses?" he asked.

It was the first thing of sense he had said since she met him, and she stopped in her tracks.

"Why yes," she answered. "You know where they are?"

He looked at her as if she was the simpleton then, and she knew she had been too condescending, which was unkind and beneath her. She followed him, walking along beside him, as he took her to a mansion about half a mile beyond the ducal gardens. The flowers bloomed right up to the mansion's gate, so she wondered if the boy had gotten confused after all and led her to the dower house by mistake.

But then the wind shifted, and she smelled the horses.

"Who put the horses in a human house?" she asked. "That's as fine a place as any in Edinburgh."

The two-story mansion filled three acres at least and glowed with the warm light of the sunshine on the windowpanes. Atlas did not respond to her question, other than to raise one eyebrow. He offered her his hand to help her over the cattle break and opened the half gate for her.

"These are the richest horses I've ever seen," Mary

Elizabeth said, startled into bluntness by the heat of his palm. He wore no gloves, as servants never did, and she had left hers behind in the carriage. His hand was hot and dry, with calluses that had long since hardened to blend with the skin around them. She discovered in that moment that she liked a man with callused hands.

Atlas laughed at her assessment, and she found that she liked the way his shoulders moved when he walked, when he was digging, and when he laughed. Such broad shoulders were none of her concern, of course, but for some reason, she found herself staring at them. When she wasn't looking into the blue of his eyes.

She had changed her mind about his eyes. They were not ice blue as they had seemed when she first met him. They were warmer than ice could ever be. They were the blue of a clear, cloudless sky after five days of rain.

She told herself to stop being a fool. She looked away before he caught her staring like a love-addled chimp, and turned her gaze instead to the horses that lived in the mansion.

They were all beautiful, and they were beautifully housed, every horse granted his own stall with oats and hay and fresh water piped in. Every stall was as large as a crofter's house back home. She blinked to see it and knew that she would speak with her father about improving the Clan's housing, as soon as Ian's next ship came in.

Then Mary Elizabeth forgot all else, for she found another soul mate standing alone, looking fraught, in the body of a great stallion.

"There now, ye wee beastie. And what might be your name?"

She crooned to him as she had seen her da croon to newborn foals. The black stallion heard her voice and shifted on his feet. The groom who had been trying to open his stall door backed away to make room for her, his eyes on Atlas.

"Don't get close to him," Atlas said. "He's mad."

"Is he now?"

Mary Elizabeth dismissed that nonsense for the foolishness it was.

"I've ridden him twice, but he is too fierce. I hope he'll breed well, for he's not good for anything but his bloodlines."

Mary Elizabeth turned on him then. He could not speak ill of a horse in its presence. Not when she was there to stop him.

"Bite your tongue. That horse there is a king and a champion and a discerning beast to boot. He'll not let the likes of you ride him, but he loves me."

"He loves no one. Please, step away from there."

His hand was on her arm then, and she raised one eyebrow, letting her eyes linger on the place where his calluses warmed her through her ruined dress. Atlas was smart enough to drop his hand, quick like, and she turned her gaze back to the horse before her.

"There now," she crooned, offering the heel of her palm. "Here's a great beastie who needs a bit of love."

The huge horse shifted toward her, and instead of taking a nip at her as she expected him to, he sniffed her hand, then snuffled along it, searching for a treat.

She kept her voice low as she spoke to Atlas. "Hand me a carrot, quick."

Atlas ignored her, but his companion groom offered her a carrot from a great sack hanging close by.

"And no wonder this one's in a foul humor," she said. "Good carrots so close and not one in his mouth."

She offered the carrot, and the stallion ate it whole. He slobbered on her hand, and when she reached up to pet his forelock, where a blaze of white shone bright, he let her.

"And what is your name, sweet boy?" she asked him.

Atlas said, "That is Sampson."

"And a fine, braw name it is," she said. "And what's yours?"

The man beside her flinched, and the other stable boy took a deep breath as if to speak. He stayed silent though, and Atlas answered her. "My name is Harry."

She felt a strange weight in the moment, as if her new friend did not often give his name. Perhaps the mad English simply called him *boy* or some other ridiculous title.

Mary did not want to embarrass him further, so she kept her hands and eyes on the horse. "Sampson, this is Harry. Be sweet to him, and he'll be sweet to you. I'll come back in the morning and ride you. Until then, eat your oats, and don't bite these boys here, or there'll be no more carrots for you."

The stallion turned one great brown eye on her, and she petted his cheek. He moved toward her quickly, and Harry jumped but did not interfere. The horse did not bite, though, but pressed his head into her palm, that she might stroke him again.

"This one just wants love," she said, instructing the groom and Harry together. "He smells your fear, and he knows he's alone. That's why he bites at you. Love him, and he will love you."

She could tell that neither Harry nor the groom believed her, and she sighed, pressing her palm once more to the warm horse before she let him go.

"I'll leave you to your work then," she told them both, not looking at the blue of Harry's eyes. She strode out and neither man spoke to her. But Sampson whinnied behind her, and she knew that she had made a friend.

She listened hopefully with half an ear for the sound of footfalls behind her from Harry's booted heels, but they did not come. She sighed and told herself not to be a fool as she followed the sound of the sea.

Four

HARRY WATCHED THE BARBARIAN GIRL GO. HE REALIZED, as the sway of her hips disappeared around the door of the stables, that though he had given her his, he did not yet know her name.

Sampson still stood beside him. The great beast had not gone after the groom close by, hoping to take a bit of flesh in his teeth. Many of the grooms had been nipped in the last two weeks, so that almost no one would come near the stallion. They drew straws now to see who would feed and water him. No one could ride him, so they simply turned him out into a paddock by himself daily and watched as he kicked at the fence.

Harry had come the first week and watched him kick. He had tried to saddle Sampson himself and had ended up in the dust. But now, in the wake of the Scottish girl with golden hair, the beast and he stood, two males united by fascination—and perhaps a hint of infatuation.

No better time than now to build on that fragile bridge.

Harry offered the horse another carrot. The stallion

reared his head back at first, the better to look suspiciously down his nose at his owner, as if affronted
by Harry's familiarity. But when Harry did not try to
pet or cajole him, Sampson took the carrot between
delicate lips and crunched it into oblivion after only
three bites.

It took three more carrots before Sampson would
allow Harry to open his stall door without charging him, another two before he could slip the bit
and bridle over his head. The saddle came next,
and Harry was sure that the great beast would force
him against the polished wooden stall in an effort to
throttle him against the wall, but Sampson did not.
He even let Harry tighten his girth and adjust the
stirrups without protest.

This time, Harry gave him an apple, which was
met with much favor and blissful eye rolling.

Sampson allowed himself to be led by the bridle out
into the sunshine of the afternoon. The sound of the
sea was close by, and Sampson's ears pricked at it as
his nostrils flared, taking in the smell of the ocean and
the fresh air together.

Harry did not hesitate, but raised himself into
the saddle. He got the beast fair under him before
Sampson kicked out, trying too late to kill him.

"Steady on," Harry said, keeping his voice low and
his tone calm, even as Sampson tried to dislodge him.

"We're in this together. We might as well make
the best of it."

For all the world as if he spoke English fluently,
Sampson stopped trying to kill him and cocked an ear
back at his rider. Harry nudged him forward gently

with one booted heel, and Sampson moved into a walk, strolling out of the stable yard as if he had not just been cutting up and bucking.

The grooms behind him gave a cheer, and Harry held up one hand to silence them. But Sampson did not take offense and bolt. Indeed, he seemed to think that his minions cheered for him, for he preened and strutted before Harry asked him to go into a canter.

Harry laughed under his breath, and turned the horse toward the rocky shore. He let Sampson have his head, and discovered at last why he had paid so much for the beast. Aside from his bloodlines, Sampson was simply the best horse Harry had ever ridden. Since they had decided to be partners, at least for one ride, the horse seemed willing to overlook the fact that Harry was a human, just as Harry was willing to forget that Sampson often tried to maim him. Both gentlemen put such rivalries behind them and simply ran, the wind in their faces.

By the time Harry brought the horse back, the grooms had Sampson's stall mucked out and fresh oats and hay brought in. Sampson still would let no one else near him, but he suffered to be brushed down by Harry, who even crooned to him a bit as he curried his hide.

The horse sighed in ecstasy, his back leg going slack. Harry chuckled and patted his flank. "You're a good one, for all your biting," he said at last. They were the first words he had spoken since they had returned from their race across the beach, and for once, Sampson seemed willing to listen.

The horse caught his eye and nipped at his sleeve. Harry forced himself to be still, knowing that the bite would hurt but not wanting to flinch and show weakness. But instead of sharp teeth, Harry felt his sleeve tugged gently between Sampson's lips. Two short tugs, and then Sampson turned from him, prepared to ignore him for the rest of the evening.

But it was enough. The bridge between them still held.

Harry, feeling triumphant, was about to return to the house for a much-needed bath before he ate a light supper and prepared his telescope on his balcony in the family wing, when the beautiful Scottish girl returned to the stable, this time with her governess and brother in tow.

He felt his breath hitch at the sultry sound of her speech with its faint burr. She was keeping her tone low and soothing, so as not to startle the horses. He wanted to take her between his hands and see what she might sound like as he drew her close against him.

Harry banished this cavalier thought, but like a siren song, her voice kept calling to him.

She ignored him altogether, though he was standing close by his stallion's stable door. "This is Sampson," the girl said to her governess, a note of pride in her voice. "He is my particular friend."

The great beast glared at the smaller lady, and she stepped back, only to come up close against the hulking Scottish man. The siren's brother drew her governess into a protective embrace, blocking her body as if the great stallion might spring over his stable door and accost her. If Harry thought it odd that the man seemed to have more of a care for the hired help than his own sister, he did not speak of it. Clearly, the Scot and the governess were lovers of long standing.

Harry told himself that he did not judge the proclivities of others, but he found himself annoyed all the same. Seducing dependents was not making love at all. It was an imposition.

He forced himself to pay attention to the beautiful Scottish girl and to forget her brother, as hard as that was with the man standing so close by.

"Mary, ye'd best step back from there," the Scot said. "He's a great brute who might take your hand off."

Harry felt a bit nonplussed that the girl's name was *Mary*, far too bland an appellation for so colorful a woman. The girl in question did not spare a glance for her brother, but extended her hand to Sampson, a dried apple in her fingertips.

"Nonsense, Robbie. Sampson is too much of a gentleman to attack a lady. All true warriors are."

The Scot snorted at that but did not move to stop his sister from endangering herself. Harry tensed, ready to intervene if his stallion's earlier good mood had flown. Unable to allow himself to be ignored in his own stables any longer, Harry spoke at last.

"Sampson won't bite a lady" was all he said.

Mary ignored them all, caressing Sampson's nose. The horse leaned closer to her, looking for another apple. The huge creature seemed to welcome the girl's touch, but Harry kept careful watch in case his pleasure turned to sudden annoyance.

"Mary Elizabeth, perhaps we had better go back to the house and dress for dinner," the governess said.

Mary Elizabeth. For some reason, the name pleased him. It had a noble ring to it and was far less pedestrian than the simple *Mary.*

His Scottish girl sighed. "Ah, well. If the duchess rings the dinner bell, I suppose we can't keep her waiting."

Mary Elizabeth gave the horse one last caress. When she stepped back and away from him, Sampson stamped and snorted loudly, as if protesting the loss of his prize. Harry knew just how his new horse felt. He felt the sudden urge to reach for her arm and keep her with him. He felt an even more bizarre inclination to take himself to the house and dress for dinner. His mother would be so pleased.

He did neither, but stayed still, almost transfixed by his sudden lust and the equally desperate need to tamp it down. He must keep his mind bent on marriage to a biddable English girl who knew the rules of polite society, who would bear his sons and do the least damage to his peace in the years to come. Lust for debutante Scottish girls, no matter how exotic and fearless, had no place in his life, that day or ever.

The girl he panted for did not notice him at all, but spoke to his horse as if the beast were the only reason worth being in the stable at all. "I'll be back tomorrow, you great bully. Mind your manners while I'm away. No biting the grooms, you hear?"

She stared the horse down, and Sampson shifted on his feet, as if being called to task by a schoolmarm. Harry could not be sure, but Sampson seemed a bit chagrined.

"Do not bite this one here, is that clear?"

She pointed to Harry then, who blinked to find her finger in his face. He wanted to take it between his teeth, to nestle it between his lips to suckle it, and then to suckle on the place where her throat met her bodice. She would not be able to ignore him then.

The hulking Scot was not as foolish as he looked, for he seemed to glean something of the tenor of Harry's thoughts from the look on his face. Her brother stepped between them pointedly and offered his arm. "Come away from here, Mary. That's an expensive beast, and you've deviled him long enough."

Harry almost laughed out loud at how true those words were, even if the man had not been talking about the horse.

Mary Elizabeth took her brother's arm. The hulking Scot nodded then with a hint of civility, but Harry saw the threat in his eyes.

"Watch out for him, Harry," Mary Elizabeth called over her shoulder as the Scot propelled both women toward the stable door. "Sampson's a bit sweeter, but he's got a mind of his own."

"God's teeth, girl, stop talking to the servants as if you've known them all your life. We're farther North, that's true, but we're still among the English."

Mary Elizabeth spoke blithely. "Don't mind Harry. He's harmless, if a bit simple."

The Duke of Northumberland opened his mouth to protest this cavalier dismissal, but her brother interrupted him.

"I do mind him," the Scot said, his voice hard as stone. "And you'll mind me. Stay away from stable lads, or I'll tan your hide."

Mary Elizabeth did not sound defiant so much as miserable when she answered. "All right, Robbie."

Their voices faded into the distance, and Harry was left alone, as he was always alone, staring after her.

"I want that girl," he said aloud to no one in particular.

"Then you should have her, Your Grace," his head groom said. "No woman can say no to a duke."

Harry smiled and clapped his hand on the groom's shoulder. He did not speak again, but headed toward the house by his secret way, through the rose garden and up past his mother's parlor. In spite of the odd, frustrating ending to his afternoon, Harry felt a strange sense of well-being. He started to whistle.

His man was right. No woman had said no to him yet. Scot or no, neither would this one...if he asked her. Since she was a well-bred girl of marriageable age, he could not ask her. But the temptation was there, beckoning to him in the sway of her hips.

Food for thought.

Five

Mary Elizabeth was bored.

She stood on her balcony, looking out over beautiful moonlit gardens. It was well past midnight, and the summer sun had finally set. The long gloaming that she loved so back home, here only made her wish for things she could not have. A quiet walk with her da beside the burn. A fresh salmon, just caught, and well-roasted over an open campfire. Harry.

She could not get the stable boy out of her mind.

Mary Elizabeth had no idea why this was so. Men had never before interested her in the slightest, save for how well they could hunt or fish and whether or not they could keep up with her when she rode. But this night, of all nights in her life, she thought of a man who had done nothing to vex her. But he irritated her nonetheless, and she did not know why.

God forbid irritation should give way and she start mooning over a man, any man, as Mrs. Prudence mooned over Robbie.

Mary Elizabeth dismissed that thought as absurd as

soon as it came into her mind. She was not a mooning kind of girl.

Since she could not escape her thoughts, she decided that she was going to ignore them. She took up her claymore, Fireheart, in its sheath and snuck down the back stairs with it clutched in one hand. She had no idea what she might do if she ran into a servant on the way, but the house was dark, save for one low-burning lamp in the kitchen. She snuck outside and stood still for a moment, drinking in the night, and the light of the moonrise.

She did not wait long, for she was wasting good darkness. She raised her sword, admiring it in the silver light, before she brought it down in one swift arc, cleaving an imaginary enemy in two. The sound of good steel whispering through the night air made her smile, and she circled her sword above her head and moved to dance with it again.

❧

Harry could not find the stars, for he had turned his telescope down into the yard, where Mary Elizabeth played at murder.

Who on God's green earth had thought it wise to give a slip of a girl a sharp piece of metal almost as long as she was Harry could not say. He watched patiently—and he was not naturally a patient man—for her hulking brother to appear and take the steel away from her. But five minutes turned to ten, and no one came, save the stable mouser, joined by the kitchen cat, both of whom sat on the wall over his mother's rosebushes and watched her antics. Neither seemed inclined to intervene, which, from the swiftness of the moving steel, Harry deemed wise.

Harry sighed, then watched in alarm as she slipped on the oyster shells that lined the walkway, as an unseen opponent forced her back in her false battle. Her battle might be a game, but the unstable shells beneath her feet were real enough. Harry calculated how far it was from his place on the third story to the ground below and told himself not to be a coward. He swung himself onto the trellis that he had used repeatedly to escape his rooms as a boy, only to find that it was still reinforced to the wall with steel rods, as his mother was never sure if he would take that way out of his room again, as he had when he was thirteen.

Once again, his mother proved right. Harry shimmied down the trellis, avoiding as many rose blooms as he might, ending up on the ground in a silent crouch. Moving swiftly on the balls of his feet, he flanked the girl so as not to startle her and approached her from the front, so that she might see him coming and hopefully stab neither him nor herself in the ankle.

She did not hear him, but she saw him clearly in the moonlight. For some strange reason of her own, she did not lower her blade. She held it in a defensive position and called out, keeping her voice low enough not to wake the house, "Who are you? Reveal yourself at once and I will not run you through."

Harry could not help himself. He laughed at that, even as he watched the moonlight gleam on the keen edge of her sword. He knew he should keep his eyes

on her weapon, but instead he found himself drawn
to the way the light fell on her golden curls, turning
them silver.

"It's only Harry," he said.

"From the stables?" she asked, suspicious. The
sword, the very one she must have raised against
Grathton in Hyde Park, was still in her hand.

"The same."

He stepped close and turned his head, so that she
might see his profile in the dim light. She smiled then
and lowered her weapon.

"And what are you doing wandering about in the
roses in the middle of the night?"

"I might ask you the same question," he answered,
smiling in spite of himself. A duke did not smile so
openly, but this once, he might make an exception,
as there was no one nearby to see him do it save two
cats, who would not tell, and a Scottish girl, who had
no idea who he was.

"I was practicing with Fireheart," she said.

"Is that your imaginary friend?" Harry heard the
condescension in his voice and wondered where it
had come from. Perhaps he was using it to defend
himself against the curve of her cheek, where one
curl rested—a curl he wanted to tuck back among its
fellows if he were free to touch her. Which, of course,
he was not.

She gave him a glower and tossed the great sword
into her left hand and then back again. "No," she said.
"Fireheart is my blade."

Now that he was closer, the sight of a blade in her
hand made his body harden, and the sound of the

word *blade* on her tongue made the situation worse. He wished to God he had never come down there.

"Might you put that sword away?" he asked.

"I might," she said. "Why are you wandering through the rosebushes in the middle of the night?"

"I came out to stop you from stabbing yourself."

She laughed at that and slid the long blade into a leather sheath that clearly had been specially made for it. She laid the sword and sheath safely on a nearby bench. The night had grown cooler, but she did not seem to notice, even in her low-cut gown and her cap sleeves. Clearly she had not changed since dinner.

A woman, alone in the moonlight, wearing cream silk and brandishing a sword.

Harry swallowed hard. He really should come down to dinner once while the Scots were in residence.

She made no move to leave and did not seem at all concerned that she was alone with a man she barely knew. Of course, the entire household was within shouting distance, but Mary Elizabeth did not seem to feel the need to call for them, or to be aware that there might ever be such a need. He wondered how many milksops she had known, that no man had ever tried to steal a kiss from her in the moonlight.

"Why are you not spoken for?" he asked instead.

Mary Elizabeth did not take offense, as any other girl might have done, nor did she seek to avoid the question. She looked pensive, a shadow crossing over the maple of her eyes that was not a trick of the feeble light. She spoke in a level tone, as if she was discussing the weather, but somehow Harry knew that the subject was a painful one.

"The men in Edinburgh were afraid of me," she said at last.

"And in London?" he asked, forcing himself to swallow hard to maintain his dignity. He knew that, even in the guise of a stable boy, he could not touch her. No matter how soft her lips looked, no matter that the lower one was a bit fuller than the one above it and fairly called for a man's teeth to bite it.

Especially then.

"They liked me well enough," she said. "But then, Englishmen are not known for their good sense."

She looked at him and seemed to remember that he was English. "Begging your pardon."

If Harry had ever heard of a well-born girl apologizing to a stable hand, he would not have believed it. And here was this lady—for a lady she was—apologizing for a slur on his countrymen. He found that the longer he stood in her presence, the better he liked this Highlander. Sadly, that liking did not stop him from wanting her, which was a nuisance. Still, he could not bring himself to walk away.

"If Scots were afraid of you, I've no doubt that Englishmen were as well."

She smiled a little then, and he felt his heart seize, as if he had been brushed by lightning. Not struck by it, for that would kill him. He felt instead as if lightning had come to hit the ground close beside him, so that he could feel the heat of it and smell the sulfur in the air. Harry blinked as if to clear his vision, but he was afraid that his sight had never been so clear.

"Lowlanders and Englishmen bear a good deal in common," she said. "Still, the men in either place were too afraid to court me openly, which is just as well. For I am not the marrying kind."

In spite of all his good intentions, Harry found himself taking two steps forward. Perhaps it was the moonlight playing havoc with his wits. Perhaps it was the fact that the girl barely seemed to notice him at all. Under most circumstances, he would thank his stars if a woman did not notice him, in the moonlight or otherwise. But for some reason, tonight, he wanted this woman's regard.

Though he was standing within arm's reach of her, Mary Elizabeth did not flinch nor did she step away. She smiled at him, a little bemused but completely unafraid. No attack of missish vapors assailed her, no fit of nerves made her back off. She simply watched him as if he were Sampson, getting up to some antics she had never seen before.

"No man ever tried to kiss you in the moonlight?" he asked at last.

She laughed a little then, while the cats watched from their perch on the low garden wall. Her laughter was as sultry as her voice. It was her laughter that did him in.

"Every man I've ever met is too scared to kiss me anywhere," she said.

Harry thought he heard a note of longing in her tone that was not completely coated over with dismissal. It was that longing that brought him to take the last step forward and close the gap between them.

"I'm not," Harry said, and kissed her.

Six

MARY ELIZABETH COULD NOT BELIEVE HER SENSES, but the stable boy's lips were on hers.

At first, she thought only of defense and reached for the dirk she had tucked away in her garter, nestled close to her thigh. But even as she reached for it, she felt a sudden warmth spreading through her limbs, as if she were relaxing in a hot bath after a long day's hunt. For some reason, she did not respond to this kiss as she would to an attack. His lips were soft against hers, not demanding at all. He seemed to be asking a question, a question she did not know the answer to.

But she wanted to find out.

Harry opened his mouth over hers, and his tongue traced the line of her lips gingerly, as if he feared to startle her. At first, Mary Elizabeth was not certain what he was about, but the warm well-being was still filling her senses, and she relaxed into it, wanting to see where it would take her.

It took her one step closer to her stable boy, and into his arms.

Harry's arms were around her, and she forgot the roles they were born to play, who in the eyes of God and Society they were supposed to be. The thought of how badly she was behaving flickered somewhere along the edge of her brain, only to be ignored as she opened her mouth to take his tongue into it.

He shuddered then, like a man possessed, and clutched her close, only to relax his grip almost at once, just when she would have drawn the dagger from her thigh. Harry seemed able to read her moods, for though his tongue danced with hers as her sword had danced alone only minutes before, he did not take any other liberties. She found that she loved the kiss and wished it might go on forever. Of course, a girl needed to breathe. She discovered this as, to her disappointment, Harry pulled away.

"You are a hellion," he murmured, as if the term were an endearment, as if he offered her the highest compliment allowed a lady. But the word was like a cold bath in place of the warm one, like a blow delivered to her sternum. Mary Elizabeth did not think but stepped on his toes even as she drew a dagger from the gathered silk flounce at the small of her back.

He let her go at once, but she felt her anger rising anyway, as if her anger might assuage the pain in her heart, a flash tide of humiliation and horror at herself and at him—at herself for trusting him, and at him for trampling that trust and for throwing a lovely moment back in her face with an epithet. She had heard that word one too many times from the gossips in London. She would be damned if she would stand by meekly and hear it from him.

"I'll thank you never to say that word in my presence again."

Harry stood staring at her as if he had been pole-axed. Mary Elizabeth stepped back and raised her dagger higher when he tried to catch her arm.

"This hellion might have put a knife between your ribs, but did not. I'll thank you to remember that when you go among the English, telling tales."

He drew himself up to his full height. "Mary Elizabeth, I will never speak of this to another."

"Do as you please," she said. "But never use my name again."

She moved to pick up her sword, keeping her eyes on him. He did not move toward her, and she felt her hurt and humiliation keenly, but she swallowed them down. They were bitter medicine.

"If you touch me again, you'll feel the taste of my steel."

"Mary Elizabeth—"

She glared at him.

"*Miss*. Please. Do not leave like this."

"I am, and I will. It serves me right for trusting an Englishman."

She turned her back on him so that he would not see the tears that had come into her eyes. There were only two of them, and she swallowed them down. She walked back to the house, a blade in each hand. She did not look back.

When she returned to her room, Mary Elizabeth did not brood about with a cup of tea as she was tempted to, but went straight to bed. As annoyed as she was, she managed to sleep. When anger and a sore heart threatened to break her reason and her good sense, she reminded herself that she was among the English, and that she should not indulge herself in too many moments of anger where Southerners were concerned. And that included stable boys who had almost become her friend.

❧

She woke to an early dawn. The light of the rising sun slanted through her second-story windows and she rose at once and dressed in breeches. She did not go seeking Harry to join her on a ride, as she had planned to do before they met in the dark the evening before. Instead, she woke Mrs. Prudence from a sound slumber and got her dressed in breeches, too.

"A lady does not wear men's attire," her companion said.

Mary Elizabeth was not in the mood to argue, that morning or ever. But that particular day she wanted only to be out riding as early as humanly possible, and she did not want to bring a groom with her. Which meant Mrs. Prudence was coming along, will she or nill she.

For as much as she wanted a ride, Mary Elizabeth would not go down to the stables alone. If she saw Harry—and she had never yet been in the stables without him lurking about in his annoying, silent manner—she might strike him. And that would be unacceptable. It was wrong to hit a man, for he, in all honor, could not hit back. Assuming the bounder had any honor.

Mary Elizabeth sniffed, as she had so often seen

Mrs. Prudence do. As a method of expressing displeasure, Mary favored her dirk.

⤨

Harry felt like a cad, a bounder, and a fool. He haunted the stables the next morning from the crack of dawn, for he could not sleep and he could not think. All he saw before him when he closed his eyes was the sweet face of Mary Elizabeth before he hurt her.

He had been fool enough to kiss the girl, a debutante who was a guest under his roof. No matter that she did not know who he was. He knew. And Harry knew that he was a man of thirty, not some ne'er-do-well or young blood of eighteen with sap rising. He had enough sense to maintain his dignity, and the dignity of the duchy, without traipsing about in the moonlight with marriageable girls. No matter how beautiful that girl might be.

Had they been caught, scandal and a hasty marriage would have been the best he could have hoped for. The worst would have been the censure of his mother.

God help him.

Harry was well into the fun of berating himself as he curried his favorite mare, Isolde, when his concentration was broken like so much porcelain on a tile floor. He lost whatever thought might have filtered through his mind in that moment, for he saw the Scottish girl.

She was walking toward the stables, as bold as a bishop, as if she were ready to conquer the world and every man in it. This early in the morning, she wielded no blade, but she was wearing breeches.

Had he not been a duke, and a man in control of

himself, he might have swallowed his tongue. As it was, he simply stared.

She ignored him, as any miffed lady might. Harry forced his gaze away from the beauty of her perfectly rounded derriere and noticed for the first time that her governess was with her. The staid lady wore glasses, but she had forgone the widow's cap. She also sported breeches and looked quite fine in them. Of course, Harry's gaze did not stay on her long, but turned back to Mary Elizabeth as if drawn by a lodestone.

She did not deign to notice him or to acknowledge his presence at all. She smiled at Charlie, the youngest groom, but Charlie was too nervous to do more than bow in her general direction and run and hide from the glory of her thighs in those breeches. The breeches were not even particularly tight, but Harry could see that no man would approach her while she was wearing them.

Before she lost her temper or got offended anew, Harry stepped up. As he was the lord of this particular demesne, it fell to him to stand in for his grooms and underlings in this regard. Also, he did not approve of any other man speaking to her when she was in such dishabille.

"Miss," he said, still uncertain of her last name. "Might we help you to saddle a horse?"

She stood looking down her pert nose at him as if he were a bug on the tip of her boot. She raised one brow imperiously, reminding him of his mother, which almost made him laugh. He had the good fortune to restrain himself, however, for laughter at that juncture would only have made matters worse between them. He already had a great deal of ground to recover.

Her companion seemed oblivious to the tension between them and thanked him prettily. He nodded to Charlie, who saddled a roan mare. Mary Elizabeth frowned at the sidesaddle.

"My companion and I will ride astride," she said. She turned her gaze on Harry. "As long as there is no objection."

Charlie blanched to hear his duke spoken to with such rude disregard, but Harry found himself smiling. "No objection at all, my lady."

She sniffed, and her companion looked at her curiously. It was not like Mary Elizabeth to be rude, and he knew it. No doubt her governess wondered why.

"I am no one's lady, I thank God," she said. "Once you have saddled my friend's horse with something that won't tip her into the dust, you can saddle Sampson over there for me."

The silence in the stables became even thicker as the men hiding behind bales of hay and behind stall doors stared at her anew. For the first time, her mode of dress was second in their minds to the fact that she wanted to ride a killer.

"Miss," Harry said, speaking calmly as Charlie resaddled Buttercup, "I am afraid that Sampson is unavailable."

She smiled then, and he saw the light of challenge in her eyes and knew that she did not smile at him but at the great beast, who, upon hearing his name, had poked his head over the door of his stall.

"Sampson and I get along well enough," she said.

Mary Elizabeth lowered her voice and stepped close to Harry so that no one else might hear. His body tightened at her nearness, and he had to remind himself firmly that, not only was he a gentleman, but there were multiple other people present. Not to mention the horses. Harry took a deep breath and tried to focus on her words, finding himself instead engulfed in the soft flowered scent of her skin.

"A ride on Sampson is my price," she said.

"Your price for what?"

"For forgiving you for last night."

"You will forgive me for what?" he asked, wondering if she had rewritten history and had forgotten that though he had kissed her, she had also kissed him back.

"For calling me names."

"I only called you one name, if you recall."

Her face darkened, and Harry regretted his blithe response.

He could not seem to step fairly with this girl, even if he tried. And he was not used to trying, for anyone. "All right," he said at last, conceding. "I am sorry to have offended you. Heartily sorry. But you cannot ride Sampson."

"Watch me."

She passed him, and her breast brushed against his arm, leaving a trail of fire that shot straight down to his loins. Completely unaffected, Mary Elizabeth opened Sampson's stall door and clicked her tongue once. The great beast obeyed her, stepping out as docilely as a lamb.

The hulking brute stood at attention, mesmerized by the girl, waiting for his next order. She did not ask for permission from Harry again, nor did she call the stallion over to the ladies' mounting block, but somehow placed her hand on his withers and vaulted onto his bare back.

"Gracious gift of God," Barton said from his place behind the hay bale.

Charlie did not speak, but crossed himself. Harry swallowed hard, certain that he had lost the power of speech for the rest of his life. Mary Elizabeth, however, had not.

"I'll race you to the beach, Mrs. Pru," Mary said, smiling at last, the feel of the great beast beneath her seeming to give her back her joy. Sampson must have been taken up by her joy as well, for she had only to nudge him with one knee and he was trotting off toward the stable door, as if wild hoydens leaped on his back every day of his life.

"Mary Elizabeth! For the love of God, you're not decent!" her brother said, appearing suddenly in the stable door. The Scot paid little heed to his sister after that, for he had caught sight of his lover in breeches and had much the same reaction as Harry had at his first look at Mary Elizabeth.

With the girl out of sight, Harry regained a modicum of good sense. He spoke low to Charlie, so as not to draw Mary Elizabeth's brother's wrath on himself, asking that another mount be brought. He watched as the pert schoolmistress rode out after her charge on the light-stepping Buttercup.

The Scot stared after the woman as if she were Aphrodite herself. Harry cleared his throat, and when the Scot did not respond, he pointed out the obvious. "If you mean to catch her, you'd best be off," Harry said.

"Aye. I'm obliged." The Scot returned to his senses only to leap onto the horse that Harry had ordered saddled for himself.

Harry bit back his smile of bemusement. He had plenty of horses, after all. "It has been my pleasure. Your family is rather colorful."

"That they are."

With that last phrase, the Scot was off to chase down the unwary ladies. But Harry knew he would find them first.

His staff did not think the Scot's theft of a good horse as amusing as he did. The grooms all stood around watching Harry for evidence of his father's temper. The old duke had been a curmudgeon in his old age and a terror in his youth. Only Harry's mother had ever been able to bring him to heel. But Harry was a gentleman, no matter where he stood, or who stood with him. He would no more take out an ill humor on a servant than he would kick a dog.

And he was not in an ill humor. All his good intentions to apologize then leave the girl alone had disappeared as soon as he saw Mary Elizabeth leap onto that horse.

He was on the hunt.

"Please saddle another horse, Charlie—a fast one. Merry ought to do," he said, naming his favorite gelding. Merry, as his name suggested, was a good soul and as sweet as maple candy, but he loved to run.

Harry mounted his latest ride and turned Merry's nose toward the sea. Merry's ears perked up at the sound of the ocean, for there was little that he loved more than riding with the sand under his hooves, racing the waves. Harry did not even have to urge Merry, but simply held on as his mount took the shortest route to the sea.

Seven

MARY ELIZABETH DID NOT UNDERSTAND WHAT ALL the fuss was about regarding Sampson. He was a good horse, with a steady gait and the manners of a gentleman. He took his jumps without balking, and when she dismounted, he followed her up the rocky hill and over to the dunes without trying to wander off, though he wore no bridle and had only met her the day before. The great beast seemed to feel protective of her and more than earned the sugar cubes she had stolen for him from her room's morning tea tray.

She stood with Sampson close by, watching the waves as they rolled onto the shore. She had rarely seen the sea, though her family made their living on it. It was not deemed proper for a woman to work onboard ship, though Ian had always let her climb the rigging with him when she was small. She had spent most of her life inland, at the family keep of Glenderrin, but the sea called to her as she stood beside it. She supposed it was in her blood. In this, as in so many things, her blood did not know that she was a woman.

The ride had left her happy, as riding bareback always did. Sampson seemed content himself as he snuffled at her pockets, and once he had eaten all his sugar, he began to crop the sea grass.

Mary Elizabeth let the wind caress her cheek. Her curls had mostly fallen from their pins, and she let them fly. What did she care how she looked? There was no one near to see.

She no sooner had that thought than Harry the stable lad rode up on a fair-gaited gelding. Mary offered her hand to the gelding at once, without thinking, but Sampson put himself between them.

"You jealous galoot. Mind your manners," she said to him.

"Any man would be jealous," Harry said.

She laughed at him, her good nature coming to the fore as it always did. She could not hold a grudge, even if she wanted to. Grudges took too much effort, and he had only called her a hellion, after all. A stable lad in the middle of Northumberland could know nothing of London rumors, nor how they stung.

"So you've forgiven me then," Harry said, swinging down from his mount's back.

She noticed his boots, polished to a high sheen. She wondered why a stable boy would have such fancy boots but knew it would not be polite to ask. Not that he had thought of politeness the night before.

"I've forgiven you," she said.

"For calling you hellion," he added, as if she needed that point clarified.

"Yes."

"So you didn't mind the kiss I gave you?" He held

both hands up as if in surrender, but stepped closer to her—so close that she could smell the sandalwood on his clothes. How would a stable boy get his hands on sandalwood? Perhaps she had made a wrong assumption. Perhaps he was a guest of the old duke himself, if an odd one. She was not the person to judge a man for being odd.

Mary Elizabeth felt her heart leap with a strange, hopeful joy at the thought of the kiss they'd shared and wondered what on earth was the matter with her. She felt her breath suddenly come short and told herself not to be a fool.

"I don't know what you mean," she lied.

"Oh, don't you?"

He smiled at her, and his face was transformed by the warmth of it. Mary Elizabeth blinked at the sight, and Harry took one step closer.

"Perhaps you won't mind if I kiss you again, here and now."

"Mind?" she asked, trying to think of some sensible way to back down. She did not want to pull a knife on him, for she liked him. She had chastised him enough for his slip of the tongue, and now she wanted to slip her tongue into his mouth again. What madness was that?

She did not rally her thoughts in time to answer him. He had closed the gap between them so that the buttons of his waistcoat brushed against the front of her overlarge shirt. She was thinking that that a stable boy would never wear a waistcoat when his lips were on hers, blocking out the rest of the world.

Mary Elizabeth knew she should not allow him, or

any man, to touch her, but he was not just any man. He was her sort-of-friend Harry. She leaned against him, feeling the contours of his chest against hers, enjoying the strength in his arms as they came around her. She knew, somehow, that he would not push her too far. She could explore with him and have a good time, with no one the wiser. Her mother would take a strip out of her hide if she knew, but her mother was in Glenderrin and would never know.

Mary Elizabeth opened her mouth, and Harry did not hesitate to press his advantage, deepening the kiss so that her breath caught and her hands started wandering.

His shoulders were truly as broad as Atlas's, and she wondered what burdens he carried beyond the occasional rosebush and the currying of horseflesh. Her fingertips searched his shoulders for a moment, taking in their breadth even as she savored the unaccountable taste of chocolate on his tongue. Her hands wandered then, down the front of his waistcoat, where it seemed a pipe was tucked away inside a breast pocket. She did not get the chance to explore further, for he caught her hands then, taking his lips from hers.

"Mary Elizabeth, that will do."

He looked down at her, and she wondered why she had ever thought the blue of his eyes icy. They were more like blue flames, small but well-lit fires that did not look like they would go out anytime soon. She stood, warming herself in the heat of his gaze, wondering if what she felt, if what she saw in him, was desire.

She had read about such things in her brother Davy's library, but she had thought it something for the storybooks, some nonsense a writer made up to cadge a living out of an unsuspecting public. But here it was, staring her in the face in the guise of a stable boy with blue eyes and red-blond hair.

"I am not done kissing you," she said.

"Yes, you are. For today, at least."

He could not seem to catch his breath, and Mary Elizabeth noticed that her chest was heaving as if she had run a fast mile in heavy boots, with a sword in one hand and a bow in the other. She supposed breathlessness came with desire. She wanted to explore the concept further but he stepped back from her altogether.

"Well," she said, her good sense returning slowly. "I suppose you're right. We might startle the horses if I were to kiss you again."

A gleam of humor came into his eyes, joining the fiery-blue conflagration of his gaze. "We would not want that."

"No, indeed," Mary Elizabeth answered. She found herself smiling into his face, though she had no idea why, as he had refused to keep kissing her or to even let her kiss him. Still, she did not feel rejected, but only as if they had put their shenanigans on hold for the moment. She wondered when she might kiss him again and knew that she should leave him where he stood.

"Well," she said. "Good day to you, then."

She vaulted onto Sampson's back, who left off chewing the greenery and reared under her—not to throw her off, but to show her that he still had his wits about him.

She patted his neck and leaned close, whispering to

him to find Mrs. Prudence, where they had left her canoodling under a tree with Robbie on the other side of the hillock.

Harry looked nonplussed to be left alone, so she winked at him as a small concession before she rode away.

&

The Scottish girl left him flat.

If that had ever happened to Harry before, he could not remember it. What woman in her right mind, or even a woman who was half-mad, would leave a gentleman standing alone, gaping after her? Harry felt yet again the unaccountable desire to reveal who he was to her. Surely even a half-wild girl from the North knew better than to treat a duke with anything less than respect.

Though Mary Elizabeth was occasionally dismissive of his persona of strange stable boy, Harry had seen no evidence of fawning on her part. Indeed, the girl seemed as if she would be the last woman on Earth to fawn over him, or over anyone. Though her kisses, while untutored, were the most delicious he had encountered in years, if not ever.

She was a quick study, it seemed.

She had commandeered his best horse, so Harry once again climbed onto the docile Merry and headed back to the stables. He did not linger, but left his mount with Charlie and made his way to the house. He did not go alone to his rooms, where Billings no doubt had set up his breakfast, but went instead up the servants' staircase to see his mother.

"Harry, I am gratified that you would join me at

so early an hour. What, may I ask, brings you to my rooms before the cock has even crowed?"

The Duchess of Northumberland looked impeccably dressed, even in her night robe, her hair in a long, silver braid down her back, the royal blue of her dressing gown bringing out the deep blue of her eyes. Even now, as old as she was, Harry could see why his father had loved her for so long, and why he had obeyed only her as if she were his North Star.

Harry wondered for half a moment what it might be like to have a marriage like that. He dismissed the thought almost at once, before it could worry him. He did not have marriage on his mind, but slippery Scottish girls.

Harry kissed his mother's cheek and sat down beside her on the settee in her sitting room. Her breakfast had already been served, as it always was at this hour. When he was small, Harry used to sneak into her rooms after his father had left and filch a bit of hot chocolate. Her habits had not changed, and neither had his. The duchess poured hot milk into the heated chocolate, stirred, and handed him the largest cup, taking a demitasse for herself.

She then put a chocolate brioche on a Sevres plate, setting it in place with gold tongs and handing it to him so that both his hands were full of sweetness.

When he did not answer her, she went on as if he had. "Well, I, for one, am glad to see you. You have been such a ghost about the place ever since my guests arrived. I thought to see you at dinner last night at least."

"I don't want to tell them that I'm the duke."

His mother raised one imperious eyebrow at that bit of nonsense, and he felt himself flush like a schoolboy. He reminded himself that he was thirty, a duke, and lord of all he surveyed. Still, in his mother's presence, he felt less than adequate when she turned that look on him.

"I see," she said. "Because eight hundred years of a proud history and service to the kings of England is something for you to be ashamed of."

"I'm not ashamed," Harry said. "These people will treat me differently once they know who I am."

She pursed her lips. "How do they treat you now?"

"Like an equal."

"But they are not your social equals, and they never will be."

"They think I am a stable hand."

The duchess laughed outright at that, snorting indecorously into a lace handkerchief that she produced from her sleeve. She set her chocolate down and wiped the tears of mirth from her eyes. "A stable hand? Harry, really."

"Mother, I have not come here to talk about them."

"No?" she looked into his eyes as if she could read the thoughts behind them. Harry shifted on the uncomfortable settee, the kind of furniture he endured only occasionally, and only then for love of her.

She waited for a moment for him to continue, and when he only drank his chocolate until it was gone, she refilled his cup.

"Well," she said at last, "I am grateful for your company, whatever the reason. I miss the sight of you at dinner. I wish you would come and take tea with us at least, before the hordes arrive from London tomorrow."

Harry winced at the thought of the bevy of marriageable ladies and their families about to descend on his peaceful haven. He pushed the thought of them aside, for none of that signified more than finding out a little more about Mary Elizabeth. If he could only bring himself to ask.

When he did not speak even then, his mother smiled on him, a new warmth coming into her eyes. "Harry, I can't pass you off as a stable boy at table, but I will be happy to tell the Waterses that you are a cousin, a distant relation that we keep about the place as an act of charity."

Harry did not like this description of himself as a mangy dog brought in from the rain, but he liked it better than owning up to the fact that the house, the lands, and all on them belonged to him. At least for now.

"Thank you, Mother."

She kissed him then, her lips soft on his cheek. "You needn't be always alone, you know. There are many people who like you very well for yourself."

He smiled and knew it was a poor excuse for one. "Mother, I think those who like me for myself alone are the two people in this room."

"The Waters family likes you," she said.

"Is that her last name, then?" he could not help but ask.

His mother froze as if she were a deer in the woodland, but it was a brief lapse before a studied casualness came over her. "The sweet Scottish girl who is visiting us?"

"I am not sure I would call her sweet," he said.

His mother smiled then, and leaned back against her cushions with an air of a cat at a mousehole. "Why yes, Harry. Sweet or not, that is the girl's name."

"Mary Elizabeth Waters," he said, musing to himself. "Indeed."

He saw the calculating look in her eye for what it was. He kissed her cheek and bolted, taking his brioche with him. "I'll be down for dinner" was all he said before he closed her bedroom door behind him.

Eight

MARY ELIZABETH SAW ANOTHER DUCAL TRAVELING coach drawing into the carriage house, and she knew that her brother Alex and his wife had come North. She let out a war whoop, told Robbie to leave off his canoodling with Mrs. Prudence, and rode hell-for-leather to the stables.

She slid off of Sampson and enveloped her big brother in a hug. She clung to him longer than was her wont. Alex was the same as he always was—tall, levelheaded, with his dark hair drawn back in a queue. He hugged her back, looking bemused at her greeting.

"I missed you," she said, laying her fist into his arm.

He laughed and caught her to him again. "You smell of horse, Mary."

"Aye. I've been riding." She patted Sampson's flank, and the horse rewarded her by slobbering in her hair.

"That beast looks a bit large to be ridden bareback," Alex said.

"Sampson is a gentleman who knows how to care for a lady in his keeping."

She noticed the wide-eyed if silent disagreement

among the stable staff, but she ignored it, as they
were Englishmen and weren't fit to ride the likes of
Sampson, that day or ever.

Her equine friend seemed to agree with her, for he
snapped at the first groom who approached him.

"I'm sorry," she said to the boy. "Sampson, remember your manners or no more sugar for you." She led
the horse into his stall and petted his forelock. "Thank
you for caring for him," she said to Charlie. "Let me
know if he misbehaves again."

The boy seemed surprised when Sampson let him
step into his stall. "Yes, miss," Charlie said, smiling shyly.

She winked at him before turning back to her
brother. "Is Catherine in the house?"

"She's at breakfast," Alex answered. "Carriage travel
makes her hungry."

Mary Elizabeth almost laughed at the blush that
came into her brother's cheeks, and she knew what had
really made her friend hungry, and it hadn't been the
jouncing ducal coach.

She winked at Alex, too, and took herself off to the
house, with only one glance behind her, to see if Harry
had come down from the beach. When she saw no sign
of him, she did not hesitate again but moved on. She
was a bit hungry herself.

There was no duchess in evidence at table, nor was the
fat duke lurking about, though the butler Billings gave
her an evil look as she entered wearing breeches. She
ignored him and wrapped her arms around Catherine.

"You're blooming like a rose!" Mary Elizabeth said.

Catherine smiled, her pink cheeks pretty against her
soft, blonde curls. "Marriage agrees with me."

Just at that moment, Mary Elizabeth saw Harry stalk by the window and enter the house through the servants' door. She was staring after him when Catherine caught her eye.

"And who was that?"

"No one," Mary Elizabeth said, filling her plate with bacon and ham from the sideboard.

"He didn't look like no one to you."

"Well, he is," Mary Elizabeth said, sitting down to pour herself a cup of tea. There wasn't a decent bannock or a pot of porridge to be found, but there were French rolls and plenty of butter. Mary Elizabeth took two and started eating, while her slender friend sat down beside her and stared at her.

"Aren't you eating?" Mary asked, starting on her second rasher of bacon. Kissing was hungry work, it seemed.

"Not until you tell me who that man is."

"He's a stable boy," Mary Elizabeth said at last.

She would have said it was impossible, but the fancy ducal butler seemed to choke at his perch beside the door.

She looked at him quizzically, but when Billings would not meet her gaze, she went back to eating her breakfast.

"He seems quite handsome for a stable boy," Catherine said.

Mary Elizabeth could feel her friend's eyes on her, as if she were sizing her for a new gown. She reached for more butter. "Harry's good-looking enough, I suppose. For an Englishman."

Mary Elizabeth was certain this time. Billings did

choke. The butler then fell into a paroxysm of coughs, so that Mary was on her feet in the next minute, offering him a glass of water.

She could tell that he was too high-and-mighty to accept, but he was choking too hard to refuse.

"Take it, man, for the love of God," she said. "I don't want you dead on the floor because of me."

He drank the water down as if it were whisky and managed to hide the glass from her once it was empty, refusing to hand it back to her. "No, miss," he said. "I shall not expire."

"Will you take breakfast with us, then?" she asked. "It seems mad for you to stand about, choking, when a bit of good bacon might set you to rights."

She was not sure, but she thought she saw a fleeting smile cross the staid butler's face.

"No, miss, but I thank you. I have already eaten."

Mary Elizabeth knew the ways of the English were queer, so she got herself more bacon and went back to her breakfast. Catherine had not been diverted by her chat with the butler, but was staring a hole into Mary Elizabeth's head, waiting for some answer she had yet to give.

"And how do you know this Harry?" Catherine asked, trying to sound nonchalant and failing.

"How does anyone know a stable hand? He helped me saddle a horse." Mary Elizabeth smiled, knowing she was not being completely forthcoming. "They've a wonderful horse, Sampson, who used to bite everyone in sight before I reminded him of his manners."

"And this stable boy saddled a biting horse for you?"

"No, he refused to. I rode out bareback."

The butler made another strangled noise when she said that, but Mary Elizabeth ignored him. "As much as I like that horse, I like Harry better."

After she made that confession, both Billings and Catherine were as silent as a tomb. Mary Elizabeth shifted uncomfortably and looked down into her empty teacup.

"Mary," Catherine said, "you are a lady. You can't be canoodling with stable boys."

Mary Elizabeth sighed, thinking of the way Harry's lips had felt on hers just that morning. "You're right, Catherine. I know it."

She pushed back from the table, not wanting to think about Harry anymore. "Let's go throw knives in the ballroom."

Catherine still looked worried, but she smiled a little at that. "Alex brought the board."

"Is Cumberland still on it?"

"His outlines might need a going over, but the good duke is still there."

Mary Elizabeth laughed out loud. Before they left, Mary Elizabeth decided to confess a little more, since there was only Billings nearby to hear. She lowered her voice, as if speaking of a conspiracy.

"I'll tell you one last thing," Mary Elizabeth said. "That stable boy is a good kisser."

Mary thought that her friend might chastise her for her behavior, but Catherine only squealed.

Catherine finished her breakfast, and then the girls went off to explore the great house. Mary Elizabeth kept an eye out for the fat Recluse Duke, but did not see him anywhere. She wondered what he got up to all day, but since it was not an interesting subject, she thanked her stars he was hiding somewhere and got on with her own business.

Mary Elizabeth had hoped to throw knives at Cumberland in the ballroom, but there was too much going on, as the duchess was hosting a dance for her come-out the next night, so Mary Elizabeth set up the outline of the evil Duke of Cumberland in the picture gallery, where no one seemed to come but the mouser who had escaped the kitchen. The little white cat washed her paws delicately while Mary went over Cumberland's edges with a charcoal Billings had helpfully provided for the purpose.

Catherine opened the knife case like the experienced caster she now was. Mary Elizabeth had taught her sister-in-law all she knew, which was a lot. Despite being a sweet girl from Devon, Catherine had taken to knife throwing like a fish to water.

For all her enjoyment of casting steel blades at a cork board, Catherine would not let the matter of Mary Elizabeth kissing a man go.

"When did you kiss him?" she asked.

"This morning, on the beach."

Catherine gasped. She was always a wonderful audience. Mary Elizabeth gave up feeling shy about her own foolishness and began to warm to her tale.

"And last night, while I was practicing my sword-play in the rose garden, he kissed me."

Catherine sighed, even as she let the short knife in her hand fly. She struck the board in her favorite place, the duke's black heart. Mary cast her own knife then, only to hear the sound of someone shuffling at the end of the hall.

"Hello?" Mary Elizabeth called. "Is anyone about? You can come out. We only throw knives at Cumberland here."

For a long moment, there was nothing but silence. Before Mary Elizabeth could go and investigate, intent on discovering which housemaid was eavesdropping with the hope of carrying tales to the duchess and, thus, to Mary Elizabeth's mother, a man stepped out from the shadows.

❧

"Ah," Mary Elizabeth said. "It's only Harry."

With a shrug, she turned back to the board and threw another wicked knife at the strange, top-hat-wearing gentleman drawn there. Her blade buried itself to the hilt in the effigy's throat.

"Not fond of dukes, are you?" Harry asked.

"I'm indifferent to them on the whole," Mary Elizabeth said. "I've never met one. That blighter there is Cumberland."

"The Butcher of Culloden," Harry said, grateful that the outline was not meant to represent anyone currently living—namely himself.

"You've heard of the bastard, then," Mary Elizabeth said, throwing another knife with deadly accuracy. Had the Duke of Cumberland been standing there, he would have been taken down by this particular Highlander.

"Once or twice."

Mary Elizabeth was as cool as ever, not the least

bit discommoded that he had discovered her pursuing unladylike ends with her friend, telling tales all the while. The fact that those tales were true—save for the salient point left out that he was the Duke of Northumberland—did not make him less annoyed with her.

Her friend—another of his mother's guests, he assumed—was struck dumb at the sight of him. He was dressed in a coat for once, along with a clean, pressed shirt, fine waistcoat, and a well-tied cravat. Much to his chagrin, the girl seemed to have an inkling—unlike Mary Elizabeth—of who he was. She curtsied deeply, as if to the king himself, and Mary Elizabeth cocked an eyebrow at her.

"Now, then, Catherine, no need to mock the man. Horses are decent work and worth a man's time—a good way for a man to earn a wage." Mary Elizabeth nodded to him, as if to congratulate him on having the good sense to care for horses. "Which makes me wonder, Harry, what are you doing in the house dressed like an undertaker?"

"I'm not a stable boy," he said.

Mary Elizabeth did not bat an eye at this revelation, but took aim at the corkboard figure again, this time with her dirk. She had drawn it from some secret pocket in her gown, and even now hefted it by the blade, as if testing its weight.

He thought with all certainty that she would drop it or that it would fall short of its mark, but in spite of it being a heavier blade, it flew straight and true, directly into the duke's throat.

Harry winced to see it.

She turned to him then. "Are you a gardener, then?" she asked. "You seem more at home among the horses."

"I'm a jack-of-all-trades, you might say," Harry answered.

Mary Elizabeth snorted at that, not seeming to notice that her lady friend and confidante had gone deadly pale. "And master of none," Mary Elizabeth said.

He flinched at her apt description, and she did notice that.

"I'm sorry, Harry. That was rude of me. But you being a man-of-all-work does not explain why you're at liberty to wander through the house at midday."

"I'm a member of the family," he said.

Mary Elizabeth raised one eyebrow and turned to face him, even as her friend tried to catch at her hand, as if to hold her back.

"So you're Her Worship's cousin, then, or some such?"

"Some such," Harry answered.

"Mary," the girl beside her said, her voice a bit choked.

He smiled at the girl to put her at her ease, but it seemed he failed, for she looked even more as if she might faint.

"Don't fret, Catherine," Mary Elizabeth said. "Whoever Harry is, he's harmless."

Henry Charles Percy, Duke of Northumberland, wanted nothing more in that moment than to dismiss her friend and draw Mary Elizabeth under him there and then. He would make love to her until she called out his name in ecstasy. That demonstration might show her exactly who was harmless. But even as unreasonable, almost insatiable lust shook his frame like a sudden storm, Harry remembered that he was a gentleman.

"I bid you both good day."

Retreat was the better part of valor. And he knew that his self-control, if not his honor, was suspended before him by a very thin thread. He bowed to them, giving the girl Catherine another small smile. Mary Elizabeth turned from him again to survey her knifeboard.

"As you will, Harry. Perhaps we'll see you at dinner, since you're some kind of poor relation."

Harry almost strangled at that, and saw that Catherine was strangling with him. Still, the girl showed admirable self-possession and did not blurt out his title. With Mary Elizabeth's back to him, he raised one finger to his lips and winked.

The lady clearly could not have been more shocked had he disrobed. But she was a lady, so she rallied and only curtsied again. She even managed to offer a small smile.

Confident that his entreaty for her silence would be obeyed, Harry left the girls in the portrait gallery and went to take a swim in the cold, bracing sea.

Nine

HARRY HAD ALWAYS THOUGHT OF HIMSELF AS LORD OF his duchy. At the very least, as someone whose authority would never be questioned in his own house. But that day, he had discovered that there were limits to what his staff would do for him.

Such as keep his identity a secret.

When Billings had given the order belowstairs that all must pretend that their duke was merely a poor relation, even the housemaids had rebelled. It seemed that they all prided themselves on serving the duchy, as he did, and that, as he was the latest embodiment of said duchy, they wanted all and sundry to know exactly who it was they served.

One housemaid had even cried.

Billings had reported back that he had all in hand, and that the household would confine themselves to referring to him as *my lord*, though everyone was displeased. Including Billings.

So that afternoon, Harry hid in his father's library, playing chess against himself and making a botch of it. He could not concentrate on any of the three books he was reading either. One was a treatise on the latest scientific developments in botany, another in astronomy, and the third on sailing. None of his usual pursuits pleased him that day, however, just as his staff did not, all because of one girl from Scotland who only came up to his breastbone and who no doubt weighed less than Sampson's saddle.

Harry was not certain what he was going to do about her family. With the help of her friend, Catherine, they had very likely puzzled out who he was by now. He hoped none of them had mentioned it to her.

He moved the white bishop, only to curse his own folly for falling into his own trap, when the door to his father's library opened and then just as quickly slammed shut. A man stood in the doorway, glaring at Harry.

"I've run you to ground," the man said.

"I beg your pardon?"

"It's not my pardon you need, Your Worship."

The hulking man crossing the vast, book-filled room did not look like a London fop, though he was dressed like one, in black superfine and a silver-gray waistcoat. He looked like a warrior. Something in Harry woke up, and he stood, smiling, not giving a thought to his father's stricture that smiles were not proper for a duke, especially with strangers. He liked the man on sight.

"I'm afraid we haven't been introduced," he said.

"My name is Alexander Waters. I've been living in your London house for the last two months, Your High-and-Mighty Lordship. With my sister."

Waters stopped short of throttling Harry where he stood only because the massive ducal desk was in his way. He looked likely to vault over it next, and while Harry would enjoy a good fisticuffs after the frustrations of kissing a girl he couldn't have, his mother would be extremely displeased if he got blood on the carpet.

"Mr. Waters," Harry said.

"Aye. The eldest Waters but two, which makes me the man to call you out." He tossed a black leather glove on the desk, in the middle of Harry's chess-board. "Name your weapons."

Harry could feel the fury rolling off the man in waves. Harry was a cool man himself and never understood passion in others. At least, he hadn't until Mary Elizabeth had climbed out of that travel-ing chaise and started treating him like her bootboy. Clearly, someone had been telling tales, and that someone was this man's wife.

"Mr. Waters," Harry said again. "I apologize."

The dark-haired man blinked, shifting his wide shoulders in his tight black coat. "You apologize for what?"

"For kissing your sister without benefit of marriage."

Waters's eyes narrowed. "You don't mean to marry her, do you?"

"No," Harry answered. "I don't."

The tension drained slowly out of the room, and Harry felt as bleak as midwinter on the moors, without a grouse in sight. He sighed and moved out from behind the desk, so that the Waters man might strike him, if he chose.

"I have certain obligations as Duke of Northumberland that require a great deal of me. I have been shirking those obligations, and as of tomorrow night, that shirking must come to an end."

"That doesn't explain why you won't marry my sister."

Harry could see that the gentleman was well on his way to working up a new fit of fury and knew that he had best explain himself.

"Your sister is a little bird," he began, then frowned, for what he had said made no sense. But for some odd reason, the other man's anger seemed to be in check.

"Go on," Waters said.

"I have seen birds caged," Harry went on. "Their lives are not worth living."

There was a long silence, and it stretched on while Harry thought of Mary Elizabeth. Harry had not known the girl long, but she was one of the most vibrant women he had ever met, that he would likely ever meet. He thought of her on Sampson's back, racing away from him, and knew that was where she belonged—on horseback, with a dagger somewhere hidden about her person, living her life with joy.

Marrying a duke would kill that joy. Even if that duke was him.

"You don't refuse to marry her because she is no one, from nowhere." Waters sounded bemused. "You refuse to marry her to take care of her."

"A coronet is a heavy burden," Harry replied, not knowing that else to say.

"It would kill her," Waters said, "to live among the English for the rest of her life." He said it, and it cut Harry to the quick, but it seemed to cut Waters more.

The man sat down heavily then, as if he had received a hard blow. Harry was not sure what to do for him, for he had only one friend, and that friend he had had from childhood. He was not sure how men went about offering each other comfort. So he crossed to his father's decanters, which Billings still kept filled, and poured the man a whisky, neat.

Waters downed it in one swallow, then winced.

"Where in God's glorious name do you find this swill?"

Harry blinked, for, as he did not drink spirits, he had no idea. "Scotland," he said at last.

Waters grimaced. "We'll be sending you three barrels of decent Islay whisky from Glenderrin."

Harry did not know what Islay was, but he knew that Glenderrin was the Waterses' seat, somewhere North, in the back of beyond. "Thank you."

Waters nodded and stood, setting the cut crystal glass down where the housemaids might find it later.

"I thank you for your honesty, belated though it is."

Waters was about to leave the room, but Harry stepped in front of him. "I ask that you don't tell her who I am. I'll tell her myself."

Waters stared him down, his dark-brown eyes boring into his skull as if to unearth his true thoughts and motives. Harry stood his ground and thought of how refreshing it was to find a man who was not afraid to look him in the eye and treat him like a man and an equal.

He had not realized how the fawning of others burdened him until he stood with another who simply wouldn't do it. Harry would have said it was impossible to find people who didn't care for rank, but his last days with the Waterses proved that he was wrong.

"My wife and I will hold our peace," Alex said, "but only until after the fancy dance your mother is throwing for Mary."

His mother was giving the ball so that Harry might look over the possible candidates for his duchess without him having to leave the comforts of Northumberland, but he did not belabor the point. He simply nodded, since he was getting what he wanted. With a houseful of London *ton*, there was no way he could continue this charade longer than that.

"Thank you," Harry said.

Waters did not leave then, as Harry expected him to, but stared him down again. "If you hurt her, I'll kill you, duke or no."

Harry felt the cold whisper of his death on the back of his neck and smiled. If circumstances were different, if the Waterses were people he might know for the rest of his life and not simply strange wayfarers passing through his mother's house, he would have been pleased to call this man friend.

"Fair enough."

Waters smiled at him then, but it was a tired smile, full of defeat. Harry watched the man walk away and was left alone, as he always was, with only his own thoughts for company.

Ten

THAT EVENING, MARY ELIZABETH WAS SORRY SHE HAD worn the insipid white-and-pink gown Mrs. Prudence had forced her to buy in London, for Harry made an appearance at dinner. He was looking morose, which was not like him, and Mary wondered if he hid himself in the gardens and in the stables because he simply didn't like company.

Food for thought.

She did little thinking that night, for the dinner laid out on the duchess's table was as grand as any she'd eaten, with fine sides of beef, carrots braised in butter, and wine to go with each course. With Robbie mooning over Mrs. Pru and with Alex glowering at her all the way from the other end of the table, Mary Elizabeth got to sample each wine as the footman poured it for her.

It seemed that not only did she like her whisky, but she also liked some of the racy French stuff as well. Wonders might never cease.

But no matter how much good food she ate or how she enjoyed talking with the duchess—whose given name was Amelia—Harry still scowled beside her, his food almost untouched. She elbowed him at one point and teased him openly, telling him to eat his greens, and he did not even crack a smile, as if he would soon be going to his own funeral.

The gentlemen did not stay back at table as they often did in English houses, but trooped into the parlor with the ladies for tea and cake. Mary Elizabeth found herself hoping that there might be chocolate cream in that cake when she stopped in the doorway to the ducal sitting room, Harry's hand on her arm.

"Might I speak with you?" he asked.

Mary Elizabeth frowned to hear him sound as strange as he looked, but before she could answer, Catherine said. "Yes, why don't we three take a turn around the picture gallery upstairs?"

"But there's cake," Mary answered.

Harry smiled then and she saw a little of himself behind whatever shadow was in his eyes. "I give you my word of honor that, after we talk, you can have all the cake you want."

"Chocolate cream?" Mary Elizabeth asked.

His lips twitched as if he was suppressing a bit of laughter. "Yes."

"All right, then," she said, leading the way up the stairs. "But I only want one piece."

Harry, who was suddenly acting the gentleman and leading Catherine on his arm behind her said, "Fair enough."

Mary Elizabeth did not know why Harry suddenly acted as if squiring her off to talk was such a necessity. They talked all the time and might easily have talked tomorrow during their ride, when she intended to take Sampson out again. But since she had decided that cake could wait, she entered the picture gallery ahead of Harry and Catherine, surveying Cumberland and the new holes she and Catherine had put in him earlier that day with a sense of satisfied accomplishment. The holes were plentiful especially in the most deadly spots on his person. She would need Alex or Robbie to get her a new board before the week was out, so that she might christen Cumberland II.

She was lost in thought over this, and over whether or not she had remembered to sharpen her blades before putting them away that day, when she noticed Harry was standing close beside her. He was not looking at Cumberland, however, as she was. He was looking at her.

"Hello, then," she said, smiling at him. She took in the lovely scent of sandalwood on his skin, grateful that the mystery of where a stable boy would acquire such a perfume had been solved.

Harry did not say anything, but continued to stare at her so long that she wondered if she had a bit of carrot on the edge of her lip. She ran her tongue over it, but found nothing. Harry's gaze became more pronounced as his eyes fastened on her lower lip, as if he might like to bite her. Still, he said nothing.

"Well," she said, making another attempt at communication. "Here we are in the picture gallery. Did you wish to show me some ancestor or other?"

"No," he answered. His eyes seemed especially blue that night, perhaps because of the sapphire cravat pin he wore, which she only just now noticed. Mary

Elizabeth had to admit that he looked handsome in his dinner dress, but she found that she preferred the Harry she had met so often in the stables—a more relaxed, less remote Harry.

She frowned and began to ask him what the matter was when she heard a shuffling from down the way. Catherine cleared her throat delicately and said, "I will step down the gallery to view the Elizabethan portraits."

Harry nodded to her, and Catherine moved down the long room until she was about fifteen feet away from them, almost hidden in shadow.

Why Catherine felt the need to make such an announcement, Mary Elizabeth did not know. She wondered if her friend made Harry nervous for some strange reason, but before she could ask him, he finally spoke of his own accord.

"I have brought you here to tell you that I cannot kiss you again." Harry said this with deadly seriousness, as if the fate of worlds rested on his words.

Mary Elizabeth knew by now that beneath his often-gruff exterior, Harry was a man with a soft heart. So she did not laugh at him as she wanted to. Indeed, when her lips twitched, she did not even let them rise into a smile. He was serious, as he so often was, but he was also in pain. He was her friend, and she would help him. But first, she would set him straight.

"Harry, if I want to kiss you, I will kiss you. So do not trouble yourself about that."

He stood even more upright than he had before, his back like an iron fire poker. "I will not allow it."

A light of challenge lit her heart. She tried to fight

it down and failed. "Oh, won't you? What else won't you allow?"

Before he could answer her with some other bit of English nonsense, Mary pressed herself against him, raising herself on her toes, and laid her lips against his.

She was not skilled at kissing by any means, but he had taught her a little since they had first tried canoodling the night before. Though he stood rigid against her, his arms not even coming up to wrap around her, she ignored his lack of enthusiasm and simply enjoyed herself.

His lips were soft beneath hers, softer than any man's had a right to be. His chest was as hard as granite beneath her fingertips, even more so than usual because he was resisting her. She trailed her lips along his jaw and up toward his ear when she finally began to feel a bit of movement beneath her questing hands. Through the layers of his clothes and through her cotton gloves, she could feel the escalated beating of his heart.

She slipped her tongue along the seam of his lips then, and his mouth opened over hers and his arms came around her, clamping her to him like a vise. She felt a moment of triumph that he had been so easily conquered, but then his tongue slipped over hers, and she forgot everything else.

The lovely warm sense of well-being that came from kissing Harry crept over her a little at a time, until she was swimming in it, as in a deep, uncharted sea. When he pulled back, she sighed against him and laid her head over his heart. It was still thundering, but she felt as peaceful as a lamb on Easter morning.

"What else did you want to tell me?" Mary Elizabeth asked, a little drowsily.

Catherine, her supposed chaperone, stayed away from them, for Mary Elizabeth did not even hear the rustle of her gown. Harry, too, was still, and for one blessed moment, all was right with the world.

And then he spoke.

"I won't marry you."

Those harsh words were an icy ocean wave breaking over her head. Mary tried to hang on to her warm sense of well-being, but it was fading, as the long gloaming must finally fade to dark. She sighed and pulled back from him, so that she could look into the blue of his eyes.

He spoke again. "I *can't* marry you."

She tried not to be annoyed with him for killing her moment of peace, as such moments were few and far between. She had found more moments of peace in his arms than she had spent since she'd left home, almost six months before. But as she looked at the line of his jaw—which was clenched as if he had brought it down on something distasteful—she knew that he was still in pain and that it was not because of her.

"I can't marry you, either," she said. "What has that to do with a little canoodling in the dark?"

She heard a gasp from Catherine then, but she ignored her as a burden for another time and kept her eyes on Harry.

He looked at her as if she were demented, as if she had lost the last thread linking her to sanity and to the daylight world. She opened her mouth to tell him to stop being an ass when he said, "But you are a lady."

"I am," she answered. "But I am not the marrying kind, Harry. I told you that the day we met."

He stared down at her as if she had grown a second head, and she wondered why it was that even the best of men never listened to a word a woman said to them, no matter how important those words might be.

"Harry, I am for Glenderrin. I cannot marry. I will not marry. I am going home, to live free in the Highlands. My family has not accepted this yet, but they will. In the end, my da will back me and fight them off, because he loves me. I could no more marry you than I might marry a bird in the sky."

Mary Elizabeth said all this gently, keeping her voice soft in an effort to soothe him, but his color only rose higher and his jaw only got more clenched.

"You don't want to marry me," Harry said. He sounded suddenly as if he were accusing her of something.

"I've only known you three days, lad," Mary said, trying to jolly him out of his funk with the God's honest truth. When he did not smile, she softened her voice again. "Harry, I don't want to marry anyone."

He turned from her, his arms crossed over his chest as if to protect his heart, and failing. Mary Elizabeth pressed her hand to his forearm, and held it there, even though he ignored her touch, even though his arm was rock-hard beneath her hand.

"Harry, I won't kiss you again if you don't want me to."

"I do want you to." His eyes met hers, and their blue was like a flame. Mary Elizabeth almost stepped back from the passion in them, but she was a strong woman for all her innocence, and she held her ground. "I want to kiss you," he said. "But I cannot."

This complete lack of reason did not make Mary Elizabeth blink. All men, even her brothers, took odd notions into their heads from time to time, and nothing save the Second Coming of Christ would force those notions out. She knew that to fight against a man's ideas at such a time was to fight the tide that was turning. So for once in her life, she did not fight. She patted her friend's arm instead.

"All right," she said. "That's as it may be. I will back you in this if you wish, even though it's daft."

He smiled a little then, and she saw his jaw soften a bit as he let loose of whatever it was he was biting down on.

"Why would you back me if you think I'm being daft?" His eyes no longer held the passion they had a few minutes before, but they were open, and more vulnerable than she had ever seen them. She knew that she must tread with care, for as lonely she was, even with her family around her, this man was lonelier.

"Because I'm your friend."

Harry stood as still as a hare, looking as if she had struck him between the eyes. She waited a long moment, but when he said nothing more, she patted his arm again in consolation, then collected Catherine and went to find a slice of cake with chocolate cream in it.

Eleven

HARRY DID NOT SLEEP THAT NIGHT. INSTEAD, HE looked at the stars from his balcony and felt the noose of his future closing around his neck.

That day, his mother's guests would arrive. The fathers, brothers, and mothers of Society would flock to his door, bringing with them their marriageable girls for him to look over, so that he might choose one at his leisure and marry her.

He knew that he must do so. He knew that he must align himself with some family or other and take a wife, so that he might have a woman to run his home, to be his duchess, to produce his heir. He knew this as he knew that the sun must rise, but instead of a beginning of things to come, such a prospect seemed like an end.

He did not change into his riding clothes once dawn had broken, but went to the stables as the sun rose up over the sea, wearing the same clothes he had gone to dinner in the night before. If the grooms thought his rumpled evening dress overly formal, they did not comment, but saddled Sampson when he asked them to.

He had just risen into the saddle from the mounting block, afraid he was too bleary-eyed to mount without one, when Mary Elizabeth strolled in, looking as fresh as a late-summer morning.

"Hello, Harry!" she said, waving to him, startling Sampson. The horse did not rear under him or try to buck him off, but docilely stepped over to his lady and accepted the sugar from the palm of her hand.

"And how is this great beastie this morning? No more biting the grooms, I trust?" she asked the horse, for all the world as if he might answer her.

Charlie stepped up, sketching a bit of a jaunty bow, cap in hand. From the glow in his eyes, the boy clearly worshipped her. Harry shifted in the saddle.

"He's not bit a one of us since you spoke with him, miss."

"I'm glad to hear it." Mary Elizabeth rubbed the stallion's nose and gave him another bite of sugar. "I see you've gotten here before me and taken Sampson for yourself," Mary Elizabeth said, smiling up at Harry.

He smiled back at her despite the fact that she was the reason he had not slept. He corrected himself. His future and its long, unturning road was what kept him awake, not this girl. But the thought of her beside him in that bed, and beneath him and—once he had tutored her in the ways of love—over him had been fantasies that he had indulged in the wee hours of the morning in an effort to forget all the rest. And now she stood in front of him in breeches, the sweet curve of her derriere begging for a man's hand to caress it. Namely his.

"Shall we ride out together?" Mary Elizabeth asked, oblivious to the way his thoughts were tending. She swung up onto Merry, who had been saddled for her without her even having to ask. His grooms responded to her better than they did to him. So much for being lord of all he surveyed.

"If we bring a groom," Harry responded, his eyes now traveling along the line of her thigh.

She smiled at him as if he were a bit addlepated. "Do you feel the need of protection from me, Harry? I promised you that I won't kiss you again, and I won't." He felt his heart seize at her words, and then sink, until she said, "Not until you ask me to."

The grooms close enough to hear her choked on what sounded like suppressed laughter. Harry waited for his anger to rise up, but it did not come. Instead, he found himself looking into the maple eyes of his Scottish friend, watching for the hint of green along the irises. When she turned her head toward him, he caught sight of that green, and it made him smile.

"Very well, then," Harry said. "If you are resolved to behave with propriety, then so am I."

Mary Elizabeth shot him a look at that bit of nonsense and nudged Merry with her knee, that they might start out of the stables and head into the sunlight. The cattle break had been covered over for the day, and she set out at a walk. Sampson followed along behind her, as docile as a lamb, with no hint of a request for motion from Harry at all.

Harry found himself watching the rise and fall of her bottom on the saddle, as well as the gentle swaying of her breasts, which seemed not to be caught up by stays at all. "Do you even own a riding habit?" he asked, hearing the petulance in his own voice.

"Yes," she replied blithely.

Harry waited, but when she did not elaborate, he asked, "Why don't you wear it?"

"Because the skirt is a nuisance, and riding side-saddle makes it more difficult to take jumps. I'll wear a habit when the fancy guests start arriving."

Harry felt his misery rising up from the ground to swamp him. He scowled.

"You don't want to see the visitors who are coming to my fancy dance," Mary Elizabeth said.

Harry wondered where on God's green earth Mary and her family had gotten the notion that his mother's ball was for them, but he did not ask. Instead, he said, "Women are coming to look me over, and I dread it."

He had not told another living soul that he hated the thought of his duty, that his certain future with a wife he did not love hung like a millstone around his neck. He had waited until he was thirty to find a woman who might brighten his days and liven his nights as well as serve as a decent duchess, and he had come to the conclusion that such a woman did not exist.

Mary Elizabeth was frowning, not at what he was thinking, but at what he had told her. "Even a duke's poor relation is a hot marriage item then?"

Harry grimaced. He needed to tell her the truth, and soon, but he was not ready to give up his friend. Save for Clive—who had beaten him soundly when they were ten even though Harry was a duke's heir—no one ever treated him as a person after they knew.

"I'm afraid so."

Mary Elizabeth sighed, as if the burden of too many suitors was something she was familiar with.

"Well, if you have need of a hiding place, let me know. I've found a few spots in that house where no one will find you."

Harry smiled at the thought of pressing into some linen closet with her. The temptation would kill him. "You would hide me away, then, and keep me for yourself?"

Mary Elizabeth laughed at that, but she did not scoff, as he had thought she might. Her brown eyes were warm on his, and he felt the moment suspended between them, as if time had stopped. He almost wished that it would, that he might ride through his park forever, with this woman at his side.

He shook his head a little to clear it of such nonsense, but Mary Elizabeth did not look away. "If I could have a man, Harry, you'd be it."

She said it simply, without affectation or flourish, and kept riding on, a steady presence at his side. The birds sang in the hedgerow as they passed, making a flurry of feathers at the intrusion of a man and a girl so close to their nest. But Harry barely heard them.

All he could see was Mary Elizabeth, the sunlight shining on the gold of her hair, which was even now coming down from its pins to curl along her shoulders and down her back. She looked like a hoyden and a scamp, and he knew that if he lived to be a hundred, he would never again see a woman as beautiful as she was.

"Race me to the beach, then?" she asked, no doubt in an effort to dispel the moment that had fallen over both of them.

"To where you kissed me yesterday?" he asked.

She laughed. "The very spot. Though there will be no such shenanigans today. I am a woman of my word."

She touched her boot to Merry's flank, and the horse was off like a shot, so quick that Harry was ten lengths behind before he took his next breath.

Sampson waited only a moment for his rider to give the order to run. When the order did not come, the beast took it upon himself to chase Mary Elizabeth down. Harry clung to his back and bent low over his neck, that the horse might go faster. He could not blame him. It seemed right that every male alive would be chasing after that girl and wanting all the beautiful things about her—things that he simply could not keep.

He found Mary Elizabeth waiting for him, her face turned toward the sea. Merry cropped the sea grass close by, and Mary Elizabeth absently ran her hand over the horse's withers. She looked deep in thought, and all Harry could think of as he looked at her was how much he wanted her and what a fool he was to moon after a gently reared virgin from the North.

She met his eyes as he climbed off of Sampson's back, and for a moment, he wondered if she knew what he was thinking. But when she spoke, it was not of the heat in his eyes that no doubt even a virgin could see, but something else altogether.

"The way to make it through this evening," she said to him, "is to have a goal beyond it."

Harry stared down at her, watching the swell of her breasts rise and fall with her breath beneath the linen shirt she wore. He saw the faint outline of a chemise beneath that, and when he wanted to look further, he forced his gaze back to her face.

"What goal would you suggest?"

"Well," Mary said, "I've never been on the sea. You might take me sailing."

"We'd have to marry after."

She laughed out loud, and Merry shifted under her hand. Sampson shook out his mane and took three steps closer to her, almost crowding Harry out.

"You're a fretful man, Harry. And I'm sorry for it."

"You didn't make me so," he said.

"No," she answered, turning her eyes back to the sea. "I did not."

He stood there looking at her, the softness of her hair flowing down her back in a mass of curls that seemed to move like a living thing. He reached out with one gloved hand and stopped just short of touching those curls.

"You would go sailing with me?" he asked at last, lowering his hand before she might see it.

"Aye." She smiled at him, giving him a wry, slanted look. "That I would."

"If I make it through the ball tonight, we'll go sailing tomorrow. Weather permitting."

Mary Elizabeth stepped toward him then and laid one hand over his heart. The muscles of his chest leaped under her bare palm. The backs of her hands were soft, but her palms were callused from riding and from playing at war.

She looked for one moment as if she might rise on her toes and kiss him. But then she seemed to remember her promise, for she patted his chest as if he were Sampson and turned away from him to mount her horse.

"I'll see you tonight, then" was all she said.

Harry did not answer, but stood staring up at her, watching the muscles of her thighs move against the brown wool of her breeches. She did not wait for him to find his manners, or for him to find his tongue, but touched her heel to Merry's flank once, gently, and let the horse have his head as she rode away.

Twelve

MARY ELIZABETH DRESSED ALONE FOR THE DUCHESS'S fancy dance party. Her Worship had sent her own maid to help her, but Mary never bought a gown that she could not put on and take off herself, so she sent the woman away, with her thanks. The little Frenchwoman looked relieved not to have to spend another moment with a Highland barbarian, but looked longingly at Mary's hair as she left.

Mary Elizabeth did have fine hair.

She did little to it, simply pinning the curls up and hoping they wouldn't fall too soon. For they would inevitably fall, as the tide inevitably turned twice each day.

Mary Elizabeth surveyed the gowns that she knew Mrs. Prudence would want her to wear. Each one was a delicate shade—eggshell pink, robin's-egg blue, buttercup yellow. Each gown was lovely, suited to a debutante. But none of them suited her spirit, and she knew it.

Instead, she drew out a vibrant-red gown with a gold baldric, a cast-off of some fancy lord's mistress that

Madame Celeste, her London modiste, had been stuck with. Mary had purchased said gown with her own money, so as not to cause an alarm among her family. For though her brothers could not care less what she clapped on her back, Mrs. Prudence definitely did.

Mary Elizabeth smiled and put it on.

She was not certain what the gold sash was originally intended to do, other than accentuate the courtesan's bosom. Mary found herself slightly annoyed by how well it accentuated her own, but she simply donned a third dagger and decided that any Englishman who was overwhelmed by lust at the sight of her breasts might be dispatched easily enough, as he would be mightily distracted.

The gold sash, it turned out, was very useful for hiding knives.

Mrs. Prudence and Catherine both protested her gown, but as they each had their own fish to fry, it did not take her long to get them downstairs to their respective men. Mary Elizabeth felt as if she had done her good deed for the day. She entered the ballroom looking for Harry, but found his mother instead.

"Well, miss," the old harridan said, raising a quizzing glass to her right eye. "It seems you have quite taken it upon yourself to don the curtains from a den of iniquity."

Mary Elizabeth felt a smile creep onto her face against her will. She was not certain, but she thought that the duchess had called her new favorite gown a dress from a whorehouse.

"I cut them down myself, ma'am," she said, determined not to rise to the bait cast out for her, nor to laugh in the old woman's face. "I had a seamstress sew them up into the dress you see here. Do you think your London friends will like it?"

The duchess swept Mary Elizabeth from head to toe, seeming to stop pointedly on her bosom. "I think the men will adore it."

Mary smiled. "Well, that's half of them, then."

"The women will be furious." The duchess looked like a cat that had just eaten a low-flying bird.

"In all honesty, ma'am, if you think I give two farthings for what any English think of me, man or woman, you are sorely mistaken."

The duchess lowered her quizzing glass. "Indeed, Mary. And that is why the men will love you and the women despise you."

Mary Elizabeth sighed. "Surely these people have more to occupy themselves with than the likes of me."

Before the duchess could comment on that, Harry was at her side, staring at Mary Elizabeth as if she had just fallen from the moon.

When he did not speak, Mary said, "Hello, Harry. Nice evening for a dance."

His voice sounded strangled when he answered, "It is."

Another silence ensued, during which the duchess gloated, though heaven only knew about what, and Harry stared. Mary Elizabeth tried again.

"So, do you dance, Harry?"

His eyes seemed as drawn to her bosom as his mother's quizzing glass had been. Mary Elizabeth sighed and adjusted the gold baldric beneath them. Harry swallowed hard, looking as if he might choke.

"I do," he answered at last, sounding as if his crisp, white linen was strangling him.

"Well, then, let's dance."

He extended his arm to her, and she took it, knowing that was the proper response when a man was escorting a lady to the dance floor. Mary Elizabeth was surprised to find the English clearing a path for them as if they were Moses parting the Red Sea. Mary thought it odd, but did not comment, so as not to offend him about the peculiarities of the duchess's guests.

She took one look around for the fat, Recluse Duke and saw him standing at attention in one corner, with everyone else ignoring him. She wondered what these English were about, leaving one of their honored lords unattended.

The band in the corner took that moment to strike up a waltz, and Mary Elizabeth forgot about the Recluse Duke altogether. This was one of the few Southern dances she liked. It had such poetry to it, such sweeping grandeur. She had never quite mastered it herself, but she loved it all the same. She hoped that she would not tread on Harry's toes, for he was not wearing his riding boots now, but slippers and breeches, as if he were at Almack's. The slippers were foolish, but the breeches showed off his fine calves.

Mary was wondering why on God's green earth she noticed that when he took her in his arms and started dancing.

She found that the waltz, with the right partner, required nothing from her at all. She found herself following his lead as if born to it when she had never followed a man's lead in her life. Most of the fops in London and in Edinburgh had simply tripped along beside her, on and off the dance floor. But Harry did not trip, nor did he mince. He soared.

"You're like an eagle," she said to him as they began their second turn around the dance floor. It seemed the English had lost what was left of their tiny minds, or had simply eaten too much before they came, for no one joined them in the dance, but watched them swirl together as if viewing a play at the theater. Not that she had ever been to a play, but she understood what happened there.

He smiled down at her. "I'm like an eagle?" he asked.

"You move on the dance floor like a hunter, but a graceful one. It's quite taking, Harry. These women really are going to be fighting over you."

He laughed, and she found she loved the sound of it. He had been so morose for the last day that she as happy to see him with a warm light in his eyes. "I'm glad you approve."

"Do you hate my dress?" she asked. "I know I'm not supposed to ask, but people have been staring ever since I got here. I don't want to offend you."

His eyes darkened from ice blue to cobalt. "You do not offend me."

He slid his hand down to the small of her back, where she had one of her blades hidden. "What's this then?" Harry asked, running his fingertips over the sheath tucked away against the silk of her gown.

"It's my blade," she said. "It's what the sash is for."

"To cover a weapon?" He looked poleaxed for at least the second time since she had met him.

"Well, yes," Mary Elizabeth said. "You don't expect me to go out among the English unarmed?"

He laughed then, a long, deep laugh that shook her where she stood, clasped in his arms. For a moment, she thought that he might miss a step in their whirling dance, but he only managed to draw her closer.

Mary's mouth went dry, and she fished for something to say. "Those girls seem right fond of you for a poor relation."

She nodded to the women scattered over the room, all of whom were staring at Harry as if he were the Second Coming of Christ, ignoring the fat duke in the corner altogether. The bloody English had started dancing at last, and the band had begun the waltzing tune over again, so that there was enough waltz time to go around for everyone. Mary Elizabeth thought that very kind of them and wondered who they were. She would find out before the hour had passed, and make sure they got a decent tip. The Scottish might be tight with their money, but the English aristocracy was miserly.

Harry glanced around as if noticing the women for the first time. He did not seem to notice the band at all. "Jealous, are you?"

She snorted. "Please! Of the likes of them?"

Harry kept smiling. Mary Elizabeth sighed, for she was nothing if not honest. "Maybe a little."

He pulled her even closer, if that was possible in that scandalous Austrian dance. "I'm glad to hear it."

His voice was low, as if someone might overhear him. He leaned close, so that his lips brushed the curls above her ear. His breath was warm on her skin, but for some odd reason, that warmth made her shiver.

"Why?" she asked, sounding breathless to her own ears, and not from the dancing.

"A jealous girl won't mind if I steal a kiss from her later."

Mary Elizabeth rallied then. She reminded herself not to be a fool, leaning back in his arms so that there was a bit more space between them. "We've had that talk, lad. You'll be stealing no kisses from me. I'm your friend, and I'm backing you in this, remember?"

"I remember."

Harry did not look at all deterred by her set down. He was smiling his new, strange smile, the one that made her hot and her innards dance. She frowned at him, hoping he might stop. But he did not. He was smiling at her even as she accepted the hand of the man who came up to her next, dancing with the first mincing fop who asked her.

❧

Harry reminded himself that he had a duty to his guests. He greeted each of them as he passed through the ballroom, allowing himself to be introduced to more marriageable girls than he thought would fit in a house, even *his* house. Harry even deigned to dance with each of them, only once, as was decorous and proper. And all the while he kept his eyes on Mary Elizabeth.

The girl had no use for the English, but she seemed to have no objection to dancing with them. She accepted the hand of every man who asked her, though she seemed to have enough knowledge of etiquette to know not to dance with any man more than once. She seemed to show no particular preference for any of them, but neither did she look his way. The entire ballroom was watching him, speculating on his actions and upon whom he might marry, but the one woman he wanted acted as if he were not there at all.

It was vexing enough to bring his warrior blood up.

Fortunately, fancy dress balls were just the thing to put a damper on warrior blood. The endless promenades, the quadrilles, the country-dances all forced him to behave as a gentleman, the weight of his mother's eye on him all the while. He thought of Mary Elizabeth and of how she had called him an eagle earlier that night. He wished fervently that he might swoop down on her now and carry her away from there.

Escaping his own party was not possible, but he did manage to find a hiding place behind one of his mother's many ferns, so that he might steal a moment to watch Mary Elizabeth in peace.

Her brother Alex found him there but did not simper or fawn, nor did he ask any foolish questions, such as why a man would be hiding from all the lovely women in the room. Alexander Waters seemed a man of few words, but when he spoke, those words were always filled with sense.

"I have kept my promise," Alex said.

"I am grateful."

"You haven't told her yet."

Harry felt the weight of his own foolishness as it settled on his shoulders. "No," he answered. "But I will, tonight."

Alex nodded and did not say anything further on the subject. The two men stood together behind that palm, watching as Mary passed by in the arms of a fool and as her brother Robert danced with his lover, Mrs. Prudence.

"Someone might tell her before you do."

"They might," Harry conceded. "But I doubt she would believe them."

Alex smiled. "True enough."

"She does not have a very good opinion of my countrymen," Harry said.

"No," Alex agreed. "But she has an excellent opinion of you."

Harry did not know what to say to that, so he did not answer. Alex went on, as if Harry had agreed.

"If you wish, you may court her openly. The family will not stand in your way."

Alexander Waters of the Back of Beyond said this as if he were offering a great gift, granting Harry a boon, as if he were the prince and Harry the man with no title and only his mother's connections to recommend him. At first, Harry felt his temper snap, and then he considered. Taken as just a man, with no titles or lineage considered, Alexander Waters was his equal.

Harry did not remind Alex of all that separated him from the woman he wanted. Her family's objections would have been the least of it. He said only, "Thank you."

Alex nodded and fell silent. Harry felt as if he should ask about their traditions, but he could think of nothing polite to ask. So as was his way, he asked something not polite at all.

"So, Waters, which do you prefer? Kilts or breeches?"

For one long moment, silence reigned. Harry

thought perhaps he had offended him—but then Alex Waters smiled.

"Kilts. Without question."

If Harry had had any sense, he would have left it at that. But being a duke had not taught him caution or prudence. He plunged on.

"Don't you find them a bit drafty?"

Alexander Waters raised one eyebrow. "A man doesn't mind that."

"Even in winter?" Harry asked.

"Especially in winter," Alexander Waters replied.

"I think a man might freeze his bollocks off."

Alexander's smile softened then, and his gaze turned to his young, blonde wife, where she was now dancing with his brother on the other side of the ballroom. "That's why it's best to marry, and quickly."

"So my mother keeps telling me." Harry caught the look said mother sent him from across the room. She raised her quizzing glass and peered at him through the fronds of the fern he hid behind. If he had not known better, he would have sworn that she knew what he was saying, even with thirty feet between them and her band from Aberdeen sawing away in the corner.

Alex saw where his gaze was tending. "Duty calls?"

"It does."

Alex nodded. "Forgive me for prying into your affairs. But it seems to me that you must make your own way, whatever others say." The statement stood between them, and then Alex said in parting, "I have a strong mother, too."

He nodded to Harry and wandered off, not waiting

to be dismissed. Harry stood behind the fern for a little while longer, watching Mary Elizabeth dance by as blithely as if she had never kissed him at all.

Thirteen

MARY ELIZABETH ENJOYED DANCING WITH THE English gentlemen who had descended on the duchess en masse, but after only two hours, she was sick of the dances themselves. If she did one more promenade, she would throw a knife, and most likely hit someone. When the band had set down their instruments for a bit of a break, she went over to them with a tray of whisky. She found that whisky lubricated the wheels of conversation with any man she had ever met, and made them more amenable to listening to her.

When she discovered that they were from Aberdeen, she gave a war whoop of joy that made all the English who heard it turn and stare. She waved to Robbie from across the ballroom so that he would know that she was not in distress. "The band's from Aberdeen!" she called to him.

She was working on talking the bandleader into her scheme when Harry appeared at her side. The bandleader blanched and almost dropped his glass.

"Harry, this is Angus. That fellow on the drums

there is Jaime, the man with the fiddle is Bobby, and the gent with the fife is William."

They all bowed to him, and she wondered why they bothered. Each man downed his whisky as if afraid someone was going to take it away from him.

"We were about to begin playing again, sir," Angus said, for all the world as if he were afraid of offending Harry. Mary Elizabeth ignored him as if he hadn't spoken.

"Angus here needs a member of the family's permission to play a song I like. Will you give it to them, Harry? I know you're only a poor relation, but I'm no blood kin to the duchess at all."

Angus choked when he heard that and almost dropped his now-empty glass.

Mary Elizabeth took it from him before he could and collected the rest of the crystal cups from the group. "There's more where that came from, lads. Good Islay whisky my brothers brought down from home."

She turned to Harry then and caught him smiling at her as if she had a smudge on her nose. Had she not been holding the silver tray, she would have swiped at it. Instead, as soon as a footman stepped over at Harry's silent bidding, she handed over the tray and carefully ran one finger across the bridge of her nose, just to be sure.

"All right, Mary Elizabeth," Harry said. "I'd be happy to dance to your tune."

She smiled and was pleased when he smiled back. Angus shifted on his feet to hear a man use her given name, but again, she ignored him. "Just the one song, mind," she said. "I don't want to frighten your English away."

Harry was still looking at her face as if he saw something new there, as if they had not just danced together two hours before. Mary Elizabeth decided not to wonder about it, for the ways of men were strange and a woman might run herself mad trying to decipher them.

"They're not my English," he said. "They're my mother's."

Mary Elizabeth did not understand the distinction, and wondered for a moment if he might be half Scot. She did not have the time to try to puzzle out who on God's green earth his mother was. But the band was tuning up by then, ready to start the new set, and she dragged Harry by the hand onto the middle of the dance floor and lifted her skirt.

"This is a simple reel," she said, "with a lively step. Watch my feet, and see if you might try it."

She moved through the steps slowly, the way she had been taught as a child. When she looked up at him, she found his eyes resting on her calves in their silk stockings.

"Harry, pay attention now. Don't be missish about seeing my legs. You saw them in breeches just this morning."

He looked at her then, and the heat in his blue eyes made her stop dead in the middle of a thought. She almost lowered her skirt and found that she had the strange, unaccountable urge to run away. But Harry acted as the gentleman he was, as he laid his hand on her waist and took her other hand in his.

"I think I see what you're about," he said. "Let's show them how it's done."

The band started playing in earnest then, and all the English around watched as Harry led her through a decent reel with only one misstep, and that one due to her. She found herself flummoxed by his easy ways with her favorite dance and wondered what else he might be good at, besides dancing and horseback riding.

She wondered if he might spar with her at swords and how she might talk him into such a thing. Then she met his eyes, and saw the heat in them, and wished to God in His Heaven that she had not given her word not to kiss him again. For Harry, it seemed, was a man born to be kissed, and she the woman born to do it.

She had little time to reflect on this, for her feet were flying, as were Harry's, and he lifted her in the air at just the right moment without her even having to tell him to. She realized then that he knew this dance, that he had danced this reel before with some other girl, and she found herself unaccountably and unreasonably jealous of whatever woman had been lifted by him in the same way, her skirt in the air and her hair falling around her shoulders, as Mary's hair had begun to fall from its pins around hers.

Mary Elizabeth told herself not to be a fool as Robbie and Mrs. Prudence joined them on the dance floor, taking up the steps, with Alex and Catherine close behind. Mary did not take the time to wonder why she was jealous, and for such a foolish reason, but stepped away from Harry as soon as her feet hit the ground once more.

"Well," she said. "You seem to know this dance without me teaching you. I'm off to find another man to teach."

Harry caught her hand and tugged her close

enough, so that he could speak low in her ear. "Don't go far," he said. "You're eating dinner with me."

She felt her heart lighten suddenly at his kind if oddly abrupt invitation. His eyes were still as hot as blue flames, and they stayed on her face, though the other women in the room were staring at him and preening, trying to get his attention for some reason known only to them.

"All right," she said. "But I'm off to dance now."

"All right," he answered, as if he had seen something in her face that satisfied him, and he let her go.

Mary Elizabeth turned to help the Earl of Grathton learn the steps to the reel. He was a kind man who had danced with her earlier, after she apologized again for attacking him in Hyde Park with her sword. Grathton was a quick study and soon had his own sister in hand, teaching her the reel as well, so Mary was free to teach each man who came forward, wanting to learn. And it seemed every man did.

Catherine and Mrs. Prudence helped with the instructing, but it seemed some of the English wanted only Mary Elizabeth. She obliged them, for they were guests of the duchess and this reel was her own scheme, but she noticed that Harry watched each man who touched her as if longing to cut every man's hand off before it could rest on her waist. When some shallow fop from Hampshire lifted her with a flourish during the final strains of the reel, Harry was at her side as soon as her feet touched the ground.

"That'll do, then," Harry said, for all the world as if he were her keeper. "I'll take her from here, Jefferies. I thank you."

The fop bowed low to Harry as if meeting the King of Sheba, and Mary smiled at him as she watched him scamper off. Then she turned narrowed eyes on the man at her side.

"Don't be rude to the English, Harry. The duchess invited them here, though God alone knows why she invited so many. And don't act like you're the boss of me, for you are not, nor will you ever be."

Harry's blue eyes caught fire when she said that, and he dragged her by the hand behind a massive fern. The dinner gong sounded, and the company began to troop into the dining room, as the duchess had arranged for informal seating and a buffet to be served.

Mary Elizabeth had worked up an appetite with all her dancing, and tried to take her hand from Harry, that she might go and eat. When that failed, and his hand clung to hers like a limpet, she tried to drag him with her and failed again.

"Harry, I'm hungry. Why have you dragged me behind this infernal plant? Let's go and eat."

Harry did not answer her, but drew her close, as if they were going to waltz. She opened her mouth again, to chastise him, when his lips closed over hers, silencing her. His tongue was in her mouth, sliding along her own in the most delicious way, and she found herself clinging to him, the muscles of his broad shoulders firm against her gloved hands, warm through the wool coat he wore.

She tried to draw back from him, remembering her oath. He did not let her go as she expected him to, but trailed his lips down her throat and then up behind her ear, making her shiver.

"Harry, I gave my word not to kiss you," she said, her voice sounding breathless, like somebody else's.

He drew back from her then, and the heat in his blue eyes was warm, but not the sparking flame it had been on the dance floor. "I did not give *my* word, Mary."

"I am supposed to be helping you," Mary Elizabeth said. "I can't help you if you kiss me."

"You help me by letting me kiss you." He kissed her again, as if to demonstrate his point, and she felt herself pressing closer to him, as to a fire in winter.

Just when she was gathering her good sense to protest again, he let her go. He let her catch her breath, as he caught his, and then he took her hand and laid it on his arm. "Let us go and get some braised beef, before the English eat it all."

"You're English, Harry."

"Then trust me when I tell you that my people are gluttons."

He did not speak again, but led her to a table and served her a plate of fine food while a footman brought a glass of wine. All the while, the English were watching them and whispering. Mary Elizabeth wondered idly where the fat duke had gotten to and why the company watched her friend Harry so closely while they ignored their own fancy lord. She tried to set the English out of her mind and eat her dinner, which she had earned, but the sound of their whispers were like a snake's hiss in her ears.

❧

Harry found himself eating braised beef with his Scottish girl, with the whole of the *ton* looking on, and he discovered that—far from feeling annoyed at being the center of attention as he always was in company—tonight, he did not care one whit. He also did not give a fig for anyone's thoughts on his dinner companion, though he could feel the tension rising among the ambitious mamas in the room as they took in Mary Elizabeth in all her red-clad glory.

Dressed as a courtesan, Mary Elizabeth had entertained the guests all evening with her antics. Leading the reel had only been part of it. Every gentleman who had danced with her to have a gander down her low-cut dress had come away half in love with her sweetness and her wit. Mary Elizabeth had also blithely led him around by the nose all evening and was the only one who seemed unaware of that rather obvious fact.

Harry felt his mother's keen eyes on him and knew without a doubt that she would soon be dressing him down for spoiling her party and not picking one of the lovely, sensible girls on offer to court with an eye toward marriage. Harry had no eye for any of them, for he kept both eyes on Mary Elizabeth Waters, the only woman in the room who seemed immune to his charms.

Harry wondered how to go about transforming her feelings of friendship for him to feelings of love. She liked kissing him, which was a good start, but it was not nearly enough. She seemed content to treat him as a sort of distant cousin, one who had a good seat on a horse and was a decent conversationalist. Of course, she did not know he was a duke. Perhaps, if he told her, she would fall swooning into his arms and allow him to take her then and there.

That fantasy lasted for all of thirty seconds. As enticing as it was to think of Mary Elizabeth surrendering to him, opening her sweet arms to him, allowing him to caress her succulent breasts with his lips and hands, he could not fathom a circumstance—any circumstance—under which his girl would swoon.

Which was why he loved her.

The fact that he loved her had come to him all in a rush as he lifted her high in the reel. He had watched her dance away from him, jigging and leaping with every man who came to her, feeling the effects of her smile even from a ballroom away. The knowledge had not surprised him, which was surprising in itself. His love for her seemed to open a door in his heart that he had not realized was closed. Now that it was open, the unbending path of his future seemed not like a burden, but an adventure. Even the path of running a duchy might be a joy for the rest of his life if Mary Elizabeth was with him. With his indulgent protection to surround her for the rest of her days, the duchy was large enough that even a bird as free as Mary might live there. And he could take her North, to her family's seat at Glenderrin, and let her roam the lands there. Not in winter, but in late spring and through the summers, perhaps. Her love for her homeland made him love her more.

Now, he had only to tell her.

"Mary," he said to the woman who held his affections. She ignored him completely, devouring a slice of spiced cake. "I need to speak with you."

She swallowed her bite and reached for her wineglass without looking at him. "Aye," she said. "Speak on."

"Not here. What I have to say is too important to say in company."

She set her glass down then and looked at him warily, wiping her mouth with delicate precision on her linen napkin. "Is that so?"

"It is."

She sighed and leaned back in her chair. "Will I be needing a tot of the whisky for this talk of yours?"

"You might."

"All right, then."

She stood up abruptly, and he had to scramble to stand with her. He felt the mamas in the room turn on him like pointers after a wily fowl. Not wily enough, it seemed, for he had been caught by the woman beside him.

"I've found a nice place for a sit and think," she said. "Come with me, and I'll show it to you."

She started out of the ballroom, and he followed, like a hound at her heels, while the ladies his mother had so thoughtfully invited for him watched their progress, daggers hidden behind their smiles as they tried to catch his eye in vain. Mary Elizabeth had eyes only for her brother Alex, who stood and glared at her as she passed, but she waved him off. Harry followed her out of the room. When his mother met him at the door with raised eyebrows, he simply kissed her cheek and kept walking.

Fourteen

MARY ELIZABETH HAD DANCED HER FILL WITH THE English anyway, so she was happy to escape them. She was less happy to sneak away with Harry, who was clearly in demand among every person present, save perhaps herself.

Not that she did not enjoy his company, because she did, but having him near that night had made her the butt of much English speculation, especially from the women present.

In the hall just outside the dining room, she saw the fat duke again. This time his blue eyes grazed over her as if over a stain on the carpet before he looked away. She felt her stomach clench. When she stopped in midstep, Harry ran into her from behind.

"Mary, what is it?" Harry asked.

She tried to whisper but saw from the stiffness of the Recluse Duke's neck that he'd heard her anyway. "It's the fat duke," she said. "I've been avoiding him for the last three days."

"The duke?" Harry asked. "And you say he's fat?"

"Lower your voice, Harry, for the love of God."

She dragged him into a darkened corridor that led around to a back staircase she had found just that morning. "He's a duke and overproud, but I don't mean to hurt his feelings by calling him names."

"You saw the duke, you say? In the hallway outside the banquet hall?"

"Well, it's his house and his party. But I don't want to see him, and I don't want to talk about him."

"Mary—"

"I mean it, Harry. Enough about the Recluse Duke."

Harry seemed to swallow something foul there on the darkened staircase, but he obeyed her. "All right, Mary. I'll let the matter of the duke rest for tonight."

"We needn't worry ourselves over him," she said.

"No. We needn't. Not tonight."

Harry's nose seemed to delve close to her cheek, and she thought he might kiss her again. Remembering her oath, she dodged his lips and dragged him up the narrow stairs behind her.

She took him to one of her new favorite spots, a sitting room on the third floor that no one seemed to use. She had been there at all hours of the day and night, and had never seen a living soul. The house was large enough that, except for the maid who dusted daily and swept the carpets, that room very well might never see another human being for a year or more.

Mary Elizabeth had seen very few maids in the house, but the house was not kept clean by fairies, so they must sneak about a great deal in order not to be noticed. Mary would have enjoyed a good conversation with a maid or two.

She did not speak to Harry, as he was acting even

stranger than usual, but opened the window and hoisted herself onto the sill without a backward glance. Harry caught her elbow before she could shimmy onto the roof and seek her favorite hiding place behind the closest gable.

"I thought you wanted your whisky," Harry said.

Mary Elizabeth smiled at him in spite of herself, for he sounded so serious. Very few Englishmen took good whisky seriously, as seriously as it had been intended when the first Scot made it.

"I always have my whisky with me," she said, and climbed out onto the roof. He followed at once, having no concern at all for his fancy dress clothes, which made her like him even more.

He did seem to have a fascination with her ankles, however, for she had to raise her skirts in order to step out onto the roof safely, and he did not speak for a long time, staring at them until she got herself situated against the roofline, which for some reason was unaccountably clean, and let her skirts fall back into place once more.

"Does the duchess have maids who sweep the roof?" she asked.

He blinked, settling down beside her but not too close, which made her sorry but also relieved. He had surprised her when he kissed her behind that potted plant, and she had thought perhaps he had gone back on his word to himself for good. It seemed now that he had not. Mary Elizabeth believed in a man keeping his word, but in this one instance, she was a little disappointed. She so liked kissing him.

"Maids on the roof?" Harry asked, a bit distracted still. "I wouldn't think so."

"Hmmm." Mary Elizabeth hummed a little to herself in agreement as she reached into the hidden pocket of her skirt and drew out her flask. Every dress she owned, even the fancy gowns, had a pocket in it despite her mother's rants about fashion, because she could not live without her whisky near to hand.

Harry laughed to see her silver flask. "Did you steal that from your brother Alex?" he asked.

She gave him a pointed look. "I do not steal, Harry. You should know that."

He wiped the smile from his face, but in the moonlight, it seemed to be dancing still in his eyes. "I'm sorry, Mary. Of course you don't steal. Why on earth do you have a flask?"

"I always carry at least one sharp blade and a flask of whisky," she said, offering it to him before she had taken the first sip. He was her guest on this roof, after all, and by rights should have the first tot.

He drank deep, as a man ought, but grimaced when he had swallowed it. She laughed at him. "I'll teach you to drink good whisky," she said. "You'll be surprised how quickly you come to love it."

"My father tried to teach me," Harry said.

He sounded musing, as if his mind was far away. He did not look at her but up into the stars above them, points of fire in a field of dark indigo. Mary turned her face away from his and drank them in, taking in their beauty as she listened to his voice.

"My father," Harry said, "was a hard man. And he believed that all men ought to be. He said that the first thing a man should know how to do is hold his liquor. He kept me up all night once when I was twelve, feeding me brandy until I was sick on mother's rug and had to be put to bed."

Mary Elizabeth did not like to speak out against the dead, so she said nothing of what she was thinking of the old bastard who had treated Harry that way. Instead, she asked, "So you hate spirits?"

"I do. I drank occasionally when I was down at Oxford, but it was never the thing. The other blokes did not seem to care if I drank or not, so I stopped."

"Why would anyone care if you drank?" Mary asked before she thought. Harry quirked a brow at her and she said, "Ach. The English."

"Aye." Harry did a fair approximation of her brogue, and then reached for her flask to take another sip of the Islay. This tot seemed to go down better, and he smiled at her as he returned the flask and watched her drink from it.

She took her own tot, then slipped the flask back into her pocket. A little whisky was warming and a gift from heaven. Too much whisky made for sore heads and an inability to rise in time for a decent ride come morning.

She did not want to bring it up, but she felt honor bound to remind Harry why they were on the roof at all, while the duchess's house was filled with guests who Harry should be seeing to. Even a poor relation must have social duties, surely.

"Harry, we've both had our whisky. Tell me why you brought me up here."

"You brought me." He sidled closer to her, and Mary felt the sudden urge to back away. But the roof was steep, and Harry was her friend. She tried again.

"Harry, what did you want to ask me?"

"I want you to marry me."

❦

Mary Elizabeth did not seem impressed with the moment, momentous as it was. She looked at him with a squint of suspicion, and then she said, "You've no head at all for whisky, do you?"

"I do not, but that does not signify. I asked you a question, and I would like an answer."

"Harry, you asked a daft question, and I will not answer it. Only yesterday you told me in the picture gallery of this very hall that you could not marry me, nor even kiss me. And now you are on a roof, asking me to wed. Are you mad, then?"

"I am," Harry said. "I am mad for you." He knew he was making a botch of it, and he wondered if he should start over, begin again by telling her that he was the duke, lord of all he surveyed, a man who could keep her happy and warm and set up with fine whisky and sharp blades for the rest of her life.

"Harry, we had better go in. You're not in a fit state of mind to be speaking with a lady."

"I am in the best state of mind to be speaking to you. You're the only lady I want to speak with. I love you. You are wonderful and funny and filled with life. Marry me, and make me the happiest man ever to walk these halls."

Mary Elizabeth sighed and moved to the window. He caught her by the skirt to hold her with him and she glared at him over her shoulder. "Let go, Harry. You're foxed from two tots, and I am going in."

"No," he said. "I'm not foxed. I swear."

They both slipped a little then, down the slanting roof. Harry caught himself with his slippered foot against the gable rim, and caught her to him so that she would not slide any farther. The heat of his body seemed to speak better for him than his words did, for Mary Elizabeth raised her arms over his shoulders and clasped her hands behind the back of his neck, burying her fingers in his hair.

"You're talking daft, and I won't hold you to it come sunrise, if you won't hold me to my promise until then either," she said.

He was not sure what she meant until her lips were on his, her luscious breasts pressed against the front of his dress coat. He could feel the heat of her body through the layers of clothes that separated them and knew that if they had been in a bed, or even safe on a rug somewhere, he would have drawn her skirt up and taken her right there. As it was, his foot lost its purchase, and they slid a little farther down the roofline.

Harry would not have cared, but Mary Elizabeth was pulling away from him.

"Harry, you daft man. Let me go before we fall."

He obeyed her at once, though his body was screaming to touch her again. Separated from her, he looked down and saw that, indeed, they were actually in peril. He turned his mind from his lust to try and figure a way to get them both safely off that roof without sliding down it any farther when he saw Mary draw out a knife from God alone knew where and slice off the gold sash that had displayed her breasts all evening.

It seemed there was a good deal more material than just the section that made her breasts stand out so beautifully. At least six feet of cloth of gold was in her hands, which she deftly secured to the roof with her dagger, placing the blade between two shingles and burying it deep in the wood beneath.

"This is what comes of canoodling on a roof," she said almost to herself as she cut away the ribbons on her dancing slippers with a second blade and kicked them off, so that they went sliding down the roofline and into the garden below.

Harry expected her to cry a little at their loss, as any other woman might have done, or perhaps simply to cry from fright at the danger they were in, but Mary Elizabeth Waters did not cry. She shimmied carefully out of her stockings, letting both stockings and garters fall down the same path as her shoes.

"Is that a yes, then?" Harry asked.

"Shut your fool mouth, Harry, and let me work."

She used her now-bare feet to gain purchase on the roof's slippery surface. She took hold of the gold sash and yanked it hard twice, as if to test its strength.

She spoke to him then as to a simpleton, slowly and clearly. "Harry, I am going to climb back up to the window. I need you to stay here and not move. At all. Do you understand me?"

He found himself smiling back at her. "Yes, ma'am." He snuck a hand toward her supple calf and ran his fingertips along it, almost meditatively, reveling in the softness of her skin.

"Harry, I swear, if we live to get off this roof and tell this tale, I may very well kill you."

"No, you won't."

She expelled her breath between her teeth and swore before climbing very carefully, one step at a time, back toward the window. For the first time, he saw how dangerous it was for her to move along the roof at all. He cursed himself roundly, first for coming out there as he had done so often in his childhood, and second, for not shouting the house down as soon as they were in danger, so that he might have kept her safe until help arrived. She would have been ruined, but she would have lived.

Now Harry was left watching her hoist herself up, using the gold sash tied around her waist and her feet and hands as purchase as she stabbed her second dagger into the roof, over and over again, drawing herself closer to the window.

She made it within only two minutes, but it was the longest two minutes of his life. She cut the sash from her and sent it down to him, where it fluttered against the house gaily, like some courtesan's forgotten banner.

"Climb up, Harry," she called. He ignored the sash and climbed up without it, his muscles remembering how to move along that roof as he had when he was a child and desperately in need of escape. He got close to the window and saw that Mary was brandishing a fire poker at him.

"Grab on!" she said.

"Mary Elizabeth, step back before you brain me with that thing."

She frowned, but looked past him at how far the drop was below and tossed the poker behind her.

Harry reached the window in a trice and managed to pull himself into the house. He lay on the floor beneath the window, breathing hard, as Mary Elizabeth stood over him like the Wrath of God.

He sneaked one hand out to curl around her bare ankle, and she stepped back, out of his reach.

"Enough canoodling for one night, Harry. We almost died, for the love of God."

"What better time to canoodle?" he asked.

He raised himself up on one elbow and found that the room was spinning, whether from the whisky or the daredevil climbing or both. He lay back down and hoped it would stop.

Mary Elizabeth squatted down next to him, close enough to look into his face, but far enough away that she could dodge his hands if he tried to reach for her. He realized how badly he had botched his proposal as she frowned down at him—and how drunk he actually was on only two shots of whisky.

"I'm going to bed, Harry. I am going to forget this nonsense, and so are you. I'll see you in the stables come morning. First person to get to Sampson is the better man."

Harry tried to speak, but she shushed him with her lips. The kiss was soft and almost glancing, but it made his body catch fire. He lay still on that rug long after she had gone, trying to calm himself. He needed to drink some water and sober up, so that he could propose again tomorrow.

He still needed to tell her that he was the duke. But perhaps he should get her to agree to marry him first.

One hurdle at a time.

Fifteen

MARY ELIZABETH WAS UP EARLY THE NEXT MORNING, dressed in breeches once again, as she could not bear to wear one of her riding habits. She rose even earlier than she was used to, for she was worried about Mrs. Prudence, who had headed off in the night, to flee in secret to help her long-lost brother in London. When Robbie caught wind of it, there was sure to be hell to pay and only Mary left behind to pay it. She wondered, and not for the first time, what it was about her brothers that made their women want to go scampering off in the dead of night.

Mary Elizabeth could not keep her mind on her friend as she ought, for she found that she was also troubled by Harry's proposal. She was troubled because, in spite of all good sense and the fact that he was as drunk as a lord when he asked her, she wanted desperately to say yes.

Had she lost the last of her mind, to think even for half a moment of marrying herself to an Englishman?

Her mother would be pleased if she did. That was the reason her mother had banished her from

Edinburgh and from home, after all, that Mary Elizabeth might make a "decent" match among her mother's countrymen and stop riding free about the Glenderrin lands and fishing in the burn.

The sting of her mother's rejection was as sharp as it had been six months before. It was more of a knife in her side, hampering her breath, which was why she tried not to think about it. But now that Harry had offered for her, giving her mother what she wanted, Mary Elizabeth felt sick to her stomach.

She wanted her mother to accept her as she was, with no husband standing beside her.

She also wanted to go home. If she married Harry, she would only be allowed home now and again, for a Gathering one year out of three perhaps, before the children started coming and she was tied to hearth and home for the rest of her life, as all women had been since Eve.

She did not even know if Harry owned his own home, as he spent all his time wandering around the lands and house of the duchess, a poor relation with little to recommend him save his connections. Not that Mary gave a fig for money or its trappings, but she had seen the way the crofters lived, and she knew that, as strong as she was, she would not raise her children to such a life. Even with her own money, if Harry had no pot of his own to piss in, she would turn him down and mean it, for their children's sakes if not her own.

Mary Elizabeth resolved to speak to Harry about it, to find out first if it had not been the whisky talking last night and he had meant what he said.

But she knew him to be a serious man and was certain that he had proposed to her in earnest. Which meant she needed to think, and hard, before she gave her answer.

She could not quite believe she was considering his proposal at all, but there it was. For she loved him, God help her.

She came to the stables and saw Charlie standing about idle, looking as pale as a gray ghost. "What's the matter?" she asked at once.

"It's Sampson," the boy answered. "He's gone missing."

She felt her stomach sink, for here it was, time to face the music that Mrs. Prudence had left her to.

"Missing my arse," Harry said from somewhere behind her. "My best horse has been stolen, and by your Mrs. Prudence, I might add."

Mary Elizabeth had to draw a breath to unpack all the nonsense in that sentence before she could respond. Harry was looking fine that morning, wearing no coat with only a fancy waistcoat over his white linen shirt. The waistcoat was a dark-blue silk, and it brought out the blue of his eyes.

She told herself not to be a fool and to attend to the matter at hand.

"Prudence Farthington is not a thief!" Mary Elizabeth said with a bit more emphasis than she intended, but Harry was standing there, looking smug and kissable, which made her want to smack him.

Robbie came into the stables then and stood listening to Harry as if the man were talking sense.

"And yet," Harry said, his voice a calm, smug

contrast to her own vehemence, "my finest horse is missing, and Mrs. Prudence, too, is gone."

"Your horse? *Your* horse, is it? Just because you feed him oats does not make Sampson yours."

"And yet my name on the bill of sale does."

"Excuse me," Robbie said, trying to piece together some sense from their conversation and no doubt failing, as she was. "May I ask, are you referring to my Lady Prudence?"

"Yes, Robbie." Mary Elizabeth turned her back on him dismissively, about to round on Harry again, but Robbie's hand on her arm stopped her.

"And she stole Sampson for a morning ride you say? Dear God, that horse will kill her."

"She did not steal him," Mary Elizabeth repeated slowly, trying to tamp down her temper. "Mrs. Prudence borrowed him, which is a world of difference. No doubt she's gone to save her brother. She will return Sampson, right as rain, as soon as she comes back from London."

Robbie took that in and turned as gray as the boy Charlie, who now had hidden behind a stall door. She thought for a moment that her brother might faint at the thought of the peril the woman he loved had put herself in, but before she could help him, Harry stepped in and placed his hand on Robbie's arm.

"You'll take my second-fastest horse," Harry said. "He's not as swift as Sampson, but then Sampson isn't likely to run his best for a stranger. She only has a three-hour lead on you, at best. You'll find her. The north road only runs two ways."

"I thank you," Robbie said. "Your Grace might

send a carriage behind me. Once I find Mrs. Prudence, we won't be able to ride all the way to London on horseback."

Mary Elizabeth felt a headache beginning at the back of her neck at the thought of Robbie running off after Mrs. Prudence on horseback with yet another borrowed ducal coach trailing behind him.

Harry smiled, clearly delighted with himself. "Consider it done. You'd best get on. You're losing daylight."

For Robbie to fall in with Harry's nonsense did not surprise her, but it did add fuel to her inner fire.

"*Your Grace*, are you?" Mary Elizabeth said, so spitting mad that she almost could not hear herself think. "I'll be damned if you are."

Harry's smile did not waver as Robbie climbed onto Merry's back and rode away. "Language, Miss Waters, please. My stable hands have delicate ears."

"Your hands? Since when have you acquired such delusions of grandeur?"

"Your Grace." The sober, calm head of the stables, Bart, came to Harry's side, cap in hand. "We've prepared the traveling chaise to send after them."

"Excellent."

Mary Elizabeth's head was pounding so now that she could barely see at all. The world was upside down with madness, and no mistake—if Harry was a duke, she was a horse's ass.

❦

Harry had not meant to tell her so abruptly, as almost an afterthought. But she knew now, and he could see by the mulish expression on her face that she was not happy about it. Mary Elizabeth did not look to see where her brother had gone but still stood staring straight at him.

"Duke, is it?" she asked.

"It is. Henry Charles Percy, Duke of Northumberland, at your service."

She stared at him for a long moment, and the silence made him hopeful. Then she grunted, adjusting the knife that she wore at her belt.

"Going to skewer me with that?" he asked.

She looked down at the pearl-handled blade as if she had forgotten it was there. "No," she answered. "I don't sully my steel with the blood of liars."

Harry felt the sting of that and watched her as she walked away from him. She mounted the first horse that came to hand, a blooded sorrel that he had bought for breeding purposes. But neither Mary Elizabeth nor the horse cared a tinker's damn for the fact that the mount was not there to be ridden. She did not even wait for a saddle but leaped onto the horse's back and took off at a canter. Harry knew he had to follow her, but he dreaded the strip she was going to tear out of his hide.

The Duke of Northumberland stood alone in his own stables, for his grooms had hidden themselves away, most likely to avoid his wrath as well as Mary Elizabeth's. But Harry knew well that he had no one to be angry at but himself. He stood in silence, feeling chagrined, when he noticed that he was not alone at all but that her brother Alexander was with him.

"Don't fret too much, Your Grace," Alexander

said. "Mary has a fierce temper, but she'll see reason soon enough."

"I love her," Harry said, almost inanely, as if the knowledge were a burden he did not know how to set down.

"Of course you do," Alexander said. "She's a love-able girl. Just don't get near her blades until she's had time to cool off."

"I only saw one knife," Harry said.

"That's because that's all she wants you to see. She never wears less than three."

Harry stood in silence, contemplating that fact as he listened to the birdsong outside the stables. He wondered what it would be like to marry a woman who wore no less than three knives on any given day. He contemplated such a fate and started smiling.

"You have your heart set on her."

Harry met his eyes. "I do."

"Well, you're a good man, though you're a duke. As I've said, you have the family's blessing. But be careful with her. She's certain that the Highlands are all she's after."

"She's all I'm after," Harry said. "If I have to follow her all the way to the end of the earth, I will."

Alexander Waters cocked a brow at him. "You might have to at that." He swallowed hard. "Your Grace."

"Call me Harry."

Alexander smiled then, and this time, it reached his eyes. "All right then. I'm Alex."

The men shook hands as if meeting for the first time. Harry was shocked at the familiarity, but only a little. He had been around the Waterses a week now, and they were wearing him down. His ducal pretensions were all but dormant where they were concerned.

His mother would be horrified.

Sixteen

MARY ELIZABETH DID NOT LIKE HERSELF WHEN SHE lost her temper. She did not like the headache that came with anger nor the feeling of chagrin once her anger had passed. She did not know why Harry had decided to lie to her, why he was intent on putting on airs that were ridiculous and did not suit him, but she knew that she had to get off the ducal lands before she sank a blade into him. So she took the road back to the village.

It would have been faster by boat, if she'd had one, but as she had only one borrowed horse, a sweet-natured creature whose name she did not know, she took the gravel-lined road all the way to the inn that sat closest to the ducal lands on the north side of the village green. She had no rope to tie her horse with, so they brought her breakfast outside, that she might eat it under a shade tree and keep her eye on her mount. The even-tempered beast cropped the grass at his feet, happy to be out in the summer morning, for all the world as if he was content to leave the palatial stables behind and never look back.

Mary Elizabeth felt a deep and abiding desire to ride him all the way to Aberdeen, but she knew that the thought was a foolish one, so she put it aside.

She wondered what was wrong with Harry, if perhaps, along with being kin to a duke, he had wandering wits. She did not understand why he thought lying to her about something so important as his identity, even for a moment, would be a good idea. If pretending to be a duke was his idea of a joke, she didn't like it. But Harry did not seem to be the joking kind.

She knew so little about him, about who he truly was and where he really came from. But that truth did not change the fact that she loved him.

God help her.

She had ordered two breakfasts, for she knew that he would not be far behind her. She was not sure how he did it, but he always seemed to know where she was headed before she did herself. And she was right. In less than ten minutes after she had started sipping at her breakfast tea, Harry rode up on his own mare, which wasn't saddled either.

"My cattle will get spoiled, riding only bareback," he said.

She felt her teeth clench as he referred to the ducal horses as if he owned them, but in deference to the peace of the morning, she said nothing. She wanted to eat her breakfast before she spoke with him again.

He seemed to sense something of her resolution, or perhaps he was just a man of few words, for Harry sat beside her and ate the oatcakes and honey that the serving woman brought. They ate in companionable silence, and Mary Elizabeth congratulated herself on her calm. She even began to think that she might be able to ask him why he was lying to her in a civil way when he reached into his waistcoat pocket and drew out a gold guinea to pay for their repast.

"For the love of God, Harry, leave off this nonsense about being a duke," Mary Elizabeth groused. She took a deep breath and tried to hold on to her temper, even as she felt it rising.

"What do you mean?" Harry asked, as innocent as any babe.

"Tossing gold to folk as if you are the lord of the realm. I like you fine without *duke* in front of your name."

Harry smiled and Mary Elizabeth looked away, keeping her gaze focused the dregs of her tea. "You like me fine, do you?"

"Aye. So there's no need for theatrics," she said. "As angry as I am with you, I still like you fine."

"I know you like kissing me."

Mary Elizabeth felt his gaze on her skin as if he were touching her. She rose to her feet and vaulted onto the back of her new horse. She nudged him with her knees, but the beast did not seem interested in running so much as he was interested in hearing what Harry had to say next. Mary Elizabeth cursed silently under her breath.

"I'm sorry you're annoyed that I'm a duke, Mary, but it will grow on you. Give it time."

"Bah!" Mary nudged her mount again, and this time he remembered himself and took off as if he had been shot from a canon. Harry gave pursuit on his own mare, but even when he pulled up beside her, she refused to slow down and continue their idiotic conversation.

"You think I'm lying about being a duke," Harry said, for all the world as if it were she who had lost her mind and not he who was acting the fool.

Mary Elizabeth got down off her horse and led him to a stream that ran clear close to the road. She let her horse drink his fill, then filled her empty flask. The cool water calmed her temper as she sipped it before handing it to Harry without a word. He looked at it in surprise for a moment, then drank after her.

"I don't want to discuss it," Mary Elizabeth said.

"Will you discuss it with my mother?"

"I've not met your mother."

Harry laughed at that, and his laughter was a warm bit of sunlight that crept up her back, up her neck, and into her hair. His laughter was as warm as the touch of his hands had been on her cheek the night before, and she shivered.

"You take tea with her every day, Mary."

Mary Elizabeth frowned. "You mean you want me to take this nonsense to Her Worship."

Harry's lips quirked. "If by *Her Worship* you mean the duchess, I do."

Mary Elizabeth sighed. She had no desire to shame him in front of his relations. She opened her mouth to tell him so when his lips descended on hers out of nowhere, stealing her breath. Her reason fled soon after it, and she found herself pressed against his chest, her breasts squished between them in the most pleasurable way as his hands began to roam down her waist to her backside. She reveled in the feel of his hard body against hers, a body that was getting harder by the moment. She shivered and knew for the first time why it was that foolish women threw away their virtue for a farthing. Those women had been kissed by a man like Harry.

When his hands caressed her backside in her buckskin breeches and drew her hard against him so that she could feel just how much of a man he was, cold reason returned like a wave of ocean water, drowning her foolishness and his in one great wave of fury. She jerked away from him and began to writhe, trying desperately to work herself free of his embrace.

It seemed Harry's mind could not quite catch up with what she wanted, for his body wanted something else altogether. Mary Elizabeth's traitorous body wanted the same thing, and she cursed him and herself roundly, this time out loud so that he might hear.

At the sound of her vehement blasphemies, Harry let her go as if she were a snake that had bitten him.

"All right, then," she said, trying hard to rein her temper in. Her new horse could hear the fury in her voice, and he stepped closer to her, getting between her and Harry. She did not chastise him for his insolence, but let him shield her. More to the point, she let him shield Harry, for her blades were close under her hand and she was afraid she might skewer the man she loved with one of them.

"I'll go to Her Worship and I'll tell her the nonsense you've been spouting. And when she confirms that you are naught but a damned fool who plagues me with lies, we'll talk again."

Harry's eyes narrowed, for it seemed she had reached the end of his good nature. "If you were a man, I'd call you out for that."

"Don't let that stop you."

Harry reached for her again, but she leaped onto her horse and turned his head toward the house. "I'll turn you over my knee before the sun has set," Harry promised.

"The devil you will," Mary Elizabeth responded, feeling her blood rise up at the fact that the man was still challenging her, even now, when any other man of sense would have given up his lies and backed down long ago. She would have respected him if he was not playing her false by handing her a pack of children's tales, when she had seen the fat, old duke with her own eyes. She would have to break him of this nonsense, here and now, if she had any hope of getting decent children out of him once they were wed.

She nudged her mount and he ran, as he was born to do, but they had not gone twelve lengths before Harry had pulled up beside them, keeping pace. "My knee, Mary," Harry growled at her. She almost laughed at his idiocy. She would have laughed had she not been so angry.

She wondered how on God's green earth he could make her want to kiss him and kill him all in the same breath. She breathed deep and set her eyes toward home. She would settle this with the duchess first, and then she would deal with Harry.

Mary Elizabeth found that her ire did not dissipate on the ride back to the duchess's house, as it usually did. Given even five minutes, Mary Elizabeth often lost the thread of an annoyance in the throes of something more interesting—practice with her rapier or a good knife-throwing session. But even the beauty of that summer day did not stop her from cradling her fury at Harry next to her heart. Did he think her some kind of simple fool, that she would immediately believe him to be a duke simply because he asked a stable hand or two to go along with this ruse?

And more importantly, why would he think such a ruse necessary? Did he think her the low sort of woman who would be persuaded to marry based on a man's title and position in the world? What kind of woman would that make her if she were?

Mary Elizabeth had the answer to her question almost with her next breath: an Englishwoman.

By the time she reached the fancy house, she did not even trouble herself to take her horse to the stables and rub him down as she ought to do, but left him with a waiting footman, who clearly had no idea what to do with him. She strode into the house, and Billings let her in. For once, the butler did not raise an eyebrow at the sight of her breeches.

Harry was close on her heels, and when the staid butler followed them into the front hall, looking concerned, Harry said, "That will be all, Billings."

"Leave off your airs, Harry, for the love of God."

Billings looked a bit shocked at her outburst, but then, he often looked shocked when she was in the room, so she paid him no mind, but went to find the duchess. She did not have far to look, for she heard the soft sound of feminine laughter coming from the front parlor. Mary Elizabeth strode in without knocking, and Harry stayed with her.

"Your Worship, Harry and I have a matter between us that you need to settle." Mary Elizabeth spoke without preamble, then noticed that the ladies sitting all around in their soft silks and muslins stared at her as if she were a Highland barbarian down from the mountains to kill them.

Mary Elizabeth sighed and hoped the duchess did not write to her mother about this incident. Still, in for a penny, in for a pound. She bowed to the ladies, making a decent leg, she thought, in her buckskin breeches, but the ladies in the room only tittered, as the duchess raised her quizzing glass.

"Do you, indeed, Miss Waters?"

She placed undue emphasis on the word *miss*, and Mary Elizabeth knew that her mother would be receiving a letter about the latest of her antics. However, she did not back down, as the damage was already done, and she still did not have her answer.

Catherine was in the room and looked as pale as death. Still, luck was with Mary Elizabeth, for it seemed to be a ladies' tea, and her brother Alex nowhere in sight. He would have bundled her out of there, tossing his coat around her like some kind of avenging angel, as if none of these people had ever seen their own legs before, much less hers.

She saw the fat duke then, standing at attention in his finery against one wall. She turned her back on the duchess and faced him squarely.

"Your Worship," she said to him. "I want a bit of something settled here, and you're the man to help me. My friend has been playing at being a duke this morning, but I know that you are the laird here."

The fat duke squinted at her, and then he blinked. He did not speak nor did he move, but a deep-puce color rose from his tight, white linen to suffuse his face. Mary Elizabeth thought for a moment that he might die of an apoplexy then and there.

It was the duchess who spoke, as it seemed the fat man had swallowed his tongue.

"That is my under butler, Miss Waters. Pemberton the Younger. I believe you have met his brother, who runs my house in Town."

The women behind her tittered but fell silent when Harry turned a glare on them. Mary Elizabeth felt her own color rise and her stomach churn. If this fat man was some butler or other, who was the duke?

She looked at Harry, and he winked at her. She did not give him the satisfaction of acknowledging that, turning her back on him to face the duchess, her stomach sinking. "I beg your pardon, Your Worship and Pemberton," she said. "My mistake."

The fat under butler did not speak even then, but bowed solemnly, before tripping over the doorjamb on his way out of the room.

The duchess spoke to no one in particular. "Pemberton has a bit of trouble with doors, as he is terribly nearsighted. But he keeps the clocks in perfect time. No one has as fine a touch with watch-works as Pemberton does."

The duchess had not yet lowered her quizzing glass and still had it trained on her. Mary Elizabeth felt a fool for mistaking a butler for a fine duke, as well as a bit chagrined for charging into the middle of a ladies' tea like a bull run mad, but she wanted her answer and she could not wait another two hours for it. Her future was at stake.

She also hoped that the duchess might give Harry the dressing down of his life, and that she could watch.

She looked at the tea cart and saw that those well-dressed women had not touched the chocolate cream cakes on it. She wanted one of those as well.

"I wonder if we might speak alone," Mary Elizabeth said.

It was not the duchess who cleared the room but Harry. He spoke only once, using a particularly arch tone, as if it were these ladies and not she who had offended him. "Leave us," he said, as if they were all his servants and as if he lived to be served.

Before Mary Elizabeth could take him to task for rudeness, the women rose en masse and filed out of the room. Catherine was the last to go. She cast one glance at Harry as she might at a marauding lion, but came close enough to him to kiss Mary Elizabeth's cheek.

Catherine did not speak but squeezed her hand in silent sympathy before she left. Mary Elizabeth was not sure she needed sympathy, but she welcomed Catherine's sweet gesture all the same.

Since playing lord of the manner seemed to amuse Harry, Mary Elizabeth did not give him the satisfaction of correcting him this time but let his false airs stand. Especially since they had been so effective in clearing the room.

She turned instead to the duchess, only to find that august lady's sights set on him. "Harry, what are you playing at, behaving with such a lack of decorum among the ladies?"

"They'll love me for it," Harry said.

Mary Elizabeth rolled her eyes, and the duchess harrumphed.

"It's my house, Mother."

"And those are your guests," the duchess replied, dropping her quizzing glass. It fell against her large bosom, dangling from its gold chain. Mary Elizabeth listened to their words and started to feel sick.

Harry was not paying her any mind at all, but had gone over to the tea tray and poured himself a cup. "Not for much longer, I hope."

"Another week, you blasted boy. Put that cold tea down. I'll ring for a fresh pot."

She did not bother to rise to go to the bell pull next to the fireplace, but instead rang a little silver bell that sat in pride of place on the tea tray. Billings appeared within the moment, as if by magic, carrying a new teapot wrapped in a cozy.

Harry thanked him, then poured for himself first, and then a second cup with cream and two sugars for Mary. He handed her a cup and a plate with two chocolate cream cakes on it. She sat down with them both and thanked him automatically. Her stomach was beginning to roil in earnest.

"Your Worship," Mary Elizabeth said at last, "is this man your son?"

The duchess blinked once, for all the world as if Mary Elizabeth had asked something extraordinary. But the old lady rallied almost at once. Taking a sip of tea that Harry had just freshened, the duchess said, "Why, of course he is."

Seventeen

HARRY WAS NOT SURE WHAT HE EXPECTED WHEN HIS mother made that revelation, but whatever it was, he did not get it. Mary Elizabeth did not shout the house down. She did not reach for her whisky or for one of her blades.

Instead, she simply sat, looking somewhat ill. She finished her sip of tea and then set the cup and her cake plate down. "God have mercy," she said.

"No doubt He will," his mother answered, wriggling her fingers at Harry, who obediently poured more tea.

Mary Elizabeth was silent a long while, and he watched her digest the information he had been trying to impart to her off and on all day. He felt the last of his anger at her slipping away, like smoke from a fire that had long since gone out. He found himself sorry that he had lied to her in the first place. He should have revealed himself on the very first day, if not on the very first evening he had kissed her in his mother's rose garden. He felt like a cad and a bounder as he sat there, watching the woman he loved come to grips with the fact that, in some small ways, he had betrayed her.

"It's good news, Mary," he said at last.

She met his eyes, and he saw the heat leap in the maple depths of her gaze, revealing the tinge of green along her irises. "It's good news that you've been making a fool of me, mocking me behind my back to God knows who all?"

Just like the strike of flint on steel, Harry felt his temper take light. He was in the wrong, so he tried to hold on to it. He managed, but barely.

"Mary Elizabeth, I think we have things to discuss in private."

"Well, take yourselves elsewhere," the duchess said. "You've run my guests off, but I am staying here until I finish my tea."

When neither Harry nor Mary Elizabeth looked to her, the duchess simply pursed her lips and ate another cream cake. She settled back against her cushions, as if to watch a show. Harry felt a blush begin to rise along his cheekbones. He did not want to air his romantic laundry in front of his mother.

"I've not been mocking you," Harry said, deciding to deal with one of his women at a time.

"Well, you're the only one, then," Mary Elizabeth said. "Those women will spread the word as far as Aberdeen and all the way to London that Mary Elizabeth Waters is such a country bumpkin fool that she does not know a famous duke when she sees one."

"Why do you care what those women think of you?" Harry asked, perplexed, his temper starting to fade.

Mary Elizabeth blinked, and he saw that there were actually tears in her eyes. "I don't," she said. "But my mother does. Damn and blast you for a lying cad, Harry."

She was on her feet and out of the room before he could rally long enough to reach for her hand. Harry sat in silence with his mother for a long moment, feeling like the stable dirt that clung to the bottom of his favorite riding boots. The only sound in the room was the ticking of the gold clock on the mantel that had been a gift from Louis XVI of France.

"You'd best settle with that one, and quickly" was all his mother said.

Harry rubbed his eyes, suddenly feeling tired and much older than his thirty years. "I'm trying, Mother. I'm trying."

"Try harder. I've word that her mother will be arriving within the week."

Another wild woman from the North. Harry did not think the household could handle two of them. Perhaps Mary Elizabeth only needed an hour alone to cool down. He sighed and rose to leave, kissing his mother's cheek.

∽

Harry watched Mary Elizabeth all through dinner from his lofty place at the head of the table, and he saw that she did not eat much of the glorious repast his mother had laid on. The handsome footman, Sam, tried repeatedly to discreetly urge more food onto her gold-rimmed plate, and the last time he tried with the candied fruit was the only moment all evening when Harry saw his girl smile.

He stayed back with the gentlemen as was seemly, for in his pursuit of Mary Elizabeth, he had let every social duty lapse. He found he had as little to say to the men who were his peers as he did to their women, save for Alex Waters, who talked a bit about the fur trade from Canada, bringing all discussion in the room to a dead stop.

"It's how we make our living in the back of beyond," Alex said.

The gentlemen did not seem to know how to respond to this, so Harry took that moment to suggest that they join the ladies in the drawing room forthwith. He saw Alex meet his Catherine close to the tea trolley, but as he scanned the room, he could not find Mary Elizabeth anywhere.

His mother raised her quizzing glass and took him in, then raised one eyebrow. He knew that she wanted the matter of his marriage settled before the girl's mother arrived. Harry looked to the settee in the middle of the hubbub, where Lady Ashleigh had saved a place for him. The good lady, a bit bolder than the rest, patted the cushion beside her with a wink.

Harry bowed to her and then to the company, saying that he needed to see to a horse that was foaling in the stables. He could not think of a better lie, and since he was a duke, and they were all there to hunt him, they let him go with only a few murmurs of regret. The women were disappointed, but he could tell by the way they looked him over like a stallion at market that the ruder he was to them, the more they loved it.

Strange creatures, women.

His mother simply laughed at him behind her hand as he left the room. He set aside all thoughts of his guests and the social demands that would be required of him as soon as Mary Elizabeth agreed to be his. He thought instead of a happier threat he had made—a promise that, this time, he would actually keep.

⤜∾⤛

Mary Elizabeth was not sure how she made it through the ten-course dinner. It seemed to go on for ages, with each course more cumbersome than the one before it. She had seen Alex frowning at her and Harry staring like a galoot, but only the attentions of a decent footman had made her feel a little better, and he was paid to pay attention to her.

God have mercy, but she was losing her mind.

She had watched all night as the women simpered at Harry, as the men tried to impress him, as all but Alex and Catherine treated him as if his every utterance were spun in gold. Mary Elizabeth could not stomach another minute of the farce and had slipped away from the ladies right after dinner. She hid now among the books of the library, knowing that no one, namely Catherine or Alex, would think to look for her there.

She could give a fig for reading on the whole, since she preferred action to sitting, but this library was the best she had ever seen, rising two stories, with a balcony that ran around the top of the room, accessible by a staircase. It was high above that she found some wonderful books on fencing translated from the French, and another leather-bound tome on the tempering of steel for sword making, that one translated from the Spanish. Mary Elizabeth took one moment to wish she had learned a bit of languages, that she might study the originals, but she lost herself in the world of Toledo steel folding almost at once, and did not look up until the door slammed below her, making her jump.

She peered down, expecting to find Alex glaring, but she discovered Harry smiling up at her instead.

"Go away, Harry," Mary Elizabeth groused. "I'm reading."

"You can keep reading once we're done talking," he answered. "Come down."

"I've nothing to say to you."

"Well, I've a great deal to say to you."

Mary Elizabeth did not respond, save to sit back in her leather wingback chair and raise her book to cover her face. She tried hard to focus on the matter at hand, namely the temperature that was required of a blaze to begin the first step in melting good steel, when she heard the tapping of Harry's heels on the staircase.

"Mary Elizabeth, I don't mean to be rude, but we've talking to do, and I've a promise to keep. The sun has not yet set, but it will within the hour."

Mary did her best to ignore him even then, but he was standing close beside her chair, looming in that delicious way of his, and the scent of warm sandalwood seemed to enfold her like an eiderdown quilt. She drew the scent deep into her nose in spite of herself, and found that she loved no other scent so well on earth. Why did the man she loved have to be a blasted Englishman? And why did he have to be born with a ducal coronet affixed to his brow like the mark of Cain? Mary knew better than to ask such questions, as they had no answer.

"What promise do you mean?" she asked. "And what has the setting sun to do with it?"

"I promised to turn you over my knee by sunset, and I am losing daylight."

She set her heavy book down in her lap and laughed long and loud at that. She did not finger her weapons, nor did she even reach for their handles. Harry might be an Englishman and a blighter, but she would not need her weapons to ward off an attack from him.

"Harry, I am reading. I am not in the mood to play games with you. Go on then, and find one of your fawning ladies to chat and canoodle with, because I'll have none of it."

"I don't want one of my fawning ladies, as you put it. I want you."

Mary started reading her book again, or at least tried to. Harry still loomed over her, and she found herself listening to his breathing, waiting for him to go away. That was, until he plucked the heavy book from between her hands as if it weighed nothing, tossing it onto a nearby table.

"Be careful of that," she said. "Books cost money."

He did not answer her, lifting her into his arms. He did not carry her like a lady, however, but tossed her over his shoulder like a sack of flour. Mary Elizabeth saw only his nicely rounded backside peeking from beneath his tailcoat as he carried her down the staircase to the library below.

"Have you lost your bleedin' mind?" she asked when she got her breath.

He did not answer her until he had tossed her onto a sofa. "Indeed, I have," he answered. "It's the only logical explanation for why I am in love with you."

"In love, are you? Is that why you've been pretending to be someone else since the day I met you, and why you carry me about like a parcel?"

"Mary Elizabeth Waters, listen to me speak, because I am only going to say this once. I am sorry I did not tell you of my title. But my true name is Harry, and I gave it to you from the first. I am a man who loves roses and horses and sailing. I have never lied to you about anything that matters, and I never will."

Mary glared up at him as he stood over her, still looming. "You apologize?"

"I do. Deeply, and with all my heart."

Mary Elizabeth stared into the blue of his eyes. She looked at him for a long moment, and decided to let her ire go. She knew in that moment that part of her anger was at herself, for being so blind and foolish that she had not noticed a duke when he was standing as big as life under her nose.

"All right," she said. "I accept your apology. And I hope you will accept my apology for calling you a liar."

"I will."

Still, Harry did not sit down beside her, and she began to wonder what he was about.

"There is still the small matter of you impinging on my honor, however."

She smiled. "Your honor?"

"Indeed. Today, on horseback, you called me a liar. I must have satisfaction."

"Shall we fight at rapiers, then?" she asked hopefully.

"No," Harry said. He was not smiling back. "I will not call you out. I will, however, turn you over my knee here and now."

She laughed out loud at him for the second time in ten minutes. "You will, will you? Good luck to you, boy-o."

She was off, sliding away from him as quick as a whippet. Harry must have been surprised by the fact that a woman was running away from him, for he did not catch her arm, though he reached for her. She had almost made it to the door when he was on her, turning her to face him, his large body pressing her back against the walnut surface.

Harry did not speak to continue their argument, but moved away from her a little almost at once, staring down at her with an arrested look that she had never seen on his face before. Mary looked down then at where his gaze was tending, thinking that perhaps he was taking a gander at her bosom, as he so often seemed to do. Instead, he was looking at the dirk she had drawn without even knowing she had done it.

She saw that the point was tilted as she had been taught from a child, the wicked sharp blade pointed just so, ready to slip between his ribs and plunge into his lung. She opened her fingers at once and let the blade drop. As close as she and Harry were standing, the blade still had room to fall between them. The dirk hit the carpet with a dull thud, and she forced herself to meet Harry's eyes, knowing that the censure she would find there was well deserved.

"I'm sorry, Harry. It's instinct. I guard my life the way your beefeaters guard the Crown Jewels. I do not think. I act."

She watched as the hard planes of his face gave way into a small smile. Harry drew her close, his hands running over the small of her back, where he found her second blade and tossed it to the carpet. "Your brother says you wear at least three. Where's the other one?"

Mary Elizabeth felt her heart begin to pound like the hooves of a runaway horse. She told herself to calm down, for the love of God, but she could not seem to catch her breath.

"On my thigh," she answered.

She watched the blue of his eyes turn to a deeper shade still, and then his hand began its slow descent down the length of her waist, over her thigh, and to her knee, where he started to draw her skirt up one slow inch at a time.

Eighteen

MARY ELIZABETH LEANED CLOSE TO HARRY, ALLOWING him to explore beneath her skirt as if he had the right. Which she supposed he did; she had given it to him without thinking, just as she had drawn her blade. Perhaps she was the one who had run mad.

His callused fingertips were hot on her bare thigh. He found the knife tied to her garter and pulled it free, leaving its sheath and her garter intact.

Harry let the last of her weapons fall beside the other two, while he smiled down at her, his azure eyes searching her face before sliding down her body. She shivered as he drew his hand away, letting her skirt fall back into place.

"I don't know if I got them all," he said. "I think I'd better search a little further."

"Where else can you search?" Mary asked, her breath almost gone.

"Let me think a bit, while you think on this."

Harry's lips were on hers. First skating across her throat and then her cheek, they came to rest on her mouth, and she felt her innards melt in a delicious puddle, like a brick of chocolate turning to soft candy over the fire. His tongue played with hers a moment, while she felt his hands glide down her sides and her buttocks, and back up to cup her breasts. That was when she pulled away.

"Harry!" she said. "Behave!"

He smiled a wicked smile, and she felt her stomach flutter. "But that's no fun at all."

He kissed her again, but this time his hands moved away from her derriere and her breasts and stayed at her waist, drawing her close so that she might feel his manhood burgeoning behind his breeches. Mary Elizabeth shuddered, but not in horror, as any proper girl would have done.

So this was what lust felt like. She had always wondered, and now she knew.

He locked the library door behind her—whether to keep her in or to keep Billings out, she did not know, but she let him do it. For the second time that night, Harry picked her up in his arms, but this time he cradled her against his chest. She laid her ear against his heart and listened to it beating. She was so enthralled by the warmth of his body wrapped around hers that she did not notice what he was up to until they were sprawled once again on the only comfortable sofa in the room, with her sitting on his lap.

"I promised you that I would take you over my knee before sunset," he said.

"I think you missed your deadline."

Harry laughed and kissed her, but when she would have lost herself in the taste of his lips, he drew back once more. "I love you, Mary Elizabeth Waters. Before I touch you again, I want you to know it."

"I know it already, Harry. Now kiss me again."

He not only kissed her, but slid his hands along her bodice again, until his fingers were delving along the modest scallop of her décolletage, as if seeking some treasure in her bosom that she had not known was there. Mary Elizabeth felt her stays tight around her ribs, lifting her breasts beneath her silk gown as if making them ready for his touch. She shivered in his arms, and he let her draw back from him, his blue eyes on hers.

"I won't let you spank me like a child, Harry," she said, trying to gather her wits even as she worked to catch her breath. He smiled, and the warm wickedness of it made her want to move closer to him, good sense be damned.

"You are many things, Mary Elizabeth Waters. A child is not one of them."

His callused thumb made its way past the barrier of her stays. The feel of the callus against her peaked breast made her almost swallow her tongue. She shivered with pleasure, and tried to rally her reason. Part of her only wanted to feel and to let reason go, but Mary Elizabeth was far too stubborn for that.

"You'll not be spanking me, Harry," she said again. This time her voice sounded faint in her own ears. Harry's thumb left off playing with beneath her gown to slide down her side. His large hands turned her over, so that she was lying across the sofa they sat on, no longer sitting on his lap like a hoyden, but sprawled on her stomach, her posterior over his lap. She raised herself on her elbow but did nothing else to bring herself up. She looked at him and saw the heated gleam in his blue eyes, and she almost forgot what protest she was going to make.

Almost, but not quite.

"Don't be daft, man" was all she could manage to say.

"Oh, I'm well past daft, sweet Mary. I've crossed over into pure madness."

He caressed her bum, not once but twice. She could feel the heat of his callused palm through the layers of silk and muslin she wore. She wondered if Alex would burst in on them and kill Harry where he sat, for she was not the only Waters to go about armed. She prayed that no one would try the locked door, and that no servant would find them, peeking at them through one of the hidden doors in the wall.

She did not move to get away, nor did she give herself over to his caresses completely. Mary Elizabeth steadied her voice.

"You should let me up now, ye wee, daft man."

"Wee, am I?" His thumb moved along her jaw then, and she turned her head toward it, taking his thumb into her mouth without thinking. She drew it behind her teeth and laved it with her tongue. The taste of his skin was sweet even there, and he drew his breath in and held it.

"Stop, Mary," he said.

She did not answer but drew his thumb in deeper. His breathing seemed more erratic of a sudden, and before she knew it, her mouth was empty and she was on her back, with a lot of hulking Harry looming over her.

"We must talk, Mary." He sounded as if his fancy linen were strangling him. He knelt beside the sofa, his hand running over her body again and again of its own accord, as if trying to memorize how she might feel if they were alone in the dark.

"I don't want to talk," she said, telling him only the truth. If they talked, they would have to deal with the fact that he was a duke and that she would rather throw herself into the sea and drown than tie herself to such a mess of burdens for the rest of her life—or so she told herself as she gazed into the blue of his eyes. His face was not the face of some English duke, but of the man she loved.

God help her.

"I don't want to talk, either."

Mary Elizabeth felt his hand on her stocking then, running up her leg, beneath her gown. His fingers caressed her garter and the sheath that was still tied to it, but they did not stop there, rising to her thigh, bringing her skirt along with it.

"I'll have to call you out, Harry, if your hand goes any higher."

He laughed at that, as if he did not believe her, and his hand kept moving. "I'll risk it, Mary."

"Swords at dawn, then," she quipped, just to prove she could still think. But then his hand slipped between her thighs, delving beneath her smallclothes in some clever, wicked way she had not thought of before, and she could think no longer.

"Mary," he said. "You can kill me tomorrow, but let me kiss you tonight."

∽

It seemed that his lady had lost her tongue somewhere, and the will to use it. At least, she was no longer able to speak, which Harry took for a good sign. She simply smiled at him and tousled his hair, which he took for a bad one.

He moved quickly, drawing her knees up to his shoulders, so that she gasped. But she trusted him, for she spread her legs wide, as free as any courtesan. But he knew that she was no courtesan, nor even a wanton woman. She was a girl who trusted him with her life, along with her virtue. He reminded himself of this, even as he committed himself to not being a gentleman.

"I love you, Mary Elizabeth Waters," Harry said. "I want you to remember that."

She blinked at him, her curls fallen from their pins to frame her face against his leather sofa cushion in shades of honey, bronze, and gold. Harry leaned forward and kissed her lips, almost losing himself in their sweet softness. But he knew what he was about, and he drew back, only to lift her hips, shifting her smallclothes out of his way.

"I also want you to remember this."

Harry bent down then and pressed his lips to the softness of her inner thigh. She gasped and tried to scrabble away, but his weight held her down. He did not speak, but put his mouth on her secret places, until she fell still beneath him, and stopped trying to get away.

The woman he loved shook as his mouth covered her, and when he looked up, his eyes traveling the length of her body, she met his gaze.

"Harry, you are daft. What in God's Holy Name are you doing down there?"

He almost laughed out loud at that, but knew his business and that he needed to get down to it before she kicked him off her altogether. He went to work over her then, and in less than a minute, she was writhing, her hands in his hair, this time not trying to get away but to get closer.

"Harry, I love you," she said, and then she spasmed beneath his mouth, her thighs clamping over his ears. He could still hear her labored breathing and her gasping moans, which she tried to stifle in the sofa cushion, and failed.

Finally she laid back, her thighs falling open, her breathing labored but slowly beginning to calm. Harry sat up then, his hands running over her body, feeling very like the cat in the cream.

She smacked him once, not very hard, on his shoulder, which was all she could reach. He felt himself smiling and knew that he was going to enjoy pleasuring this woman for the rest of his life.

"So, Mary, is it pistols at dawn, then?"

She smacked him again, but this time she spoke. "Don't be cheeky, ye wee bugger. What the devil did you do to me?"

"I'd say that was fairly obvious. You were there, beneath my mouth the whole time."

As he watched, his lady blushed, pushing herself away from him and drawing her knees together. She also drew her dress back down, but Harry left his hands on her calves. He was not willing to surrender that ground, not all of it. Not yet.

She stared at him, and he knew that she would not quit giving him that arch look until he answered her.

"Mary Elizabeth, I gave you pleasure with my tongue."

"I believe your thumb was in there as well," she corrected.

He raised one brow and sat beside her on the couch, drawing her close to him, his lips pressed to her temple. "I believe it was."

At first she did not yield, but before he had taken his next breath, she had settled against him, tucked into the crook of his arm, her soft curves splayed against his body like the answer to every prayer he had ever spoken—and some he had not been wise enough to make. Harry kissed her then and lingered over her lips a long while, until he felt his own desire rising to a peak. He knew that he had to let her go, but he did not want to, not yet.

"Come sailing with me tomorrow," he said.

"Hmm?" She was drowsy and did not seem to be heeding him.

"On the ocean, tomorrow morning. Come sailing with me."

"What of your house full of English?" she asked.

"They are not invited."

She smiled at him then, raising her face to his to kiss his cheek. "All right, Harry. I'll go sailing with you. Just don't bring Billings along at the last minute."

A feeling of warm triumph rose in his breast, but he hid his smile in her hair. "As you say, Miss Waters. The illustrious Billings will stay here."

Nineteen

MARY ELIZABETH HAD A GOOD DEAL TO THINK ABOUT once Harry let her go. The first thing she thought of was how lovely it would be to invite him to her room, so that he might truly ruin her on one of the purgatorial ducal settees. Or better yet, on the comfortable bed.

She had come to know her man a bit over the last week, and she knew him well enough that had she managed to get him alone in her room and naked, he would take it as a declaration on her part. Harry would be certain she meant to marry him, and that would never do.

She was simply not duchess material.

She thought of the women who had scoffed at her during the ball and after, and she thought of their mothers, their fathers, and their English kin, all of whom would sit in judgment of her for the rest of her life, muttering behind her back about how the nobody from nowhere had appeared out of the back of beyond and stolen a young and handsome duke off the marriage market.

Mary Elizabeth swore under her breath and brandished the fire iron, as her sword was too long to fight indoors. She put herself through her paces but was no calmer afterward. A duchess would have to spend time in London, time at court, God help her, and be a support and a succor to Harry while she did it.

Mary Elizabeth cast the fireplace poker back on its stand, listening to it clatter against the spotless brass, swearing again, this time a bit louder.

She put herself to bed in the vain hope that she might sleep, but when she lay down, all she could think of was Harry's mouth and how he had used it on her lips...and other places. This was certainly a more delicious line of thought, but she still did not sleep. With her candles blown out and her fire banked, she watched as the moon rose and crossed behind the windows, casting milky light over her borrowed bedchamber. She watched as the room turned dark, and then light again only a few hours hour later and knew she must get up.

She was down in the breakfast room alone, hoping that the other ladies would not rise so soon. She was right in that, for even Catherine was not there to greet her, as Alex no doubt had not let her out of bed yet. To her surprise, the duchess joined her, though she did not think the older lady ever rose before noon, guests or no guests.

Mary Elizabeth watched as Billings poured hot chocolate into a demitasse cup for Her Grace and did the same for Mary. "I'd like a mug of that, if you please, and a bit more milk poured in," Mary Elizabeth said.

Billings raised one eyebrow but rang for more chocolate and more milk, while the duchess eyed her over her own bit of porcelain.

"My boy is going to offer for you," the duchess said. "I want to know what your answer will be."

Mary Elizabeth fidgeted in her chair, tearing a bit of brioche apart between her fingers. The duchess stared pointedly at the ruined roll, and Mary Elizabeth ate the shards of it without butter, wondering where the porridge was.

"I just discovered he's your boy," Mary Elizabeth said. "I am not sure I want to make him mine."

The duchess did not turn her blue-eyed gaze away from Mary Elizabeth, but mixed the new chocolate with milk when it came and poured it herself. Decent mugs had not been brought, but slightly larger porcelain cups had. Mary Elizabeth made do, wishing she might spike hers with a bit of Islay to soften this conversation but knowing that it was far too early to exercise such a remedy. She was a Scot and no English sot. No whisky until afternoon, unless she was in peril of her life and needed the whisky to dress a wound. Her father had taught her that.

She thought of home with a desperate pang, and as she always did, she fervently wished herself there, wading through her own streams, fighting back her own bracken, fishing her own waters, left alone and in peace. But for the first time, the vision was an empty one, because Harry wasn't in it.

Mary Elizabeth would have cursed but did not, only because she feared sending Billings into an apoplexy. Instead, she drank her chocolate, noting that it was quite fine, though her mood was not.

"I've more for you to consider before you make your decision," the duchess said. "I warn you that I will not let you dally and trifle with my son. He is a hard man, but he has a soft heart. If you break it, I will break you."

Mary Elizabeth smiled for the first time that day and raised her chocolate cup in a salute. "Agreed, Your Worship. I will have a care with Harry's heart, and he will no doubt have a care with mine."

Billings filled her cup while it was aloft, and Mary Elizabeth thanked him for the kindness before turning back to the matter at hand.

Before she could speak again, the duchess asked, "So you love him then?"

Mary Elizabeth did not flinch. "I do."

"But you will not marry him."

"I don't see how I can and remain myself. If I try to be the woman you English want, Harry won't want me anyway."

The duchess smiled then, and tossed a bit of vellum across the creamy expanse of the table. The older lady sat back, smiling into her chocolate, for all the world as pleased as if Mary Elizabeth had given a different answer. Mary did not touch the vellum, for God alone knew what it was. She had never known paper to bring good news, and vellum, expensive as it was, usually brought worse. Still, she fingered it as she met the duchess's eyes.

"I will be honest with him, always," Mary Elizabeth said. "I will have a care for his heart. But I do not know yet what my answer will be."

The duchess smiled at her as if she could see into her soul and knew what her answer was already. Mary Elizabeth sighed and lifted the vellum, wondering what fresh hell it contained. When she stripped away the outer cover, she saw her mother's slanted, glancing hand. Mary Elizabeth dropped it as if it were a hot coal. She had had no word from her mother since March, when she had first been sent away.

"Open it, girl. Don't be missish."

Mary Elizabeth shot a glare at the other woman, duchess or no, but she did pry open her mother's seal, a band of heather with a buck's horns inside it. The missive contained no greeting, no salutation, and no signature. It held only one line, terse but to the point.

If you can't bring the duke to offer for you, I shall.

Mary Elizabeth felt the sting of the one-line note as if it were a slap on her cheek. Her appetite gone, she rose to her feet before the footman standing by could even pull out her chair.

"Your mother is on her way here," the duchess said, eyeing Mary with something that looked like sympathy. "It seems she has decided to no longer leave your matchmaking to others and is coming to see to it herself."

"My mother prefers her own opinions to anyone else's."

The duchess smiled a little. "Don't we all."

Mary Elizabeth moved to the door. A footman opened it for her, but before she crossed the threshold, the duchess spoke one last time. "Choose for yourself. Stand up to her, but don't let her ruin your choice. If Harry is what you want, take him, and damn them all."

Mary Elizabeth smiled grimly but did not answer. She met the man in question in the hallway before she had taken three steps.

"Mary, you're not wearing breeches. I believe I am shocked."

Mary Elizabeth made to walk right by him, but Harry caught her arm. "You're meant to go sailing with me."

She faced him then, not able to muster even the hint of a smile. Her mother's letter lingered like a bad taste in the mouth, the vellum burning a hole in her hand. She crumpled the letter, but still felt its sting.

"I'm not fit company for the dog kennel, Harry, much less a fancy duke."

He drew her close, heedless of the footmen standing by and the guests who might any moment come traipsing down the staircase to find them standing together. "I'm no duke with you, Mary. I'm your friend."

She met his eyes and saw that he meant what he said. No one had ever stood with her against her mother, not even her da. If her family would not stand with her, she could not expect Harry to do so. But his friendship was a salve on her pride, and on her heart, even so.

"Let's have that sail, then. If you'll let me onboard in a skirt."

"I prefer it."

She laughed, in spite of her overwhelming feeling of darkness. Harry's blue eyes seemed to gleam with mirth, but beneath that was concern. She did not want to talk about her mother's note, nor what her mother's intentions were for her future. Mary Elizabeth found that she did not want to think at all. Perhaps some time on the sea would be good for that.

⌘

Harry did not know what was wrong with his girl, for she had been smiling when he left her at the door of her room the night before. She was not smiling now.

Mary Elizabeth picked up a heavy stone on the way to the dock, and instead of casting the stone into the sea, she took a ribbon from her gown and tied the rock inside a letter she was carrying. As soon as he had her in his sloop and the sail raised, taking in the wind, she cast the rock and the letter together into the sea.

"What was that?" he asked her.

"Ill news that needs must be cast away," she answered him. "My mother is coming."

"Is that bad?" Harry asked, feeling like a bit of a fool. "Do you not like her?" He had heard of girls and their mothers being at daggers drawn, but he had never seen it for himself, as he did not have a sister.

"I love her," Mary Elizabeth answered him, looking grim in spite of the sunshine on her face. "She tears at my heart as no one else can."

Not for the first time, Harry was humbled by this woman's honesty. He wondered if he could ever match it if he knew her for a hundred years. He could try, but it was in his nature to keep his own counsel, and his father had beaten the truth into him that a duke never showed weakness, not before a woman, nor anyone.

Harry wondered if he could learn to see simple honesty not as a weakness, but as a strength. This woman, at least, deserved nothing less.

"I am sorry she hurt you."

She did not answer him, but looked out to sea, the wind in her face, teasing the hair out of her braid.

Harry trimmed the sail to take them into shore. He owned an island not far from home, and he was taking her there to get away from his houseguests, so that he might enjoy her company alone. He knew that he should have brought her brother Alex along on their sail, or even her friend Catherine, but when it came time to set off for the docks, he hadn't done it. He told himself that while they were alone, he simply wouldn't touch her again. At least, not until he had convinced her to marry him. He wondered, should he ask her there, on the sea, with the sun shining on her golden hair? Before he could, she had leaped out of the boat and into the shallows, wetting her skirt to the knees. He jumped off after her and helped her pull his light teak boat into shore.

"This is a fine craft," Mary Elizabeth said. "I am not allowed on my family's ships anymore, but I love the sea. I have loved it since I was a child."

The crashing waves helped them bring the skiff onto the beach, and Harry pulled it away from the tide line. He took a burlap sack out of the hold, which contained their lunch of bread and cheese.

"I will teach you to sail, then," Harry offered. "You are welcome on any ship I own."

She smiled at him, and the maple brown of her eyes shown with that familiar hint of green around the irises.

Harry stood looking down into her face, knowing that no matter how many years he shared with her, he would never grow tired of looking into those eyes and watching their color change. Mary Elizabeth did not go farther up the beach, nor did she look away, but she set her hand over his heart and leaned up and kissed his cheek.

"I promised your mother that I would have a care for your heart," she said. "I must not break it."

"You won't," he said.

She looked at him, her fingers caressing his cheek where his whiskers had already started to grow in from his morning shave. "I will do my best not to bruise it," she said, "but I am not sure that I can marry you yet."

"I'll wait," Harry answered. "I'll wait until Doomsday, if I must."

"You must secure the succession and have a son." She answered him with his mother's argument.

"Bugger the succession, and damn the duchy. A cousin can have it. I would rather have you."

Mary Elizabeth did not believe his declaration. He would not have believed it himself, if he had not made it. But his pulse was steady and his mind sure. He knew himself. After thirty years, he damn well should. This woman was his future, and his future mattered more than his mother's wishes, more than the pressure the king and his cronies might bring to bear. He was the king's cousin, though a distant one, and His Majesty took a sporting interest in his well-being. Damn the man for an interfering ass.

"I was not allowed to fight in the war," Harry said suddenly, speaking of the thing he had never mentioned to another soul, the shame that he had done his best to forget. He had failed at that, as at so many things, and had come home to grieve his failure—until his mother brought Mary Elizabeth here to draw him out of the fortress he had built around himself. Harry knew that he would never be the same again. Mary Elizabeth might leave him on the morrow, but he had changed for knowing her, and for the better.

Mary Elizabeth could not hear his thoughts. She was focused on the words he had spoken and frowned. "Who can stop a duke from doing anything?" she asked.

"His kin," Harry answered her. "The king. He was Prince Regent in those days. And, ultimately, the Duke of Wellington. He refused my service, not once, but twice."

"Were they all daft?" she asked, scoffing at English foolishness as she so often did. But this time, her censure had a keener edge, and he knew that she would defend him against Wellington, even against the king himself.

"Show me where these self-righteous bastards are and I'll run them through."

Harry laughed and drew her close, so that her soft hair tickled his chin as he held her against him, his cheek resting on her braid. Harry lifted her chin then, and kissed her, knowing that he should not take advantage of her again, but not being able to resist the soft pliancy of her body against his own.

Mary Elizabeth kissed him back, but would not be distracted from her ire. She leaned away from him. "These English bastards told you not to fight because you are a duke?"

"Yes," Harry answered her. "I am an only son, and the duchy has been passed from father to son, unbroken for eight hundred years."

Mary Elizabeth looked more thoughtful then, and less angry. "My God, Harry. You must marry. I cannot be the one to break that chain, even if it is a line of English."

Harry pressed her close to him, feeling his body respond to her nearness as it always did, as he knew it always would. He did not speak of the things he would like to do to her down on that sand. He did not want to continue speaking of his duty and his honor, and all the burdens that came along with them. Instead, he kissed her cheek and drew her by the hand farther up the beach, away from the tide.

"We'll eat," he said. "We'll enjoy the sunshine of this beautiful day and forget mothers and princes altogether."

He tossed a blanket down for them to sit on and meant to draw her onto it with him, but she stood still, staring at him, as if trying to solve a riddle that eluded her. "All right, Harry" was all she said, as she sat down beside him and opened the sack to find their bread and cheese.

Mary Elizabeth leaned close to him then, handing him a bit of food, and her lips brushed his of their own accord, opening over him as if to devour him. "I love you, Harry. We'll forget the rest, if we can."

Harry felt as if his heart were a seabird that, caged all its life, had only now just taken flight. He kissed her back, but gently, so as not to frighten her with his ardor, if such a thing was possible.

"That is all that matters, Mary. You'll see."

Though she did not look convinced, she did not argue with him either. For blessed once, he accepted her silence as a temporary victory.

Twenty

HARRY HAD NOT KISSED HER ONCE ON THEIR JOURNEY back to his house, not even when she had leaned close to him on the skiff. He had pressed his lips to her temple when she had asked him how long he thought it would take for her mother to reach them from Edinburgh, but after that, he had not touched her but to hold her hand. She wished he had, for his mouth was the most beautiful piece of distraction she had ever beheld, and she might have used a bit of distracting.

She had no idea how much distraction she needed until she returned to the duchess's house in time for tea and found her mother waiting for her.

Mary Elizabeth stood, with her braid bound to the nape of her neck like a farrier's daughter, her pink gown wrinkled and smelling of salt from her afternoon at sea. She wondered to herself idly why she had never acquired the sense to change her clothes when coming in from outdoors. Her mother had tried to make her learn that small lesson for years, since she was a child. The lesson had not taken, not even among the fancy

Lowlanders in Edinburgh. It did not take now, among the English elíte in the duchess's parlor.

There was one bit of blessing, however. The Englishwomen who had come hunting Harry were not in evidence as Mary Elizabeth faced her mother down. They were off on the terrace, being entertained by some young cousin of Harry's, a bright, young girl who seemed at ease among them. Mary Elizabeth supposed that was as it should be, since the girl was among her own people. She remembered what that ease was like, when she had been home among her own in Glenderrin.

She wished herself there now, as her mother took in her dishabille, from the top of her braid with its escaping curls, to the toes of her muddy boots. Mary Elizabeth felt Harry shift at her back, before he stepped forward and sketched a decent ducal bow.

"My lady of Glenderrin, welcome to Claremont."

Mary Elizabeth watched as her mother smiled at Harry, the warmth of her eyes betraying little of the simmering anger that waited just beneath that smile's surface. Harry was a smart man, though, for he was not taken in by it. After he kissed her mother's hand, he returned to Mary Elizabeth's side, as if to stand between her and whatever storm her mother's anger might unleash upon her.

Mary Elizabeth loved him well, and never so well as in that moment. But this confrontation had been a long time in coming, and he could not shield her from it, nor from its aftermath, no matter how many coronets he offered her.

It was his mother who spoke. "Harry, be a dear

and leave us alone for a bit. The ladies have a bit of catching up to do. They have not seen each other since March."

Harry touched Mary's hand once, low down and close to her side. He did this swiftly, in an effort not to be seen, but both the ladies present saw him do it, for they had eagle eyes. Harry did not notice this, however, for his eyes stayed on Mary Elizabeth's face. She wanted to kiss him, there, in front of both their mothers, and toss a bit of defiance in both their faces: her mother's, for breaking her heart, and his, for helping her to do it.

But Harry had nothing to do with this fight and, truly, his mother did not either. So Mary Elizabeth did not kiss him but smiled at him instead. "I will see you at dinner," she said.

"I will escort you in."

He left her there, much against his own will, it seemed. He bowed once more to her mother and nodded to his own, and left, the door shushing closed behind him as Billings pulled it to.

Mary Elizabeth crossed the room to the tea tray and poured herself a cup. She added sugar and a bit of milk, pleased to see that her hand did not shake. Though all she wanted to do was cast the tea in her mother's face, she took a sip of it instead, before lifting a sugar biscuit and placing it neatly on the saucer beside it.

She sat down in one corner of the sitting area, with her back to the French doors and the beauty of the day beyond. Mary Elizabeth ate the biscuit, every crumb, though she tasted none of it, the mass of it turning to sand in her mouth. She swallowed it down and finished her tea. All the while, her mother stood still, staring at her.

"I see that with all the money I sent for your upkeep in London, none of it went for a decent gown."

The first shot over the bow went wide, as her mother had meant it to. Her ladyship was simply warming up, as Mary Elizabeth well knew. Getting her range, as a gunner might say.

The duchess shifted on her settee and cleared her throat. "For God's sake, Anna, sit down. How can a woman take a second cup of tea with you looming about like Athena watching over a battlefield?"

Mary Elizabeth's mother smiled again, this time with more genuine warmth. She did sit and even accepted the cup that the duchess refilled for her, though she did not drink from it. Mary Elizabeth set her own cup aside and fingered her dagger beneath her gown, though against her mother, she was unarmed, as always.

"The duke seems quite attached to you," her mother said. "I had been given to understand that he has not yet offered for you. Since taking you out alone without a chaperone this afternoon, has that situation changed?"

Mary Elizabeth did not think of what her answer should be. She did not plot or plan, for plotting and planning was not part of her nature. She was an honest girl and an open one, though that honesty had never been appreciated by her mother, nor was anything else about her for that matter. Mary Elizabeth felt the sting of that truth in her heart, as she always did, but this time, it was followed by the salve of another truth.

Harry cared for her and would no matter what her mother said or did. And the love of Harry Percy, duke or no, was no small thing.

"Harry has offered for me," Mary Elizabeth said.

Her mother's shoulders relaxed, but only a little, as she sipped a bit of her tea. She did not have long to recline against the cushions of her stiff settee, however, for Mary Elizabeth went on.

"He has asked me, but I have not answered him."

Her mother's eyes fastened on her again, and the august lady set her teacup down. Mary took in the beauty of her mother's face and wondered if that was where her own beauty had come from. Her mother seemed more hard planes and angles than Mary had ever been, in spite of all her exercise and knife throwing. Mary Elizabeth tried to remember a time when she and her mother had not had their men as a buffer between them. Even that last dark day in Edinburgh, Alex and Robbie had been there. And now they were alone, sitting with a stranger, with only a tea cart between them.

Her mother's coiffure was perfect, as it always was, her curls smoothed into obedience, caught up at the nape of her neck in a French chignon. Her blue eyes were as brilliant as polished sapphires, in spite of the anger that lurked in them now. Her jaw was too genteel to be clenched, but it did hold a line of tension—tension that Mary Elizabeth had put there.

For the millionth time in her life, Mary Elizabeth wished that her mother had a different daughter, one who wore muslin and danced prettily, who ate dainty cakes and never walked out with a gentleman, much less rode to hounds, hunting deer. But, as her old nurse was fond of saying, if wishes were horses, all men would ride.

Mary Elizabeth loved her mother, but she knew with unwavering certainty that she was herself, and no other. She never could, nor ever would, be any mincing, quiet, obedient girl. There was some freedom in this, as she sat and looked at her mother, and let her hopes for reconciliation go.

"I'll go dress for dinner, then," Mary Elizabeth said, making her curtsy to the duchess, who sat in silence, for once without one blessed thing to say.

Her mother rose when she did, and the blue of her eyes pierced Mary Elizabeth, cutting her to the heart, as it always did. Mary did not waver, but faced her down, certain for once that she was in the right. Or if not, if she was in the wrong yet again, there was nothing to be done for it.

"You will give him your answer tonight," her mother said.

Mary Elizabeth squinted at her, as if a narrowed gaze might change the view. It did not. Her mother was as beautiful as she ever was, and as remote as a distant mountain that Mary would never climb.

"I'll answer him when it suits me, Mother."

She curtsied once more to the duchess and walked out before her mother could say anything else. She almost expected her mother to follow her, to rail at her, even though they were in public, even though the fancy English were close by on the terrace to hear. But of course, her mother did not. Mary Elizabeth stepped out into the hall alone, only to find Billings there, ready to close the door to the duchess's sitting room behind her.

Mary Elizabeth looked around the hall, hoping for some reason she could not fathom that Harry might be there, waiting for her, though of course, he was not. He loved her, but he was a duke with a houseful of guests, and had better things to do than loiter in a hall, waiting for the likes of her.

Mary Elizabeth took herself upstairs to change her gown, and to have a bath, that she might soak away her depression in one of the many ducal bathing rooms.

Harry loitered about in the hallway, ignoring Billings's inquiring gaze, trying desperately to hear what was being said in the sitting room beyond the stout oak door. He was just thinking of walking out along the terrace and trying to listen from the glass doors, or perhaps at one of the windows, when his only friend, Clive, appeared from abovestairs, sliding on one hip down the last three feet of the polished banister, landing like a cat on booted feet, swaggering as he winked at Billings's disapproving stare.

"And what is this I find? The great Duke of Northumberland standing about like a footman in his own hall? Harry, come and give a man a hug, and a drink, for the love of God."

Before Harry could answer him or hit him, Clive Owain, son of a small baronet from Wales, hugged him tight and then let him go. They had met as schoolboys at Harrow, and had been fast friends ever since. Harry had watched Clive's back among the evildoing sons of the elite, and Clive had watched Harry's whenever they went down to London for a bender. Harry was never much of one for benders of any kind, but Clive had always managed to get him to unbend, if only a little.

Harry smiled at his friend and thought how lovely it was that he would not have to send for him to stand up as his best man. Where such a nonsensical thought had come from when Mary Elizabeth had not yet consented to be his, Harry was not sure. But he had it none the same, and the joyous sense of well-being that went with it.

"Billings here tried to make me come in by the servants' entrance, but with the house filled to the rafters with Scots, it seems a mere Welshman goes barely noticed."

Billings did not glower, but his face became impassive, the closest to a glower he ever gave. Harry thanked Billings and took his friend by the arm, dragging him along the corridor to the library before his mother heard that he was about. Not that anything slipped past the duchess, not even the arrival of Harry's only undesirable connection.

Harry closed the door behind them once they were safely tucked away in his library. He poured Clive a whisky, neat, and watched as his friend smiled appreciatively as he drank it and poured himself another. Harry sprawled on the only comfortable sofa, thinking of how he had made love to Mary on it only the night before and when he might get her back onto that sofa, with a good deal fewer clothes, once they were engaged.

"I see you finally got some decent whisky in," Clive said, sipping his second glass as he sat down across from Harry in an armchair.

"You have the Scots to thank for that," Harry answered.

Clive raised his glass to them in a silent salute. "I will thank them when we meet. Over dinner, perhaps?"

"There will be at least two Scots present for the meal, I believe."

Harry heard his own voice stiffening in what Mary Elizabeth would have called "fancy ducal fashion," and Clive laughed out loud at his prim tone, as no one else living would ever do save for Mary herself.

"So who is she?" Clive asked.

"I beg your pardon?"

Clive smiled but this time did not laugh at him. "The girl you're in love with."

"How do you know I'm in love with anyone?"

"Because I'm in love myself, and I know what it looks like. Who is she?"

"She's one of the Scots."

"God help you, man. A Scot?"

Harry found himself smiling as he caressed the back of his comfortable sofa with one hand. "A Highlander."

"And that is a different breed, then?"

"Quite."

Clive downed the last of his whisky but did not get up to pour himself another. "Well, if she brought decent drink into your house, I'm inclined to like her."

"And what of your lady? This is the first I've heard of it."

Clive set his heavy crystal glass down on a side table

and leaned back into his armchair, spreading his long legs out before him. He smiled a bit like a Cheshire cat, and Harry realized that for once, he was not going to get this particular story out of him. "Romance is a tedious business to all save those most directly concerned. Let us just say, for now, that it is a tale for another day."

Harry opened his mouth to needle his friend further, but something about the set of Clive's gaze made him change his mind. "All right. I'll leave you be, for now. Just don't cause a scandal in the middle of my house party."

Clive sent him a wicked smile. "But, Harry, isn't that what house parties are for?"

Twenty-one

THERE WAS ONE LAST GOWN THAT MARY ELIZABETH had bought from Madame Celeste with her own money while in London, a gown that she had gotten for a song, as a courtesan had been between patrons and had reneged on her bill. Mary Elizabeth loved the gown so much that she did not simply shake it out and put it on, but called in an upstairs maid to press it for her.

Mary Elizabeth stood at the top of the ducal staircase in her royal-blue gown, preparing herself for the screeches she might soon be hearing from her brother Alex and the deathly pallor that would no doubt come over her mother's lovely face, undermining her rosy complexion. Mary Elizabeth squared her shoulders and walked with some semblance of grace down the stairs. One must begin as one meant to go on.

"Mary!" Catherine said as she entered the drawing room. Her friend and sister-in-law could no more contain her exclamation than she could have stopped the sun from rising. Catherine recovered, though, and moved away from Alex to embrace her. For a moment, Mary Elizabeth thought that the sweet girl might offer her shawl.

"Good evening, Catherine. Have I missed anything?"

Catherine opened and closed her mouth like a fish, and Alex began crossing the room, his face as dark as thunder. Before he could reach her side, however, some Englishman she had never seen before sidled up to her and bowed over her hand. "Madam, what a vision you are in blue."

The man was not as tall as Harry, nor were his shoulders as broad, but his green eyes gleamed with mischief that made her smile. "Call me Mary Elizabeth," she said.

"My lady, it would be my honor."

"And you are?"

"Harry's friend from Wales. Clive Owain. And you must be his friend from the Highlands."

Clive caressed the word *friend* with a hint of something else beneath it. Mary Elizabeth thought to call him on it, but when he smiled at her, it seemed to be in good-natured fun, so she let the moment go.

"Where is Harry?" she asked instead.

"Trapped in the corner by his mother and some young lady I have yet to meet."

"Lady Ashleigh," Catherine supplied helpfully.

Mary Elizabeth caught Harry's eye from across the room. He looked like a man who was going down for the third time. "Get over there and help him, man, if you call him friend."

"I would, but I have more pressing business of my own—business I hope you can help me with."

Catherine gasped at that bit of buffoonery, and Alex

came up beside her, taking his wife's hand. "I see you've met Clive of North Powys."

"I have, Alex." She quirked an eyebrow at her brother, waiting for his comment on her gown. He said nothing, as a nonmember of the family was present. She had to give her brothers points for loyalty—as long as their mother was not around. She wondered where their mother was and had just started to look for her when Clive took her hand and placed it on his arm for a turn about the room.

"I've never understood the object of the promenade," Mary Elizabeth said.

"To see and be seen, of course," Clive answered.

"By whom?"

"Ah, now, in the answer to that lies the mystery of the ages."

She laughed a little at him, catching Harry's eye again. Her man raised one eyebrow at her and she shrugged one shoulder at him, as if to say she had no idea what his friend was about but might soon find out. He nodded as if he understood her, and turned back to his mother and the lady at his side. A patient man, her Harry. He would need that patience if he was to deal with her and hers for the rest of his life.

"I've never been to Wales," Mary Elizabeth said. "Do you love it there?"

"I hate to leave it."

"I hate to leave Glenderrin," Mary Elizabeth said. She caught the eye of Harry's cousin, Clarice, a young lady who seemed to always know what was going on in every corner of the house without even being told. Mary Elizabeth wondered if the girl kept spies and, if so, how much she paid them.

She hoped the girl had had no one peering in at her and Harry when he'd been under her skirts in the library the night before.

"I need your help with a small enterprise," Clive said.

When Mary Elizabeth nodded to him, he went on.

"I need your help to make a certain young lady jealous."

Mary Elizabeth laughed out loud at that, and a few of the gentlemen's heads turned to listen to her. Not a few of the women glared at her, and Mary Elizabeth had to curb the urge to glare right back. She saw Harry smile, and her irritation lifted.

"If you're trying to devil Harry's little cousin, Clarice, she is already jealous. She is watching us like a hawk with a mouse."

"She is indeed my intended target," Clive said. "How astute you are."

"Don't blow smoke, sirrah. The lady has not taken her eyes off you since I came in this room. It takes no genius to see that."

"Perhaps not. But the lady is stubborn. She will not admit her feelings for me, not even to herself."

"You ought to cease foolish game playing and carry her off. She'll thank you after."

Clive laughed out loud. "If I were a man of Harry's stature, I might do just that. But as a lowly baronet's son, and a Welsh baronet's son at that, I find I must employ more stealth."

Mary Elizabeth found herself growing bored with the whole thing. "Well, good luck to you, then. I hope you win your lady."

"This promenade has served my cause well." Clive

stopped in front of Harry, bowing to the duchess. "A pleasant dinner to you, Miss Waters."

"Mary Elizabeth," she reminded him.

He bowed over her hand. "Mary Elizabeth."

The duchess looked down her nose at him, raising her quizzing glass. Clive simply smiled broader and kissed the lady's hand before whisking Lady Ashleigh toward the door, where Billings had just rung the dinner bell.

"I see you've met Clive," Harry said, his smile warming her heart as nothing else had since she had seen her mother. She stood in the light of it and drank it in.

"Colorful company you keep" was all she said.

The duchess snorted upon hearing that. "You ought to know, missy. You're the best example of it."

With that, the older lady swooped down on a handsome young man from Devon and asked him to lead her in to dine. It was the very reason the duchess allowed informal procession in to dine at her country house: so that she might swoop down on a different young man at each seating.

"I like your gown," Harry murmured in her ear.

Mary Elizabeth was about to whisper to him that she'd rather hide in the library with him than eat, but then she met her mother's eyes across the drawing room. If the ice of the North Sea was colder, Mary would have been surprised.

"I wore it for you," she said, telling only half the truth as she drew him with her toward the dining room. Harry fell into step beside her, flanking her as if for battle. He had seen her mother, too.

"I'm with you," Harry said.

Mary Elizabeth looked into his sky-blue eyes and smiled at him. The very sight of him seemed to tug at her heart—not hard enough to tear it, but strong enough to remind her that she loved him. "Thank you," she answered him, as he seated her at the far end of the table from her mother and Alex both.

She felt safe for the moment, but knew that she had more work before her that night. She squared her shoulders and raised a glass of white Burgundy to her lips, sipping the French stuff without tasting it. Which was a shame, for Harry's mother had only the best wines brought to table. Mary Elizabeth should savor it. She tried to savor the exotic wines and the meal that went with them, but all the while she felt the heavy gaze of her mother on her like a stone.

Harry loved to see his woman in royal blue. He had not known it until he saw her swan into his mother's drawing room wearing yet another low-cut silk confection. He had been trapped with his back to the wall, speaking idly with the Lady Ashleigh, able only to gaze across the room at his Mary, almost swallowing his tongue with lust even as he did his level best to make polite conversation.

Clive had rescued him, as he always did, and Harry spent a pleasant dinner gazing down his intended's gown to the beautiful curves of her breasts and the hint of lace that edged her stays.

He would give her a sapphire pendant to go with that gown, as soon as he might order one from his jeweler in York. It would be surrounded by tiny diamonds and rest low in her cleavage, just between her breasts. Harry wanted to put his lips there and taste her, where her skin would have the flavor of darkness and soft flowers. He remembered, for he had tasted her there the night before.

His pleasant thoughts were interrupted after dinner when Lady Anna of Glenderrin cut him and his girl off from the herd, cornering them in his mother's salon. The lady did not look at him at all, but kept her hard, blue eyes on her daughter.

"I see that you have used my money to purchase a courtesan's gown."

The ice in her voice ran along his skin, and Harry stepped closer to Mary Elizabeth, wishing they were already married, that he might shield her from this woman for the rest of his life.

"I purchased it with my money," Mary Elizabeth said. "It would have belonged to a courtesan, but as she could not pay, I bought it. I prefer jewel colors, and it had the convenience of hidden pockets so that I might hide my smaller blades."

The love of his life said all this as a matter of fact, as she might comment on the weather or the state of the roads. He braced himself, for he knew women well enough to know that her mother would not let that pass.

"I will not discuss the wearing of blades, much less the use of them, in company. I will only say that you have disgraced the family long enough, and it is far past time that you behave with decorum, like a lady."

"Like an English lady, you mean."

Harry wondered for a moment if perhaps his girl did not need protecting after all. Her mother drew up as tall as a goddess, and, as if she feared that she might say something she would regret, left abruptly to join the duchess where she was holding court once more beside the tea cart. Lady Anna's only concession was to nod at him briefly before stalking off.

Mary Elizabeth released one long breath, staring after her mother for only a second before she turned to smile at him. "That is getting easier, I believe," she said.

Harry touched a stray curl that had come loose from her topknot to rest against her cheek. He knew that he should not touch her so in company, with all of the ladies of London looking on, but it seemed he could not stop himself. Even as he stood there, more than one ambitious mama looked a bit depressed, with a couple of the more enterprising ones turning to the eligible Earl of Grathton to chat him up, dragging their daughters with them.

"What is getting easier?" he asked.

"Standing up to her."

There was a pounding at the piano as someone struck up what sounded like a reel. Harry turned to find Catherine seated at the instrument, pounding away with more enthusiasm than talent, though she seemed to hit all the notes in correct succession, more or less. Her husband Alex stood beside her, smiling down at her as if she were producing the music of the spheres. Mary Elizabeth sighed as she looked at them.

"They are well matched," she said. There was a longing in her voice that he wanted to kiss away.

"So are we."

Mary Elizabeth smiled at him, and the shadow that had come into her eyes since she had first seen her mother that afternoon faded, if only a little.

"Come and dance with me," Harry said.

"You know the steps, then?"

"Aye, lass."

She laughed at his ridiculous attempt at a brogue, and then he had her in his arms, her waist under his hands as he spun her up and over a useless ottoman. A few of the mothers clucked and gasped, but the young people did not wait long before following behind, joining the dance, as he knew they would. Without bothering to lift up the carpets, he and his guests, at least all those under thirty, spent the next half hour jigging and leaping and drinking like lords. Which he supposed was what they were.

Mary Elizabeth was breathless with dancing and laughter. When the reel was over, the entire company applauded Catherine, even the duchess. Harry looked to see what reaction Lady Anna might have had, but when he scanned the room for her, he could not find her. It seemed she had already retired.

"Come into the garden," Harry whispered, leaning so close that he caught the scent of roses on her skin.

Mary Elizabeth cut her eyes at him. "What for? I've seen the moon and the flowers. Both are pretty, but why see them twice?"

He laughed a little, a low sound that vibrated in his chest. He kept quiet, so as not to draw too much attention, but he watched as Mary Elizabeth shivered at the sound of it.

"Come outside so that I can seduce you in the moonlight."

She laughed a little herself, but she was breathless as she looked up at him. "All right," she said. "I'll meet you by the fountain in the rose garden in ten minutes. But you won't seduce me."

"No?"

"No. It can't be done."

Harry did not remind her of their stolen hour on his library sofa the night before. He simply smiled, and watched her eyes change from maple to darker hazel as she looked at his lips.

"We'll see," he said.

She disappeared through the door to the hall, which Billings closed discreetly behind her. Harry went to his mother's side and made his excuses, but from the gleam in her eye, she knew exactly where he was going, and why.

Twenty-two

MARY ELIZABETH HAD MANAGED TO HOLD HER OWN at dinner and after, which was more of a victory than she had ever been able to expect when dealing with her mother. But she knew her mother well, and knew that the lady had not given up her goal. She would see Mary and Harry engaged by week's end, or there would truly be hell to pay.

Mary Elizabeth sighed as she sank onto a bench tucked inside the duchess's folly. The rose garden spread itself below, the moonlight casting the petals in shades of silver and gray. There was nothing wrong with marrying Harry, save for the facts at hand: he was an Englishman, and he lived four days' drive by the swiftest coach from the only place in the world she called home.

Mary Elizabeth had grown up free on her father's lands, forgotten by her mother altogether until her sixteenth birthday. Only then had her mother brought her indoors, given her a bath, and made her learn to be a lady.

She had listened to the lessons, most of them,

though she had not always heeded them. And when her mother had dragged her down to Edinburgh, she had gone willingly, even though, as always, she would rather have been at home.

Her mother was English, and thus could not understand the love Mary Elizabeth felt for the land that had borne her. Her father's people had lived at Glenderrin since before the Vikings had come, and would live there forever after, God willing. Mary Elizabeth knew that she was a girl and, as such, should marry and move away. But to do so would be to leave her heart behind, along with the best part of herself. Mary Elizabeth might be considered wild among the English, but since she had come away, she had been only a shadow. She would never possess the whole of her soul anywhere but Glenderrin.

Harry came upon her in the moonlight and caught her brooding. She was in his arms before she thought, taking comfort from the only man in the world who would ever make her consider leaving her home behind. He seemed to sense her urgency and her desperation, and that they had nothing to do with desire. Harry held her close and caressed her hair, kissing her temple, all the while keeping her tight against him, a bulwark against the world.

"You're sorrowing, Mary."

"I am."

"I brought you out here to woo, not to weep."

She drew back just far enough to smile up into his face. The harsh planes of his cheekbones were softened in the moonlight, making him even more beautiful, if such a thing were possible. She kissed his jaw, the only part of his face she could reach, before she laid her head back on his chest, resting over his heart. "I am sorrowing for home, Harry. Do you love this place as much as I love Glenderrin?"

"Yes." He answered without hesitation, and she leaned back to look at him again. "There is no place on Earth so fine as here, nowhere I find the sky as blue or the sea as beautiful. The roses elsewhere never bloom as they do in my mother's garden, and now that my father is dead, there is no ogre to loom over the castle keep and darken any corner of it."

Mary Elizabeth felt tears come into her eyes. When one slid down her cheek, her man kissed it away. "Is that how you feel about Glenderrin?" Harry asked.

She nodded and swallowed hard, so that she would not sob. "Yes."

He drew her away from the bench, deeper into the shadows of the folly. His mother had ordered it built, he had told Mary Elizabeth, to resemble a Greek temple that had long since fallen to ruin. The duchess had built not the ruin, but the temple in its glory, smaller than the Parthenon by far, but an elegant place, fit for the goddess Aphrodite. Harry did not give Mary time to admire much of the interior by moonlight, but kissed her.

Mary Elizabeth felt his lips on hers, a fiery caress that teased at her sorrow, drawing out a bit of her inherent joy. It seemed her reaction was not what he had hoped for, however, for his arms tightened around her, and his lips slanted over hers until her mouth opened beneath his. Mary Elizabeth shivered then, and felt his hand on her breast, caressing her flesh through the silk of her royal-blue gown. His long, callused fingers teased the fabric down and the lace beneath that, until there was only her breast, swelling to fill his hand.

Mary Elizabeth felt as if she had lost the last bit of her reason, that she would let him touch her, there, like that, in the middle of his mother's garden. But that thought flitted away like the flight of a butterfly as his hand moved to her other breast to free it, as his lips came down on her, drawing her straining nipple into his mouth.

She gasped in pleasure and felt her knees begin to weaken. She shored them up, but had no self-possession other than to cling to him as he kissed and caressed her by turns. Before long, she was writhing against him, moaning his name. It was his name on her lips that seemed to bring him back to himself. He stopped kissing her, and his caresses grew less demanding and more soothing.

Mary Elizabeth's body would not be soothed. She shook and strained against him, reaching for the place he had taken her last night, frustrated, knowing that she could not get there.

"I'm sorry, Mary," Harry said. "I did not mean to take this so far."

She drew on her reserves of pride and inner strength and forced herself to stop writhing. His body was hard against hers, and when she pressed herself against him one final time, she felt him stiffen against her, his breath hissing between his teeth.

The fact that she was not the only one suffering calmed her down as his caresses and his apology had not. "Harry, I love you. But you can be a right pain in my arse."

He laughed at that and held her close, but not too close. She could no longer feel the evidence of his desire for her against her belly, but she could hear it in his breathing, which was still as ragged as her own.

"Marry me, Mary Elizabeth Waters, for the love of God."

As if a wave of cold seawater had swamped her, Mary felt the warm desire and her joy in it disappear in a trice. She sighed. She should not encourage Harry's attentions until she gave him her answer—if her answer ended up being yes. She was tempted to tell him yes in that moment just to have the matter settled.

But when she closed her eyes, she saw not Harry's face, but the sun rising over the burn, the mist rising off her river. She tried to move her tongue, but it would not obey her. She could not do it.

She loved him, but she loved herself, too.

Her silence was his only answer. He sighed against her, and she could feel the edges of his seemingly infinite patience beginning to fray.

"I'm sorry, Harry."

"Don't be sorry," he said. "You haven't said no. Until you say no, there's nothing for either of us to be sorry for."

Mary Elizabeth kissed him then, pouring all of her love, if not her desire, into it. He kissed her back, but she knew from the taste of his lips that he was not satisfied, and she knew how little room there was between her love for him, and her love for home. She tried to push the opposing thoughts of

Glenderrin and of her mother out of her mind, but they both seemed to weigh on her, even as Harry walked with her back into the house, his hand on hers. There was a shadow over them, and she needed to dispel it, one way or another.

She must choose which part of her heart to live with.

But not yet.

❧

Mary Elizabeth woke early the next morning, as she always did. And as always, no matter the crisis in her life, she woke hungry. She dressed in a gown, though an older one, out of deference to her mother's sensibilities. She knew that the Lady Anna would take a tray in her room as she planned her day, and as such, Mary Elizabeth had at least a half hour to eat and to get out of the house.

At worse, she could cadge a bit of bread and flee. At best, she could devour some eggs and a rasher of hot bacon.

Mary Elizabeth was surprised to find a pile of English up and milling about in the entryway and down along the front steps of the palatial house. They had their horses ready to mount, and every gentlemen and lady were dressed as for a hunt. She asked a young buck who seemed eager for the saddle, "What are you riding out for this morning? Will you be hunting deer, then?"

The boy smiled at her, his excitement clear in every muscle of his body. He fairly shook with the need to be gone and riding, just at the hounds outside bayed and called for their freedom. "No, indeed, miss. Today, we are hunting fox."

Mary Elizabeth frowned. "Are foxes a great trouble to the farmers hereabouts?"

He almost started to laugh, but swallowed it down, so as not to offend her. "No, miss. The gamekeeper raises foxes, and we hunt them."

She felt a chill when he said that. "So one of you will shoot this fox?"

"No. The dogs will tear it up once we've run it to ground."

Mary Elizabeth felt cold again then, but it was the cold of fury. She turned on her heel, her breakfast forgotten, and walked straight to Billings, who was handing out cups of mulled wine in silver goblets.

"Where might I find the gamekeeper, Mr. Billings?" she asked.

The stately man blinked at the title she gave him, but he did not comment. "He might be found in the stone building closest to the stables."

"I thank you."

She did not leave by the front door, but slipped through the duchess's sitting room, which was empty this early in the morning. She let herself out by the terrace door and went out into the rose garden. Once she was well clear of the house, she lifted her skirts and started to run.

❧

Harry greeted his guests, dressed in his red hunting coat, as his valet had remembered that there was a hunt that morning. He had been so consumed with his pursuit of his Scottish bride that he had forgotten all about it, though he had planned the entertainment himself.

He greeted the company, speaking with each man he saw and bowing to each lady. He was surprised to find Mary Elizabeth absent and not dressed in the mythical habit he had yet to see. He was thinking of how she might look with a jaunty feather trailing over her shoulder from her riding hat and her long skirt hitched up over her arm when Billings came to stand beside him.

"My lord duke," Billings said.

"Yes?"

"I believe we are in for a bit of trouble."

"Why, man? Has some horse thrown a shoe?"

"No, Your Grace. Miss Waters asked after Mr. Bartlett."

"The gamekeeper? What on earth for?"

Billings only raised one brow, but Harry had his answer.

"She's after the foxes."

"I fear so, sir."

"Has Sampson been brought up?"

"Yes, sir."

"Have him brought around to the path by the rose garden. And keep these people here for at least another ten minutes if you can."

"They were hoping you might lead the hunt, my lord."

"So was I, Billings. But I fear Miss Waters has other plans."

"She often does, sir."

Harry mounted Sampson out of view of all his guests, grateful that his best horse had been returned to him the day before. He slipped away so that no one would see him and follow, thinking that the hunt was on. Harry rode hell-for-leather to the stalls where the foxes were raised. Sampson thought a morning gallop through the primroses great fun, and took joy in leaping one of the duchess's boxwood hedges. Though Sampson was the fastest horse he owned, Harry was still too late.

Mary Elizabeth stood in front of the empty cages. A bit of fur was left behind in one of them, but every living fox was gone.

Harry simply stared and wondered what on God's green earth he was going to say to his guests.

"Your prey is gone," Mary Elizabeth said. "If you hope to kill them, they've got a fair chance, seeing as all twelve of them are free now, and even your pack of dogs won't find them all."

"My God, Mary Elizabeth."

She did not speak again but waited in patience for his judgment.

"I love you, Mary. But you are a pain in my arse."

She smiled at him then, and he leaned down and offered her an arm. She swung up onto Sampson behind him, and they rode back to the house together, that he might tell his guests the hunt was off.

Before he could open his mouth, however, Mary Elizabeth waved to the company and shouted them down. "Gentlefolk! Gentlefolk all! One moment, if you please."

The entire company fell into a dead silence. It was Harry's presence alone that kept them from turning their noses up at her, and their backs to her. She was his choice as duchess, and they knew it. So they swallowed their irritation at being shouted at by a Highland barbarian and listened to her.

"Your foxes are run off," she said. "I freed them all myself."

"All?" Lord Grathton asked, looking dazed. Harry knew, as the entire *ton* did, that Grathton had run into Mary Elizabeth and her wild ways before.

"Aye," she answered. "Your prey is scattered, so there will be no easy kills today."

The company murmured among themselves, milling about a bit restlessly, but it seemed Mary Elizabeth was not finished. "The good news for the true hunters among you is that there are now twelve foxes where before there would have been only one. If you've skill or luck, you might get a muff for your lady."

The men laughed at that, and the few women who were awake at that hour smiled a little at the mad girl Harry wanted as his wife.

"So good luck to you. The man who bags a fox will get a silver cup as prize, courtesy of our grand duke here."

The gentlemen, none of whom needed a silver cup but all of whom loved a chance to compete for any reason whatsoever, applauded her largesse. Harry sighed as he watched the men ride away, the hounds released in all directions, after different foxes or perhaps simply just happy to be freed from their restraints.

The Earl of Grathton raised his hat to her before he rode away. Mary Elizabeth smiled as if she had been awarded a great prize, and Harry felt a little jealous.

"Mary," he said. "I think I will turn you over my knee again."

She smiled at him and kissed his ear quickly, clearly hoping that no one else would see. "I'd like that, Harry. If it turns out as well for me as it did the last time you tried it."

Twenty-three

AFTER LETTING MARY ELIZABETH DOWN OFF OF Sampson, Harry left to ride out with a few of his guests. Mary Elizabeth wandered into the breakfast room, where a giant repast still waited for the hungry folk returning sporadically from the hunt. She lingered over her tea and a chocolate brioche, talking with the English guests as they ate. If she was considering living among these people for the rest of her life, she supposed she should try to get used to them.

Some of the English, preferring the ease of a controlled kill, came back right away. But others stayed out for hours, chasing foxes and their phantom tails all over the countryside. The Earl of Grathton was one of these, and he smiled as he took his seat beside her.

"You gave us good hunting today," he said. "I never saw a fox, much less shot one, but it was a roaring good time."

"I'm glad, my lord," Mary Elizabeth answered. "I've been meaning to apologize again for threatening you with a claymore in the park."

Grathton laughed out loud at that, spearing a bit of egg with his fork. "No apology is necessary, Miss Waters. You were contrite on the day, and there was no harm done. I was reintroduced to an old friend through the encounter, so it was all to the good."

He looked a bit forlorn, and Mary Elizabeth realized that he meant her friend and companion Lady Prudence, who had lately married Robbie. Mary Elizabeth did not know him well enough to interfere with his affairs, but for a moment, she wished that he was one of her kin, that she might find a decent girl for him. He was too kind a man to be alone.

Mary Elizabeth was distracted from her quarry by a summons from Billings.

"Miss Waters," the stately butler said. "Lady Anna of Glenderrin requests your presence in the blue drawing room."

"Does she, now?" Mary sipped at her tepid tea. "And where might this room be?"

"On the second floor, miss. In the guest wing. Shall I call a maid to take you there?"

"Don't trouble yourself, Mr. Billings. When my mother summons, I had best make haste."

Mary Elizabeth downed the last of her Darjeeling, wishing fervently for something stronger. But hard drink had never done more than take the edge off for her, and when dealing with her mother, she needed all her wits about her.

"Good day to you, then," she said, nodding to Grathton and to Billings, straightening her skirts as she stepped into the hall. She checked her hair in the downstairs mirror and saw that it was falling from its pins, as it always seemed to do. She sighed and left it alone. For once in her life, her mother would have to accept her as she was.

Still, Mary Elizabeth had to shore herself up with the thought of Harry and a pleasant evening to come spent at his side as she climbed the stairs slowly, as if headed to her doom. She was not far off. Her mother had an edict to impart, and even Alex was not present to soften the blow.

Mary Elizabeth found the blue sitting room that Billings had mentioned. The door was standing open. Without knocking on the jamb, Mary stepped inside and closed the door behind her.

"Good day, Mother," she said, focusing on the intention of remaining civil, no matter what her mother said.

Lady Anna turned from the window, where she had been gazing out over a sheep-dotted lawn. The sea was not far distant from this side of the house, and Mary Elizabeth could hear the soothing sound of it through the open window.

"Is it? I understand the Duke of Northumberland has offered for you, and you have refused him," her mother said.

As always, Lady Anna did not stand on ceremony or greet her pleasantly but stood glowering at her, her beautiful rose-colored gown bringing out the soft-golden highlights in her hair. Mary Elizabeth sighed before she answered. If she lived to be a hundred, she would never look as beautiful as her mother did without even trying.

"No, ma'am," Mary Elizabeth answered. "I have

not refused him, as such. But I have not accepted him either."

"Such an offer does not last forever," Lady Anna said.

"This one might," Mary said. She could not resist the urge to be flippant. "A marriage must last forever, or so Father Malcolm tells me."

"Do not try your winsome ways with me, Mary Elizabeth. I am not your father."

Mary did not speak again, but let the silence lengthen. She thought perhaps to take her leave, as she had nothing more to say, but her mother was not finished with her yet.

"Daughter, I came down here to help you persuade the duke to declare himself. Now that he has done so, I feel my work here is done."

Mary Elizabeth felt hopeful, but only for a brief moment. Her mother spoke on.

"I had hoped that you and the duke might reach an understanding without my intervention. But as it stands, I see that, as usual, my good intentions have been thwarted. As you refuse to marry His Grace, you'll go back to London until you choose someone to marry. You may suit yourself in your choice, as long as Alex approves of him and he has a pulse and a decent purse."

Mary Elizabeth felt the light go out of the day. She wished that, just once, her mother might speak to her as a human being, instead of issuing orders and edicts like a god on high. She bit her tongue until she tasted blood, so that she would not curse her mother to her face. The first wave of her temper washed over her and passed by, leaving only pain in its wake.

"I love you, Ma. I wish you loved me. I wish you would accept me as I am and leave me be."

Her mother's granite facade softened, and Mary Elizabeth felt a second hint of hope rise. The hope did not last long, but her mother's words offered more comfort than she had expected to find.

"I do love you, Mary. I will always love you, whatever you do." Her mother took one step forward, and Mary Elizabeth held her ground, wondering for one mad moment if her mother might reach for her and take her hand. Of course, her proper mother did nothing of the kind, but for the first time since Mary Elizabeth had been a little girl, she looked as if she wanted to.

"But you are a woman grown, and as such, you must take your place in the world, as I did when I was your age."

"You ran away with Da when you were my age. You caused a scandal among your own kind and have lived in the Highlands ever since."

Her mother smiled, and Mary Elizabeth watched as the hard woman she thought she knew softened a little more. "I love your father. I loved him then. I ran away with him because he was my choice, and my father would not give his permission for us to wed. I want only the same for you."

"For me to run off?" Mary Elizabeth asked, knowing she was not so foolish as to hare off across the countryside alone on horseback, as her friends Catherine and Prudence had done.

"No. For you to find the man who holds the key to your heart. You will never find him among the men of Glenderrin. You did not find him in Edinburgh. Perhaps you will find him in London, if we give that city a bit more time."

"Ma, I was in London almost two months. I found nothing worth seeing there."

Her mother touched her then, very lightly, on her cheek, but drew back almost at once, as if the softness of her daughter's skin burned her fingertips. "You will return there and give it a few more months. There is bound to be someone worth marrying."

"No, Ma. There's not." *Save for Harry*, she thought to herself.

"You will return there tomorrow anyway."

"Without going home for the Gathering?" Mary Elizabeth asked, not quite believing that even her mother could be so cruel as to deny her the fabric of her family at the yearly call of the clan.

"No, Mary. London for you, until you marry."

"Ma, you're being daft."

Her mother's face hardened again as if the softness Mary had seen there had never been. "Insulting me will not help your cause, Mary Elizabeth. You will go to the center of the empire and live until you find a man worthy of your love, since you feel the duke is not the man for you."

"I never said that."

"Well, you have the rest of the day and tonight to decide. If you do not accept his suit, you will leave tomorrow with Alex and Catherine."

Mary Elizabeth wanted to scream in frustration. She wanted to throw the ugly porcelain shepherdess that sat on the table near her hand. She wanted to rail at her mother, to insult her in earnest, to scream at her until she made her see reason. But Mary Elizabeth knew from the shouting matches of her sixteenth year that her mother was implacable once her mind was made up.

Mary Elizabeth sighed, letting a long breath out. Her anger went with it. Her mother did love her. She had said so. Though she had a funny way of showing it. But then, she was English after all.

"I love you, Ma" was all Mary Elizabeth said. She kissed her mother's cheek. She took in the sweet hyacinth on her mother's skin before she walked away.

❦

Mary Elizabeth went to the stables, where Sampson stood in his stall, eating warmed bran and oats. She petted his neck, then slipped into the stall with him to hide. When he was done eating, she got out his fancy currycomb and went over his coat, making him shudder with pleasure. He checked her pockets for sugar and found all three lumps she had hidden from him. She petted him awhile, even after he was a glossy as an Arabian. He must have sensed that she was out of sorts, for he let her.

Harry found her close to teatime, and stuck his head above the stall door. Sampson whinnied when he saw him, but moved so that Harry could not come inside.

"Let him in, ye wee bugger," she said, and Sampson moved just enough for Harry to slip through the door.

"What are you doing in here, Mary? It's almost teatime."

"I've been currying Sampson. And he's been a gentleman all afternoon."

Harry patted the horse's neck, and Sampson allowed the liberty. Mary Elizabeth was glad that these two would have each other when she went away.

She was not some dramatic lady, to flee at the first sign of trouble. Nor did she discount ever marrying Harry. For if she ever married a man, English or otherwise, it would be him. But she would not be dragged into a wedding as if she had disgraced the family by falling into the family way. Nor would she allow her mother to dictate the terms of her life to her anymore. That time was done, and forever.

So she was leaving for the Highlands in the morning. She would not tell Harry, for he was silver-tongued and would talk her out of it. At the very least, he would want to go with her, which would be as good as an engagement. She wanted time alone, to think beside the burn. She wanted to be among her own kind and remember who she was. If she still loved him then, next to the loch behind the castle, then she would wed him.

Mary Elizabeth could only hope that he would still want her then. But it was not for her to dictate to Harry any more that it was for her mother to dictate to her. If he loved her now—and she was certain he did—he would love her when she was ready to marry. He was no flighty Englishman, to take offense at her caution and refuse to marry her to spite himself. Or so she told herself as she leaned her head against his chest and pulled him to her.

He was no longer dressed in the garish red coat of the morning, but wore indigo superfine with buff breeches. His waistcoat was threaded with silver and the same blue of his coat, which brought out the sky blue of his eyes.

"You've spoken with your mother again," he said.

"I have." She did not tell him of her mother's plans to send her away on the morrow. She knew he would only fall into a temper and ruin both their days. He might even confront the Lady of Glenderrin and cause a ruckus that only the duchess might sort out. All the while, it mattered little what her mother said or Harry thought. She needed to go home and think with a clear head before she decided once and for all the course of the rest of her life.

His house was filled with the evidence of that choice. She had seen London, and how the entire city bowed and scraped when they saw the ducal carriage driving by. She could only imagine how that bowing and scraping would increase if Harry were actually in that carriage with her.

There were myriad things about being a duchess that she did not know. Some of them she could learn, with his mother as her teacher. Others, she would never know, and likely never do, even if she lived to be a hundred. She thought of her children, more than half English, growing up in the South, surrounded by privilege, but without ever knowing what it was like to be a true part of a clan. If she married away from home, her children would not have her childhood. If she married Harry, her sons would be taught to hate her own people and her daughters to fear them. She would never teach them this, nor would Harry, but the English *ton* would.

Harry did not speak, but let her lean against him

and think. When she was done listening to the sweet sound of the beat of his heart, Mary Elizabeth pulled back and smiled at him.

"Shall we go take a cup of tea with your mother?" she asked.

"I thought you'd never ask."

His smiled pierced her heart, and the thought of leaving him, even for a month or two, made her ache. But she knew herself and knew that when she saw him again, she must give him her answer. Her mother was right about one thing at least—Harry Percy was too fine a man to leave dangling for long.

"Will Her Worship mind that I smell of horse?"

He laughed and touched her lips with his. He lingered over her, and she drank him in, for the true water of life lived in that man's kisses.

"She will mind, as will all the other ladies."

"Perhaps I should change, then," Mary Elizabeth said.

"I will do the same," Harry offered.

"I will even wash behind my ears," she said, trying to outdo him, watching the smile play across his lips.

"Such largesse, my lady. My mother will be honored."

Mary Elizabeth laughed, as he had no doubt meant her to, and let him lead her out of Sampson's stall. The horse tried to block her passage, but let her by when she crooned to him.

"I'll see you again, wee beastie, by and by."

She let Harry take her hand, and looked over his grounds and gardens, trying to imagine that she belonged with him there. For the first time, it was not as hard to do as she had feared it might be. When

Billings opened the front door for them, she climbed the stairs two at a time, so as not to miss all the chocolate-filled cakes. Harry was close on her heels and kissed her again before releasing her to the darkness of the guest wing.

"Be there in ten minutes, and I'll give you something," Harry said.

Mary Elizabeth laughed out loud. "Show me your telescope," she said.

"I'd do that for free."

"I'll think of something else, then. But show me the stars tonight."

"I'll have the telescope set up in the garden."

"No need. I'll come to it."

"It's in my room."

Mary smiled, a flash of wickedness running down her spine. "Is it, now? And do you have a sofa as comfortable as the one in your library?"

Harry's blue eyes had darkened to indigo with desire. She wondered for a moment if he would seize her then and there, his guests below be damned. But he did not.

"I do."

"I'll definitely come to you, then."

She did not wait for him to answer her, but strolled away, swinging her hips. She looked over her shoulder to laugh at him and saw he was still watching her. She blew him a kiss and kept moving, for as beautiful as Harry was and as much as he made her fill with desire for his touch, she had a powerful hankering for a chocolate puff, too.

Twenty-four

HARRY SPENT THE REST OF THE EVENING IN A VALIANT effort not to watch Mary Elizabeth Waters every waking moment, and failing.

She seemed more at ease among the *ton* gathered in his home, almost as if her last talk with her mother had freed her somehow, almost as if she was trying on being English for size. Of course, she would never be English, which was part of her charm. She did not behave as any duchess he had ever known, and it seemed unlikely that she ever would.

Thank God.

She was unfailingly warm, and while she did not suffer fools gladly, she did not treat anyone gathered in his mother's drawing room with disdain. She was kind to the young pups who had accompanied their sisters to see the Recluse Duke. She talked hunting with the older gentlemen and gowns with the ladies, going so far as to show the Earl of Grathton's sister, Lady Sara, a secret pocket where she hid one of her smaller daggers.

Lady Sara blanched a little, but even the sight of

cold steel could not horrify the gently reared girl completely, for the force of Mary Elizabeth's personality seemed to soften even that. Harry watched his mother smile benevolently on his chosen wife, and he knew that he would stop at nothing to make her his.

How to persuade her was the question. As a duke, he had rarely had to ask for anything in his life. Before he had needed a thing, his people had provided it without question, knowing his desires beforehand. His needs were simple, as were his wants. A simple man, he had thought himself, until he first set eyes on the woman of his life.

Life did take odd turns when you least expected it. A Scottish girl becoming necessary for his next breath was just one of those turns. Better not to question it.

Mary Elizabeth made an elaborate effort to yawn. Her mother, brooding beside the duchess, seemed to notice it and to despair. Harry hid his own smile behind his hand as Mary tripped out of the drawing room early, off to bed. He knew, of course, that she had no such destination in mind.

With the sky still lit with the last of the gloaming, when all of the ladies had followed Mary Elizabeth's example, Harry settled the remaining gentlemen in the smoking room with the billiard tables and the ever-steady Billings at their disposal before retiring himself. He thought to sneak by Mary Elizabeth's room to bring her to his own, but he decided to use his tooth powder first, on the likely chance that he could not resist canoodling with her, at least a little.

He stepped into his sitting room and was surprised to discover not Philips, his valet, but Mary Elizabeth reclining in one of his wingback chairs.

"I thought you'd never get here," she said, smiling at him.

She had not changed out of her gown, which for once was a charming confection any debutante might have worn, made of soft-peach silk and rosettes of silk and lace. But Mary Elizabeth wore it as she wore all her clothes, with a casual elegance that no one else could duplicate. Mary Elizabeth rose from her chair and crossed the room to him, rising up on her toes to kiss his cheek. She smelled of flowers, as she always did, and the scent lingered in his nostrils even after she had drawn back and wandered away again.

He watched her as a lion might his prey, trying to tamp down his lust and failing. There was something about seeing her strolling in his rooms, where she had no right to be, strolling among his things, where no woman had ever been before, that made him want her more. He had not thought that possible.

For the first time in his life, the feeling of possessiveness came over him, and he began to understand what the poets wrote of and why men died for love—and killed for it. Had some other man stepped into the room in that moment in an effort to take Mary Elizabeth away from him, all his civilized manners and common sense would have fallen away, and he would have killed the man where he stood.

Harry took a deep breath, trying to dispel his unreasoning lust along with his sudden mad bloodlust. His man chose that moment to step into the room from

the bedroom beyond, and Harry felt himself reach for
a weapon that was not there.

Philips blanched at the look on his face and
retreated at once. Harry sighed, knowing that his
man was discreet and well paid and, as such, did
not need to fear for his very life from his suddenly
pillaging employer.

Mary Elizabeth spoke at last, blithely unaware of
the struggle Harry was having with his baser self.
She did not look at him at all, but dusted off a fine
mahogany clock that rested on the mantelpiece—yet
another gift from the doomed King of France.

"Harry, your man there is afraid of women, it
seems. I chased him out of here about half an hour
ago. You might want to see to him."

Harry almost laughed out loud. He would send for
a special license first thing in the morning. The Bishop
of York was reticent with them, but he understood
that the Bishop of London gave them out like candy.

He adjusted his falls and strode across the room,
staying as far away from Mary Elizabeth and her sweet
curves as he could. The peach silk that encased those
curves would be so easily dispatched, and would be so
warm under his hands as he peeled it off of her. He
could almost feel that softness beneath his palms, and
then the softness of her skin beneath that.

He had touched her too much already for his own
peace of mind. He knew what her curves looked
like when bared to his gaze. He knew the sounds she
made when she came apart beneath his mouth. He
had watched her two nights before, as she almost wept
with pleasure on his favorite sofa—pleasure that he

had given her. He knew from her tiny gasps and the way that she had clutched him that she had never felt such pleasure before.

He had been the first, the only man to give her such bliss, and he knew that he would make it his life's mission to be the only man to ever give her such pleasure for the rest of her life. The thought made him smile, so Philips looked less frightened when he looked in on him. Philips was arranging the hairbrushes on his dressing table and flicking away bits of nonexistent dust.

"Forgive me, Your Grace," Philips began. His man was well trained, and fell silent as soon as Harry raised one hand.

"There is nothing to forgive, Philips. You are understandably chagrined to find a lady in my chambers. I admit that such an arrangement is a bit unusual, but my fiancée is a bit unusual, being from the far North region of the Scottish Highlands."

The ramrod shoulders beneath Philips black coat relaxed a fraction. "Of course, sir."

"Miss Waters is here to have a look through my telescope. She will be leaving within a quarter of an hour."

"Very good, sir."

Philips did not blink an eye at that blatant lie, and Harry remembered why he paid him as well as he did. But this was not some widow come for a bit of evening frolic. This was his future wife.

"Our engagement is of a peculiar kind, Philips. The rest of the company, including her mother and mine, are not even aware that it has been contracted.

To be completely frank, the young lady herself does not yet know."

That last bit broke once more through Philips icy reserve. "Indeed, my lord? The lady does not know that she is to be the next Duchess of Northumberland?"

"She is a bit stubborn. As I mentioned, she is a Highlander."

Philips had nothing to say to this, as the idea of a woman refusing his duke had simply never occurred to him.

"She will give her consent," Harry said. "She just does not know it yet."

"Scots are an odd lot, if I may say so, sir."

Harry smiled. "That they are."

"Will there be anything else tonight, sir?"

"No, Philips. You may go to bed. I will see you in the morning. And, Philips?"

"Yes, sir?"

"As always, I count on your discretion."

"It is my honor, Your Grace, to serve both you and our future duchess."

Philips bowed formally and, with that, vanished into the dressing room and out of the suite through the servant's door. Harry waited a moment, then carefully locked the door behind him.

He would do his level best to get Mary Elizabeth out of his rooms as soon as he might, as soon as he could bear to, but he did not want anyone else discovering them in the meantime. He girded his loins, so to speak, rearranging his falls once more, before stepping into the room where he had left the object of all his desires.

Mary Elizabeth wondered what was taking her man so long. She was not going to accept him that night, but he was hers and always would be, at least in her heart.

For the first time in her life, she felt nervous when in the same room with a man. Even with Harry a room away, conferring with his manservant, she was fit to jump at every sound she heard. It seemed there was a bit of energy surging along just beneath her skin. She would have said it felt like little jolts of gentle lightning, but she had never been struck and, God willing, never would be. The feeling made her skittish as a long-tailed cat in a room filled with booted feet, and she had to work to stay still. She dusted one clean clock on the mantel and then began to circle the room, keeping her eyes averted from the door Harry had disappeared through and the bedroom beyond.

She wanted this man. God knows she did. She had a bit of knowledge from the farm of what desire entailed, at least among the animals. She had gotten more than a glimpse of what might be between a man and a woman in Harry's arms in his library. But she found that she did not want to leave him without making him hers completely.

She wanted to make love to Harry Percy.

The very idea made her a wanton, and no doubt a fool, since she had not agreed to wear his ring for the rest of her life and still would not, at least not that night, even if he was amendable to her plans. She was a wanton for certain, for she did not care.

Making Harry her own would serve another purpose: no other man—no fool from London, no

Lowlander in Edinburgh—would want her after that. Her mother would leave her in peace.

She knew her da would not be best pleased if she ever was forced to reveal the fact that she was ruined for good and all. He would rail and rant a bit, but she was his only girl and the apple of his eye. He was a man who loved women, was her da, even when that woman was a fool.

She did not think of the shame of being ruined, or at least, she tried not to. She told herself that she would stay in the Highlands, far from anyone, and live free. If she did not choose to marry Harry in the end, or if he chose not to have her for a wife, then she would make her own way on her father's lands for the rest of her life. She had enough kith and kin to see to herself, whatever her own mother might say.

Mary Elizabeth felt a bit wrong in using Harry in such a way, but she loved him, and knew that she would always love him if she lived to be a hundred, whether they ever married or not. And there was something about the predator in his eyes that night that made her flush and feel the edges of her stomach tremble. She would give her left arm to have him touch her only once, but she need make no such sacrifice, for he was here, in the room with her.

Harry had come back from seeing to his man. His valet must have vanished out a back door, for he did not emerge. Harry did not speak, nor did he come to her as she hoped he might, but crossed the room to the door and locked it, leaving the key. When he turned back to her, his blue eyes were not the color of a sunny sky, but a darker blue. Mary Elizabeth shivered as his gaze moved over her gown, as if he was figuring the quickest way to take it off her.

"So you want to see the telescope?" Harry asked.

Even his voice sounded different—darker—there alone in his rooms, with his bed only a few steps away behind an open door. Mary Elizabeth straightened her back and forced herself to look away from the fine lines of his shoulders beneath his tight coat, and met his eyes.

"Aye," she said. "I'm in the mood for a bit of stargazing."

She could feel her bravado crack a little as Harry stalked across the room to her, moving slow, giving her every chance to skitter away like the rabbit she felt. She stood her ground and waited. He stopped close to her, close enough that the buttons of his waistcoat brushed the bodice of her gown. The little peach rosettes that Lady Prudence had thought so fine in Madame Celeste's dress shop followed the edge of her scalloped neckline, and one of them got caught on Harry's ivory button. She leaned closer, raising her hand between them to wrest herself free, while Harry laughed.

A little of the tension between them dissipated, but only a very little. He was watching her as a cat might watch a tempting bird that had come to roost a bit too close. She wondered what a woman had to do to make a man kiss her.

She supposed that she should just kiss him, but for some reason, she wanted to see if he would do it. She wanted him, and she knew that he wanted her, but for some perverse female reason beyond her own understanding, she also wanted him to make the first move. So she bided her time.

Harry did not kiss her. He did not draw her into his arms or touch her in any way. Instead, he took two steps back and gestured to an open window. "The telescope and the night sky awaits. After you, my lady."

For one daft moment, Mary Elizabeth thought that he meant for her to leap before him out of a window to the ground three stories below, but when she crossed the room, she found that the window was not a window, but a door leading onto a small balcony that had a view of all the estate, all the way down to the sea.

"How beautiful," she said. She was not one much given to flowery talk, but the night was too lovely not to remark on.

"The most beautiful thing I have ever seen," Harry said agreeably.

Mary Elizabeth felt his arm brush her own, and she shivered and looked up to find him staring not out to the ocean beyond, but down at her own upturned face.

He leaned down then, and kissed her once, very gently, and she thought, *At last*. But when he pulled away almost immediately, she frowned like thunder.

"Harry, what in God's name are you playing at?"

Twenty-five

IF HARRY HAD NOT BEEN FIGHTING EVERY URGE IN HIS body, every fiber of his being, to stop himself from picking his girl up and carrying her inside, he might have laughed. For Mary Elizabeth stood close, smelling delightfully of some spicy, unknown flower, dressed in peach silk, which was quickly becoming his favorite gown on her, and waiting for him to kiss her. She might even be waiting for him to make love to her as he had done down in the library not two nights before.

She looked so annoyed, so beautiful, and so delightfully his, that instead of picking her up as he wanted to, Harry spoke. "Marry me, Mary. Don't make me wait."

She sighed then, her annoyance replaced by a flash of guilt. "Harry, I cannot. Not yet. I am very sorry."

"You love me," he said.

"I do."

"Then you'll marry me."

"I might."

Hope filled him, followed by joy. Then she spoke again.

"I'm just not certain yet, Harry. I need more time."

He drew her close, his telescope forgotten. The hulk of wood and metal stood beside them, a tool that had opened another world for him when he first received it from his mother at the age of eighteen. And now, he could not care less about it, or about much else, save for Mary Elizabeth's answer. He had clearly lost his mind.

He supposed he would have to learn to live without one.

"What if I seduce you into saying yes?"

Mary Elizabeth pulled away far enough to smile at him. "You threatened to do that before. Do you think you might try?"

"I won't try. I'll succeed."

He heard the arrogance in his own voice and her laughter that came after it. He could not remember any other woman who had dared to laugh in his face, nor man either, save for Clive once or twice. He would have to follow her about like a pup until she agreed to marry him for that reason alone. He needed a woman who could make him laugh at himself.

Her body was soft and warm against his, and Harry found himself wanting to forget all that had come before that moment—her run-ins with her mother, her constant refusal of his suit, the fact that she had released his foxes. Harry wished that he might start the day from scratch, and spend it only with her. Or perhaps go back further than that, and stop his mother from inviting all and sundry to his home save for Mary Elizabeth and her kin, that he might woo her with no distractions.

It occurred to him then that he had never really wooed her at all. Perhaps he might try that. Perhaps a little tender loving care might sway her where his kisses and declarations did not.

The wheels of his mind spinning with delight in his newly hatched scheme, Harry left his lady on the balcony. Mary Elizabeth only clung to him for a moment before her arms fell away, and she let him go. He knew that he would spend the rest of that evening making it harder for her to turn from him. As it was, she simply sighed and looked into the garden below, watching the kitchen mouser on her way to visit her friend, the stable tabby.

Harry stepped inside and rang for Philips. His man appeared without delay, still immaculately dressed, in spite of the fact that he had dismissed him for the night.

"Forgive the intrusion on your evening, Philips."

"No intrusion at all, my lord."

"I have need of a few items from the kitchen, as well as a bit of discretion."

Harry was not sure, but he thought he saw his man repress a smile. "It will be a pleasure, sir."

Mary Elizabeth could not see a blasted thing through his bloody telescope. When Harry was gone for longer than five minutes, she got tired of watching the antics of her friends the cats down below and started fiddling with the machine that held pride of place on the small balcony.

The walnut casing gleamed in the moonlight, as did the brass fixtures. It was a lovely piece, and looked a good deal like Ian's spyglass, save that it was large enough to need a stand of its own to bear its weight.

But when she peered into the eyepiece, all she could see was unrelieved black. She was about to climb onto the balcony railing, that she might look into the lens of the telescope, to see perhaps if it had a cap covering its glass, when Harry reappeared, looking like a mouser that had been in the cream.

"You're up to something," she said in lieu of haranguing him about the defects of his telescope.

"I am," he said. "Come inside and see."

She looked at him suspiciously. She reminded herself of the fact that she had invited herself to his rooms, after all. It was she who wished to make love with him and ruin herself in the eyes of the world for any other man. She told herself not to be missish and squeamish, but to step through the door and see what he was about. But the predatory gleam in his eye, a gleam so unlike Harry, gave her pause.

There was a great deal about this man she simply did not know, things that she had never seen before that night. That gleam was one of them.

Mary Elizabeth squared her shoulders and moved to step into the room beyond him, giving him as wide a berth as she might. The french doors were narrow, for Harry was still standing in them, taking up most of the space. As she passed, Mary Elizabeth took in a deep breath of the scent of his skin and the warmth of his body beneath his evening dress. She had the sudden unaccountable urge to peel those fancy clothes off him, one layer at a time.

Clearly, Harry was not the only predator on that balcony.

She told herself not to be daft, and slipped past him as quick as an eel. He laughed a little under his breath, no doubt at her. She would have taken him to task for it, and had even opened her mouth to do so, when she saw what was arrayed in his sitting room and fell silent.

On his tiny table, drawn close to the fire, was a pile of strawberries covered in chocolate. There was a pot of chocolate, gleaming silver, set over its own warmer, with a pitcher of milk beside it. There were bits of cheese, all arrayed on a plate in the shape of a fan, and champagne bubbled in two glasses, just poured.

Mary Elizabeth did not know what to say, so she stepped into the room and approached the feast slowly, hoping to think of something.

"You look as if it will bite you, Mary."

She did not look at him but smiled distractedly over her shoulder for one moment before turning back to the banquet before her. It was as if the fairies had come and left every good thing for her delight there. She did not sit in a chair, but crouched low next to the table that she might take it in better.

"You want a picnic on the carpet, then?" Harry asked. His voice came from very close behind her, for he was no longer standing in the door at all. The apple wood fire gave off a cheerful light and smelled delightful, but for one odd moment, Mary Elizabeth wished it were a peat fire and that they were home, so that she might show some of the delights of Glenderrin to him. She pushed the thought aside as ungrateful and met his gaze at last.

"No," she answered. "Such fancy food must be eaten on a chair."

"Or a sofa," he said, lifting her by the waist and seating her on his lap on the sofa in question. She wondered for a moment if the sofa in his sitting room was as comfortable as the one in his library, but she did not wriggle down to find out. Instead, she leaned against Harry and let the bulk of him surround her in warmth. This is what home would feel like when she got there.

She pushed home out of her mind again and turned her face to Harry's cravat, drawing in the sandalwood scent of him, sighing.

"I was hoping you might like at least a bite or two of this," Harry said, sounding a bit peeved. "I am trying to woo you."

Mary Elizabeth kissed his cheek, her lips lingering on the edge of his cheekbone, where his beard was beginning to grow back. She rubbed her nose along the rasp of it, and then her cheek, sighing again at how delightful he felt against her and how sorry she was to leave him behind, even for a few weeks.

But she must see if her feelings for him were some South-addled dream, or if they were real. Only home could tell her that.

"You're doing a fine job," she said by way of soothing him, and herself. When she looked up at him, he was still frowning at her, so she reached over and took up a glass of champagne in one hand and a strawberry in the other.

"These berries are from the hothouse," she said.

Somewhat mollified, Harry watched her take a bite.

The annoyance in his face soon turned to desire. She could tell because his eyes darkened. But she could not be bothered with his changing moods now, for the combination of chocolate and fruit on her tongue made her close her eyes in ecstasy.

They did not have strawberries in Glenderrin.

Nor did they have Harry.

She opened her eyes and found him watching her mouth as if she might impart the wisdom of the world to him at any moment. She had no wisdom to offer him, but she loved him. She supposed she might offer him that.

She sipped from the champagne, since he had brought it to her, and the fizzing dry wine bit at her tongue, making her blink. Harry took the glass from her and drained it before setting it behind him on a table. It was her turn to frown at him.

"I want more of that," she said. She turned to pick up the second glass from the low table in front of them when she felt Harry's lips on the skin of her throat, just beneath her ear. She shivered and almost dropped what was left of her strawberry.

"Leave it for later," Harry said. "I've another way to woo you."

Her wicked thoughts turned to the sofa they were sitting on, which turned them to the sofa down in the library and the things he had done to her down there. Mary Elizabeth had not been able to make much sense out of pleasure like that, pleasure she had not known existed before Harry touched her. She had tried to put the pleasure out her mind, but now, with Harry's lips on her skin and his large, warm body tucked close against her, she found that she wanted to feel that pleasure again.

Harry ate the last of her berry in one bite, tossing the bit of green cap into the empty champagne glass behind him. He smiled at her, and she shivered, because his eyes never left hers as he sprawled out on the sofa beneath her, drawing her with him.

"It's bigger up here," Mary Elizabeth said.

Harry raised one eyebrow, his eyes growing even darker. Mary Elizabeth felt the flush from the fire and the flush from her skin come together in a conflagration, and she fought to keep her good sense about her, knowing all the while that she was failing.

"The sofa, I mean," she said. "This sofa is bigger."

Harry ignored her words, his fingers sliding down along the scalloped bodice of her gown. He did not peel it off her as she hoped he might, but simply slid one finger, and then two, beneath the silk, letting the calluses on his fingertips ride along the edge of her soft skin, caressing the swells of her breasts—first one and then the other.

She wriggled against him, hoping that he might kiss her and that his hand might take one whole breast into it, but he did neither. His eyes lingered on her body, and his fingers lingered on her breast until one of them dipped lower, caressing her nipple until it was standing firm, pressing hard against the silk and lace of her bodice and stays.

Mary Elizabeth was sure he would kiss her then, and touch her other breast, but he smiled, not meeting her eyes, letting his own eyes linger on her body, on the swell of her hips where they pressed against his, over the swell of her behind where it rose and fell, riding his breathing as she might ride an ocean wave. Mary Elizabeth felt the evidence of his desire for her against her stomach, so she did not understand why he did not do something more to make her his.

"Harry," she said, not sure how to ask a man to kiss her. Instead of asking, she leaned up and tried to kiss him, but he dodged her lips easily, his own landing not on her skin but on her hair.

Mary Elizabeth had begun to smell a rat, but she tried again, wriggling against him. He sucked in a breath, and his arms clamped around her to hold her still. She was sure he would kiss her then, and maybe even draw her down beneath him, but he did not. In less than a moment, his breathing was even again, and while one arm held her still, his other hand explored the curves of her body over the silk of her gown.

"Harry," she tried again. "I need you."

"Need me, do you?"

She was not sure, but she thought she heard a little laughter in his voice. If either of her hands had been free, she would have hit him. As it was, she could not even writhe. His body was hard and hot against hers, and a heat was building in her nether parts that needed his attention, and quickly. She had no idea what to do about it, but she knew very well that Harry did.

"And what do you need me for?" Harry asked.

Mary Elizabeth strove for patience, working very hard not to grind her teeth.

"I need you to kiss me," she said.

"Oh," Harry replied. "Is that all?"

He kissed her cheek as she had just kissed his. His

lips lingered, but when she turned her head to meet his mouth with hers, he pulled away.

"No, Harry, not like that."

"How, then? You'll have to show me."

Mary Elizabeth tried to move, tried to free herself so that she might crawl up his body and take his lips with hers, but he held her fast, and easily, with only one arm. His other hand kept sliding over her, this time caressing the curves of her derriere as if it were new country he was intent on exploring.

She could barely think, but she forced herself to rally. "I canna move, Harry. You've got me trapped."

"Oh, do I now?" He looked down her body as if only just that moment noticing that he held her prisoner. His arm tightened around her. "I like you trapped," Harry said. "You're more reasonable when I have you trapped."

"Now, Harry," Mary Elizabeth began, trying to sound as reasonable as she might and failing.

He laughed a little then, and she glared at him. "Might my lady wish to do a bit of...what is your word? Canoodling?"

Mary glowered at him, but just then his free hand drew her skirt up a good six inches, so that she could feel the heat from the fire on her stockings and calves. She shivered, almost overwhelmed by that one touch. She wanted Harry so badly that she might swallow her tongue in a minute and not be able to speak at all.

"Yes, Harry. She might."

"Ah, well, then," he said expansively, stretching beneath her as a great cat might stretch in the sun. His arm still held her clamped down. He did not let her go. "We'd best come to terms," Harry said. "Before my lady becomes annoyed."

Mary Elizabeth did not want to tell him that she was already annoyed and why did he bloody well not kiss her already, but in the interest of success, she held her peace.

"What terms need we discuss?" she asked, making an experimental wriggle. She could not budge at all, save for a bit along her hips. When she used them to brush against his manhood, Harry's smile did not falter, but he did clamp down on her harder, even as he shifted himself away. All the while, his free hand kept moving, driving her mad.

"Well, now. For starters, we must both concede that you are my lady and that you will be for the rest of your life."

Mary Elizabeth did not want to think of him with any other, even after she left him, even if he decided he no longer wanted her once she was home in Glenderrin. She also knew that she would never love anyone as she loved him, nor would she want to, whatever the outcome.

"All right," she said. "I agree. I am yours, for the rest of my life. God help me."

Harry grew very still at that. His hand stopped moving and rested on the curve of her bum, cupping it so that his fingers rested along the inner curve of her thigh. Distracted by that touch, Mary tried to wriggle against his hand, but he held her fast.

He did not smile but stared at her, as if looking into her soul. "And you must concede that you will marry me."

"I might one day, Harry."

"You will. Within a week. As soon as I can get the special license in hand."

Mary Elizabeth leaned her cheek against the softness of his black coat so that she would not have to meet his eyes.

"You will be my duchess," he said. "And I will love you for the rest of my life and beyond."

Mary Elizabeth sighed, for she would not lie to him—or to herself. She realized in that moment that she should have been a barrister, so easily did the answer come to her. Perhaps Davy would let her have a look at the next contract they would sign with the East India Company, for she clearly had an eye for detail.

"If the license and I are in the same room at the same time as you, Harry, I will marry you. I give you my word."

"That is the strangest answer to a marriage proposal I have ever received," he groused.

"Asked a lot of women to be your duchess, have you?"

"Only you, Mary Elizabeth Waters, and you know it."

"It's a better answer than no, isn't it?"

She raised herself up to meet his eyes.

"Yes," he said, looking wary.

He stared down at her, as if certain he could see past the hazel of her eyes to her inner litigator. Harry seemed to see something else there, something that gave him hope, something that calmed him.

"I will hold you to your word, Mary, if I have to follow you to the end of the earth to do it. You will marry me."

"All right, Harry," she said. His body felt even harder against hers than it had before. His grip had loosened just enough so that she might writhe against him a little—not enough to satisfy her hunger, but enough to let him know that she was still there.

"I love you, Harry. I agree that I am yours for the rest of my life. What else is there to settle between us?"

His blue eyes were as dark as indigo as he stared up at her. His arms loosened just a little, and then he shifted his weight, and hers with it, so that she was sprawled beneath him on the comfortable sofa. He was as quick as a tiger, so quick she did not see the movement coming until he was over her, pressing into her, his great body and all its heat and muscled beauty making her forget her own question and everything else.

"Only this."

Harry kissed her.

Twenty-six

HARRY DID NOT KNOW WHY HE STILL FELT A NIGGLING bit of doubt at the back of his mind as to his fiancée's intentions toward him. Mary Elizabeth was a woman of her word. She would never break it. But the strange way she had agreed to marry him made him wonder what detail he was missing.

But then he turned over and had her under him, and his body could not care about any detail but the way she felt against him, pressed soft between him and his sofa cushions.

Harry stopped trying to figure a way around this woman and her stubborn pride. He simply gave himself up to the curves of her body, the way her mouth tasted beneath his, the flavor of chocolate and champagne on her tongue. He pushed away his doubts to be dealt with on the morrow.

He knew suddenly, as he drew back for air, that he would solve his own problem. He would rise with the dawn, announce their engagement to the entire household, and then keep her tethered to him by a length of silk cord if he had to until the special license arrived from London.

Or he could always lock her away, like a prisoner in some Gothic novel. That would please him, especially if he locked himself away with her.

Such scandalous actions would set the *ton*, not to mention his mother, on a roar. Not that he cared, so long as Mary Elizabeth was his.

Being a duke had its privileges.

"I'm not over your knee, Harry."

Her sleepy words did not match the fire that burned in her eyes. Harry wondered if this woman he loved would ever quit challenging him.

He hoped not.

But Mary Elizabeth had yet to learn that there were times when he was going to be, as she put it, the boss of her. It was time that she found out.

Harry kissed her lips before she could say anything else. The sweetness of her tongue beneath his spoke of dark chocolate and even darker thoughts. He did not linger there, but kissed his way down to her breasts, encased as they still were in peach-colored silk.

Harry raised his head long enough to look into her face, and when she offered no objection, he slid two fingers inside her bodice, while his other hand deftly searched out the ties to her gown. He knew his girl well, and knew that she kept no lady's maid. Her gown was tied up underneath her arm with silk ribbons, and it took him less than a trice to loosen them and for the silk of her bodice to slide away from her body like a tide slipping over sand.

Mary Elizabeth did not seem to notice or care that her bodice was going, so Harry raised himself off her long enough to let it slip down to the carpet at the foot of their sofa.

His lady smiled up at him, stretching, her breasts straining against the lace of her stays. "That is a world more comfortable," she said.

Harry felt his hand begin to shake with lust, and he stilled it, as his father had so often stilled his hand against strong drink. He smiled at the woman who would be his duchess, taking in the devilish light of challenge in her eyes. He had not subdued her yet. He thought then that it would probably take the rest of his life to teach her who was in charge in their bed. And he would enjoy those lessons, however long they spun out.

He unfastened her stays then, loosening her laces even as his fingertips played over the soft peaks of her breasts. His lips joined his fingers until she was writhing under him, her hands in his hair, drawing him down to her, urging him on.

He had forgotten all about lessons and dominance as he feasted on her, kissing and fondling first one breast and then the other. The stays simply became a barrier between him and the woman he loved, and he tossed them aside, so that they landed a little farther away from their perch on the sofa.

Harry knew that he was quickly reaching the point of no return, and as he scanned the flushed, pleasure-filled face of the woman he loved, he found that he had to be sure. Dominance in bed was amusing, but he would guard this woman, even from himself and his own selfish desires, for the rest of his life.

So he spoke, breaking the mood like shattered crystal. "Are you certain, Mary? Are you sure you want me? That you want this?"

Mary Elizabeth opened her eyes. Their usual maple brown glittered with buried bits of green. She smiled at him, as if she were twelve years his elder and not the other way around. As if she had seen the world, or all she needed to see of it, and out of all the lands, near and far, he, Harry Percy, was her choice.

For blessed once, the woman in his arms cared nothing for his money, his lineage, his so-called power, or his title. For blessed once, the woman in his arms was there for him, and him alone.

"I love you, Harry," Mary Elizabeth said. "I choose you."

∼

Mary Elizabeth felt a little guilty about the fact that though she was not lying to the man she loved, she was leaving him on the morrow and he did not know it. She wondered if he would take a page from her brothers' book and follow her into the wilds of Scotland, intent on making her his. He would not be able to catch her and drag her back, as they had done with their errant women, for she was not so foolish as to travel alone. Even Sampson, as fleet as he was, could not catch up to the mail coach to Aberdeen.

Mary Elizabeth pressed herself against her man, sighing as the hard heat of his body touched her naked breasts. Harry's hands were everywhere, unfastening her clothes in a trice. She would remember to devil him about how he had learned his way around a lady's undergarments, but she would do it later.

She pushed aside all thoughts of the dawn as well, and opened her mouth to feast on his. When Harry pulled away to trail his lips down to her breasts, she wriggled against him, her own fingers seeking the warmth of his skin as her mouth could not. Her fingertips brushed his manhood, rising hard and proud against her hand, and he hissed, drawing back.

"Did I hurt you, then?" she asked, a little concerned that he would be so missish at such a time. But she should have known her man better by then.

"Pleasure hurts as well as heals, my lady," Harry said, trapping her fingers inside the heat of his palm. He drew back and sat up, looking down at her as she sprawled on the sofa. A few cushions had found their way to the rug along with her bodice and stays. With Harry gone, she wriggled out of her skirts and petticoats as well, and pushed them over the edge with all the rest.

One flounce caught under his thigh, and she let it dangle, for all she wore now were her stockings, and they did not get in her way. She wondered if she ought to take them off, as it was her first time, but when she reached for her garters, Harry caught her hand again and stopped her cold.

"Oh, no," he said. "You'll keep those on."

"I will?" Mary Elizabeth asked. She lay back against the soft cushions, feeling like the Queen of Sheba. "You sound as if you think you are the boss of me."

"In bed, I am."

Mary Elizabeth laughed out loud at that, and sat up. She went to reach for the second untouched glass of champagne, but Harry was there before her, taking it up in his hand.

He took a swallow, his eyes never leaving her

face. Mary Elizabeth reached for it again, but he held it out of reach. "Harry, I want a bit of that fancy French wine."

"Do you, now?"

"I just said I did."

Mary Elizabeth wondered why she was sitting there arguing with him in the altogether when she simply could have reached behind her, taken up the first glass, and refilled it herself. But there was the light of joy as well as challenge in Harry's eyes, and she found that she wanted to join with him in whatever game he was playing, even if she did not yet know the rules.

"Say please," Harry said.

Mary Elizabeth laughed and grabbed for the glass. Harry kept it out of her reach, pouring a bit of the wine down the front of her, then licking it away, spending a bit of extra time lapping at her nipples, even when she was sure that all the champagne was long since gone. Mary Elizabeth lost herself for a moment in the motion of his tongue, but when he pulled away at last, she remembered her wine.

"Please," she said.

Harry did not hand her the glass as she thought he might, but raised it to her lips and tipped it back, that she might take a drink. She sipped at it, and he held the glass for her as delicately as any lady's maid might have spooned broth into her when she was ill. He was nothing like a lady's maid, however, and nothing like a nurse. His great body, which did not seem that large when he was talking, now seemed to dwarf her as she sat beside him.

Mary Elizabeth did not find herself troubled by her

nakedness, nor embarrassed, which she supposed did mean she was a bit of a wanton. That did not worry her, for Harry would keep her secret. Whatever game he was playing at, he loved her and would defend her against all comers.

Of course, that did not change the fact that she did not know the rules to this game, and she was getting tired of waiting for him to touch her in earnest.

So Mary Elizabeth did as she always did in any situation in her life and took matters into her own hands. She pushed him back against the sofa cushions so that he was sitting a bit reclined, and she rose up over his lap, swinging one leg over him as she would a horse.

"There now," she said. "That's better."

Harry did not bat an eyelash nor did he drop what was left of their wine, but his voice was a bit strangled when he answered her. "Is it, now?"

Mary Elizabeth wriggled against his manhood, the open, wet warmth of her pressing into the fine wool of his trousers, filling her with the approach of the bliss that Harry had given her in the library. His eyes filled with blue fire as she did it, and when she leaned down to kiss him, he dodged her mouth.

"Mary, you are baiting the bear," he said.

"No," she answered. "I am baiting you."

She could not reach his mouth, so she trailed her lips along the side of his neck. She felt his hot breath next to the softness of her breasts, and she wriggled again, this time not to tease him, but to find his manhood beneath his clothes.

Before she could begin to unfasten his falls, Harry caught her hand in his. He set the wine down and caught her other hand, too, drawing her wrists behind her so that she could not touch him at all.

"Mary," he said, his voice calm and his eyes blazing. "I am the man here. As on the dance floor, I will lead, and you will follow."

Mary Elizabeth shivered at the way his voice changed. She looked into the blue of his eyes, wishing he might touch her, but not certain that she had the courage to ask.

"I want you, Harry. Show me what to do, and I will do it."

He smiled then, and pressed a kiss to her breast where it rose higher with her arms behind her back. He held both her wrists easily in one hand, loosely, for she did not try to get away. His lips trailed across to her other breast and suckled there, but only a little, not drawing deep, not giving her even a glimpse of satisfaction, but making her lust rise higher.

"Harry," she said. She did not sound polite to her own ears, but demanding, and he laughed a little against her breast. She wriggled then, and he stopped laughing, beginning to suckle her in earnest.

He still did not touch her in any other way, and with her hands behind her back, she could not touch him. Mary rose up, trying to brush herself against him. When she did, her breasts made contact with the buttons of his waistcoat, and she shuddered. She had forgotten that he was still fully dressed. Somehow, his clothes made her nakedness seem even more erotic. She was sure that if he did not touch her soon, she would die.

But she did not die. Harry's free hand slipped

between her body and his, caressing first the tops of her thighs and then the juncture between them. He found what he was seeking almost at once, and he did not make her wait, nor did he play at wooing her. Harry's callused fingertips found the place between her thighs that was the fountain of all bliss, and he pressed there, hard, while one of his fingers slipped inside her body and did something else that made her come apart completely.

Mary Elizabeth screamed then, the pleasure was so great. Harry caught her scream with his mouth to muffle the sound, but she did not care if the whole house heard her. There was no one else in that house, nothing else on earth, but Harry and herself, and the music their bodies made together.

The pleasure did not recede all at once, but trickled out of her, one spasm at a time. She found herself draped across the man she loved, her cheek pressed against his heart, which was thundering as loud as if he had run a mile. He gasped, as she did, and he had not had any pleasure yet at all.

This concerned her, but only a little, as something to be dealt with as soon as she got her breath back. But before she could breathe deep, Harry had her tossed over his shoulder, one hand caressing her bum and the other bracing her legs.

"Harry, what devilry is this, then?"

"I'll not have you on a sofa," he said. "My wife deserves a bed."

The word *wife* on his tongue thrilled her as she knew the word *duchess* never would. Mary Elizabeth hung down, contemplating his fine derriere before he tossed her on the bed. How they had made it into the next room so quickly, Mary Elizabeth was not sure, but the bedclothes had been turned down, and the linen sheets were cool against her heated skin. She wriggled against them, making a snow angel she could not see, as she watched the man she loved undress before her.

He was quick about it, so she could not see everything as she would have wished, but what she could see, she savored. The light was a bit dim, being only candlelight, but she could see the width of his shoulders and the smooth tapering of his hips. She followed the trail of hair from his chest down to his manhood, and when he lay down beside her on the bed and covered her body with his own, she swirled her fingers in his chest hair even as she kissed him.

He kissed her long and well, but his hands were busy, positioning her the way he wanted her, tucking a pillow beneath her hips and then a second one beneath the small of her back, until she felt a bit strange. She did not have time to feel foolish however, for he was between her thighs then, the whole beautiful, muscled Harry-ness of him, and he kissed her, his fingertips exploring her again, making her sob with need though she had only just reached the peak of pleasure.

He slid inside her just as she was beginning that climb again. He was a large man, which was a good thing, for he surrounded her on all sides, so that she could not have gotten away if she had wanted to. She did not want to, but her body was hungry for the pleasure again and seemed to want to climb him of its own accord to seek it. But Harry knew what she needed, so that even as he breached her maidenhead in one clean stroke, she felt only the smallest bite of pain before the larger wave of pleasure rose to swamp it, taking her reason with it.

He moved against her as a battering ram might take down a fortress wall. She did not stand against him, but welcomed him in. He battered her all the same, taking her step by spiraling step higher into pleasure, until she screamed again, this time saying his name. His lips clamped over hers, and he shuddered against her until he too lay still.

They lay together then. Mary Elizabeth wondered for one brief, odd moment if she was dead and he with her, for surely such pleasure could not exist anywhere on the earth.

For such a thing to be, the world was a far different place than she had ever known it to be. It made her wonder.

She lay there, wondering, until Harry raised his head and smiled down at her. He kissed her, her gentle Harry once more, the passionate barbarian asleep for the moment behind the blue of his eyes.

"And that is why you will marry me."

Harry said that, and then nestled down beside her, his body still over hers, and promptly fell asleep.

Twenty-seven

WITH A BIG GALOOT LAID OUT ON TOP OF HER, MARY Elizabeth did not sleep. She did wriggle into a more convenient and comfortable pose, turning onto her side. Harry seemed obliging, even as he slept, but when she deemed it time to rise and find her clothes, his arm clamped around her like a vise, holding her fast.

Mary Elizabeth sighed and looked into his face. Harry was smiling, as he had been since they had made love, but now his hair was mussed and the strawberry blond of it had fluffed a bit around his head, making him look like a golden hedgehog. He was her hedgehog, and she loved him, but she needed to get out of that bed.

He did not wake and did not seem to wake even if she whispered to him. She tried to offer him a pillow in her place, but even sleeping, Harry was stubborn. He held on to her as he might have held on to a prize won in war. She had to wait an entire hour, until his sleep deepened and he turned over of his own accord, before she was able to slip away from him.

He almost woke then, and she supposed it was a good thing that his king had refused to make him a warrior, for had he been one, she never would have been able to get away. He would have woken and tied her down, or at least locked her in. But as it was, Harry had not a warrior's instincts, and he slept on peacefully as soon as she slipped a piece of her tartan into his hand.

The sight of the blue and green muted tones tucked into the palm of her Englishman made her smile. She wondered if, by some chance, one of his marauding ancestors had gone North and plucked a Lowland woman away from her embroidery and her peat fire to make her his wife. Perhaps somewhere down the line of the lineage that he was so proud of, there was a bit of Scottish blood. She would ask him when next they met.

She hoped that would be soon.

Mary Elizabeth knew that by going home without her mother's leave—indeed, by doing the exact opposite of what her mother said—she was stirring a hornet's nest among the men of her family. For the most part, Da and the boys let Mother do as she pleased, in the hope that peace would be kept, at least until the next crisis. Mary Elizabeth had done her best to go along with this scheme for the last two years, but she found that she was done with that, and forever. For once, the men of her family would have to stand with her.

She had little doubt that they would. Well, perhaps a niggling doubt that ate at her heart. But if that doubt was right, and the men of her family forced her yet again to do as her mother wished, she would simply come back to Harry and hope that he would have her. He did love her, Englishman though he was.

And she loved him.

But she would not think of that now. The mail coach came into town at four in the morning, and it was closing in on three. She donned her gown, her bodice and skirt, but carried her under things in one hand. It was too early to meet a servant, and she was stealthy. If she could hunt deer in the bracken, she could avoid the ducal household.

She kissed Harry one last time before she went. His lips were soft under hers, relaxed in his sleep, and she thought for a moment he might wake, like a prince in a fairy tale. He snuffled into the blanket, but slept on, which was just as well. She had hours of riding ahead of her, and had he seen her, Harry never would have let her go.

❧

Harry woke around seven to find that Mary Elizabeth had slipped away. He was on his feet at once, checking the sitting room and the bathing room beyond his bed, but she was nowhere to be found.

He cursed himself but did not think anything of it except that he should have hidden the key when he locked the door. He dressed with Philips's help. He might have done a quicker job of it on his own, but his man took pride in his appearance, and he had not used him often since the Scots had come to stay.

Harry found all of them, even the married women, eating peacefully in the breakfast room. The English guests were still abed, it seemed, or perhaps they were simply afraid to break bread so early with barbarians. Harry had no such qualms, and he greeted both Mrs. Waters with a smile.

The sweet, young girl, Catherine, bowed her head to him as if in church, and the second Mrs. Waters, the former Lady Prudence Farthington, nodded to him and smiled as if he did not have a ducal coronet plastered to his temples.

Alex and Robert Waters nodded to him, caught in a discussion of London and the roads out of there. Robert and his runaway bride had just returned from Town that very morning. It seemed they were not fond of the capital city on the whole, heart of the empire or not. Harry could not fault them, for London was not his favorite spot, either.

He thought of his favorite spot—the little bit of soft skin just behind Mary Elizabeth's left ear. The place that, when he touched it with his tongue, made her go limp with desire in his arms. He wondered how long she would sleep and when he might touch that place, among others, with his tongue again.

He supposed he should go through the formalities and ask Alex, as her eldest brother present, for her hand. Harry was about to do so when Robert Waters asked, "Where in God's name is Mary?"

His wife gave him a look that failed to silence him.

Alex finished chewing his brioche and took a swig of tea. "I thought she was sleeping still."

"This late?" Robert scoffed. "I doubt it."

"Have you checked the stables, if you're so concerned?" Lady Prudence asked. "She has a brute of a stallion that has fallen in love with her. Maybe she's down there, giving him treats."

The talk of stallions and treats made Harry blush, until he reminded himself that he was a duke, and dukes did not blush. And that Mary Elizabeth was marrying him as soon as he might get the license in hand.

Catherine met his eyes and smiled. "Good morning, Your Grace. I hope you enjoyed a pleasant night."

Harry felt his skin flush again, and he cleared his throat before taking the tea a footman brought him.

"Yes," he said, trying to sound calm and ducal. "Very pleasant."

"You've something to ask me," Alex said, his brown eyes gleaming. Mary Elizabeth's brother smiled at him, and Catherine squeezed Alex's hand on top of the table, a new light of joy coming into the blue of her eyes.

"I had thought to have a bite of bacon first," Harry said. "But as it happens, I do have a question for you, when you are at leisure."

"Let us withdraw so that you may speak freely," Alex said, still looking pleased but also managing to look like the Wrath of God. Harry figured he had best marry his girl, and quickly, for if this one discovered their liaison, he would kill him first and bundle Mary into a carriage after.

So that her brother and his wife would not have to make a bolt for the border with Mary Elizabeth in tow, Harry nodded and began to rise as well, with only one last rueful look at the bacon and eggs even now growing cold on his plate. He stopped cold when Robert Waters spoke.

"The devil you will withdraw. Mary's our family, too. You'll eat your breakfasts like civilized men and ask your questions here."

Alex Waters paused for one long moment. He looked not to his brother, but to his wife, who was dimpling at him, a picture of feminine loveliness in soft-blue muslin. Alex sighed then, and sat back down. Harry followed suit and fell to his breakfast. Thank God for the intervention of women.

"You wish to ask me for Mary Elizabeth's hand," Alex said.

Harry sighed, even as Lady Prudence and Catherine Waters squealed together, as if in concert. He drank another sip of tea, and this time, it was Billings who refilled his cup. Harry could not be sure, but it seemed his butler was almost smiling.

"Yes," Harry said. "I love your sister, and I think I can safely say that she loves me—"

"Nothing's ever safe with Mary. You'd best know that now," Robert Waters said.

Harry simply looked at his future brother-in-law, nonplussed, and Alex said, "Hold off for a bit, Robbie. Let the man speak."

Robert leaned back in his chair, his hand going to his waist. Harry found himself wondering if he wore a dirk and who had been the one to teach Mary Elizabeth to throw knives in the first place. Motivated both by the desire to finish his breakfast and to save his skin from puncture holes, Harry spoke.

"I would marry her, with your permission, as soon as I can get a special license."

Alex was going to say something then, but Robert

spoke for him. "Well, it's about time, lad. While I was in London, the family carrier pigeons brought nothing but letters from mother and from this one, telling me of your amour and speculating on whether or not we'd have an Englishman in the family or if we'd have to emigrate to Nova Scotia to save our skins after we shot you. I'm not fond of the English," Robert said. His wife slapped his hand with a fan that had suddenly appeared from beneath the table, and he winced. "But, as I was saying"—he raised both brows at his wife—"I have recently come to know one or two English a bit better—"

"More than a bit, I'd say, husband," Lady Prudence whispered loud enough for all the table to hear.

"As you say, wife." Robert Waters kissed his woman full on the lips in front of God and the butler. Billings, used to these shenanigans since the arrival of the Scots, did not even raise one brow.

"I find," Robert Waters continued his oration, "that not all English are half-bad. You may marry our sister, if you wish and she consents. God help you."

Alex stood and offered Harry his hand. Harry was finished with his bacon by then, and rose with good grace to shake it. Billings did blanch at that familiarity, but Harry supposed that his butler would have to get used to that, too.

Not to be outdone, Robert Waters rose as well, and Harry shook his hand for good measure. "As for the special license, I have it here." Robert tossed it onto the table, next to the silver butter dish. "Uncle Raymond thought you might be needing it. It seems that even the Bishop of London has heard of the romance between the Recluse Duke and the Hellion of Hyde Park."

In the midst of this unseemly Scottish display in the breakfast room, a footman appeared at the door. "Mr. Billings, sir."

The butler frowned like thunder. "Do not interrupt, Franklin. His Grace is at table."

"Yes, sir. It's only that, the housemaids were just cleaning the library. And they found this."

Harry turned to see a slim leather volume held in Franklin's white-gloved hand. It was a volume of poetry by Robert Burns that he had hoped to give Mary Elizabeth, but had not yet had the chance. He accepted the volume, wondering why his well-trained staff had thought to interrupt his breakfast over a trifle, when he opened it to find a bit of blue-and-green plaid tucked into it like a bookmark. It was the same plaid he had woken to find in his bed that morning.

"Our hunting tartan," Robert Waters said.

"How lovely," Catherine said.

Harry thought it pretty, too, and was pleased to know that it was a gift from his bride. But it marked a place in the book over a maudlin song about a lover who would return to his beloved, though "it t'were ten thousand miles."

He felt a bit sick even before he opened the letter from Mary Elizabeth pressed into the book. She had written in a fine hand, much better than he would have expected her ever to acquire, with all her hunting and fishing and riding horses to their doom—and his.

He did not have to read the words aloud. Indeed, he could not, so it was just as well that Robert and

Alex knew their sister well enough that he need not speak at all.

"She's done a runner," Robert groused. He swore aloud, and his wife whacked him a second time with her otherwise useless fan. She must have kept it about her person for the sole purpose of chastising her errant husband when he went astray, which no doubt was often.

Harry found himself thinking these inane things, trying to repress the knowledge that Mary Elizabeth had left him.

In spite of his best efforts, he failed.

Twenty-eight

HARRY SENT DOWN TO THE STABLES TO MAKE CERTAIN that Sampson was still there. He did this, though Mary Elizabeth had written in her note that she had taken the mail coach to Aberdeen. She hoped to find a cousin to take her the rest of the way from there to Glenderrin. Harry was not sure why he believed her, since she had also said she loved him, and the night before she had said more than once that she would marry him. He was not sure what he believed now, other than that his heart hurt and he did not know what to do about it.

He left the breakfast room and retreated into the duchess's sitting room, where no one would come that time of day, not even the duchess herself. The south-facing lawn touched the rose garden, where he'd had his first real conversation with Mary. He knew he should make plans to go after her, but what was to stop her from running a second time? If she did not want him, she did not want him. Or if she only wanted to be his friend, who occasionally rolled around with him in his bed, he could not change that either.

Harry stood watching the sunlight move across the green of his mother's lawn, trying to remember the last time he had felt like this. Perhaps when his father had died and he had been left with the burden of the duchy once and for all. But there had been relief in his father's death, too, the peace of being released from a burden of loving a man who would never love him back. There was no relief in Mary Elizabeth's desertion. Only pain.

"So you've come in here to sulk."

He tensed. "Hello, Mother."

Harry did not turn to her but continued to look out the french doors. He knew that he should rouse himself to pack, that the journey to Scotland was a long and cold one. He supposed he should take the carriage, as he would need it to bring her back. Part of him wondered if he should simply follow her on Sampson and deal with matters of carriages and returns once he had her in hand and her signature on the marriage license in his pocket. He made these plans halfheartedly, for he was not sure he could bring himself to chase a woman who made love with him one hour and fled him the next—a woman who did not love him as she had said she did.

His mother had not left him alone, as he had hoped she might. Why he had taken refuge from the prying eyes of his guests in one of her rooms, and not down at the stables, Harry could not fathom. Though his mother leaned heavily on her gilded cane, she looked as fierce as she had when he was small and she had defended him to his father. He waited for a tirade about the faithlessness of foolish women, but it did not come.

"Licking your wounds is all well and good, I suppose, Harry, but you're losing daylight."

He felt the sting of her censure but distantly, as he felt everything but the ache over his heart. He turned to contemplate her, knowing that she was trying to bait him into action. He found that he loved her for it.

"It's summer, Mama. There is plenty of daylight left."

"You think she's left you of her own accord because she does not love you enough."

"She does not love me at all."

"Balderdash!" The duchess rapped her cane once, hard, on the black-and-white parquet floor. The floor was of polished tile and gave off a nice ring. Neither her speech nor her noise impressed him, however. He knew what he knew.

His knowledge did not keep his mother from speaking, however. "Anyone with eyes in their head can see that she loves you. She never does any outlandish thing but that she looks to you to see how you'll take it. She leaves her precious tartan with no one but places it in a book for you to keep. She loves you more than she should after only a few days' acquaintance, just as you love her."

Harry listened to all this, acknowledging it. These facts were not evidence in his favor but simply ideas his mother spouted to make him feel better. He wanted to be moved by them, but found that he was not.

He was trying to find a way to let his mother down easy, while also motivating himself to make a decision, when he heard a second, quiet voice from the doorway.

"Your mother is right."

Harry turned to look at Lady Anna of Glenderrin. She was more beautiful than any woman her age had a right to be, her blonde curls untouched by time, her face cut only here and there by subtle lines—lines that did not detract from the curves of her face but softened them. Her blue eyes, dark as the sea in midwinter, stared at him.

He felt he should rouse himself to acknowledge her, as she was Mary Elizabeth's mother, whatever conflicts passed between her and the woman he loved. He bowed to her. He found that he could not force even a false smile. He tried to fall back on good manners and failed there as well.

"Good morning, Lady Anna. And how find you the ducal hospitality this morning?"

"Lovely, I thank you. But I am not here to discuss the marmalade. I am here to take the blame for my daughter's folly."

Harry listened for a moment, to see if she might say something more. He did not think that Mary Elizabeth was driven by folly, but by desperation, though he was not ready to argue the point with her relations.

"You are not to blame, my lady. Mary Elizabeth is a free woman, with freewill, and she excels in using it."

Lady Anna smiled a little then, and for the first time, Harry saw the light of love come into her eyes. He had thought perhaps that Mary Elizabeth and her wild ways were nothing but a burden to this refined woman, but he began to see in that moment that perhaps he had been wrong.

"I ordered her to marry you or to go back to London."

Harry listened to those words, then replayed them in

his head, wondering why they should sound so strange. "You ordered Mary Elizabeth to marry me?"

"I ordered her to choose. I gave her an ultimatum: she must marry you or return to the South to find a different husband."

Harry felt a bit of the ice around his heart begin to melt. Some of the ache in his chest began to ease, even as anger, like distant thunder, called for his attention. But the most important words—*ultimatum* and *ordered her to choose*—were the sounds that he heard most clearly.

"To do such a thing would be to assure yourself that Mary does the opposite," Harry said. "Do you object to our alliance, then?"

"No," Lady Anna said. "I thought she would obey me. In important things, she always has."

"Until now."

"Yes."

"Madam, I fear you do not know your daughter as well as you should."

He saw that there were tears standing in Lady Anna's eyes and that one had lost its way, winding down her cheek. Those tears did not garner his sympathy, but they did make his anger burn a little less. He worked to keep hold of his temper, knowing from past experience what the fires of his wrath could do.

"I do not know her at all, I fear. I never have. And with this last debacle, I fear I never will. Her father will be furious with me for driving her to such a pass. As he should be. As you are."

The lady sank onto one of his mother's uncomfortable

settees and drew out a handkerchief. His mother sat beside her and patted her arm.

"I know I seem a monster. I do not mean to burden her or you. But she is a headstrong girl, and left to herself, she truly would have lived out her life on her father's moors, chasing deer in the bracken and hunting grouse, until one day she woke and found herself thirty years old and childless, and that the love of her family, such a comfort in her youth, was only a burden. She would watch her nieces and nephews grow and thrive, and never have a child of her own. And she would have been miserable, all because I did not intervene and make her marry when I should have."

Harry could almost see Mary Elizabeth climbing through thickets in breeches, a gun in the crook of her arm, a game bag over her shoulder. Had she stayed in Glenderrin, as her mother had said, he would never have known her. He would never have known that love was possible for him. He would have selected one of the most sensible women he could find, and he would have made her his duchess. No doubt he would have come to love that phantom woman, over time, after a fashion, but he would never have known a love like the one he felt for Mary now.

And if Mary Elizabeth had ever thought to come down from her Scottish fastness at all, he would have seen her and loved her and been able to offer her nothing.

Harry swallowed hard. His anger had gone. "Thank you for bringing her out of the bracken," he said.

He crossed the room and offered her his hand. Lady

Anna took it and wept harder. He sat down beside her, almost crowding both women off the settee with his bulk. He did not stand on ceremony, but took Mary's mother in his arms and held her while she wept.

"I'll go and find her," he said. "I'll bring her back."

Robert and Alex Waters had both been standing in the doorway, it seemed. They came in then, and their wives with them. Both ladies seemed to be sniffling into handkerchiefs as well, and Harry knew he had lost control of the situation entirely, if, indeed, he had ever had it.

"No, Your Worship," Robert Waters said. "You won't bring her here. You'll go to her. And we'll come with you."

Alex Waters shot his brother a look, which silenced him briefly. In the interim, Alex nodded to Harry. "I would like to officially invite you and yours to our place in the Highlands. Come to Glenderrin for the Gathering, and bide awhile with my kin."

The duchess opened her mouth to speak, but Harry spoke for her. "We accept. I thank you. Might I trouble you to see to it that my mother and yours are safely brought to Glenderrin?"

"Of course," Alex said. "And where will you be?"

"I'll be riding ahead on Sampson. I've got a stubborn woman to catch, and as my mother mentioned an hour ago, I'm losing daylight."

Twenty-nine

MARY ELIZABETH MADE IT TO ABERDEEN IN TWO AND a half days, which was why she had taken the mail coach in the first place. She had wanted safety and speed and a chance to think. One out of the three eluded her.

All she could think of was what Harry's feelings must have been when he woke up and found her gone. Slipping away in the night had made perfect sense when she was still with him, his body and his love a stalwart bulwark around her. But now she was alone, away from her kin for the first time in her life. She was not frightened, for she never met a man she did not make ten of, and she had her blades with her. The world was not as big as she had thought it was. It was simply lonelier.

Of course, she had not come away from Harry to embrace the world, nor even the road to Aberdeen. She had left her man to come home and to find within herself if she had the strength to leave it, to discover whether or not she could live among the English for the rest of her life.

The Lowlanders were little help, for they seemed

to her simply English with a different accent. But when she reached Aberdeen and the edge of the Highlands, she began to relax a little and remember why she had come.

She found one of her cousins in the farmers' market, as she knew she would. There was never a day in summer when one or another of her kin wasn't in town, save perhaps on Sunday. Michael McElraes, one of her favorite cousins, was waiting there almost as if she had sent for him.

"For God's sake, Mary Elizabeth Waters. What took it into your head to travel without one of your brothers? Even Davy will have my ballocks for this, and he's the mildest of the lot."

"Michael, calm yourself," Mary said as she hoisted herself into his wagon. The last of her cousin's summer wool was sold at market, and he was heading back to Glenstock, which was only one loch away from Glenderrin. "I'll defend you to Davy," she said. "It's my harebrained scheme that brought me here. You're simply rescuing me from myself."

He groused and clucked to his mules, who knew the way home blindfolded and were happy to go there. Michael's little son, Bran, was too small to be missed on the farm, so he had been allowed to come along to town. He peeped at her from the back of the wagon, where he had set up a fort of burlap and oilskin hides against the English.

"Good luck to him," Michael said.

"It'll hold as well as anything does when the English march their Hessians in and lay waste to the countryside."

"Aye," Michael replied. "I need to remind him that oilskin burns hot and fast."

Mary Elizabeth laughed at that, but she felt a hollow place in her chest. Where once nothing had lived but her hope for good fishing and her freedom for a clean hunt, now in her heart lived Harry's image. With him gone from her and she from him, the memory of his strawberry-blond hair and sky-blue eyes made her sad.

"You've run from a man, then," Michael said, looking out over the open road, which was dry enough this time of year.

"Who said so?" Mary Elizabeth wondered if her mother had sent a bird and if the whole clan was searching for her already. Michael did not seem particularly alarmed, but was as calm as the McElraeses of Glenstock always were.

"No one had to tell me, lass. You've that hunted-rabbit look about you. It's the same look I wore when I met my Mags. Nigh on ten years ago that was. She got me in her grip, and I settled in fine and proper. But it was a fight there at the end."

"You fought her?" Mary Elizabeth asked.

"Aye." Michael McElraes took a bit of dried mutton from his shirt pocket and chewed it, after offering it to her. He handed a bit of it to his son in the back, and little Bran fell to without a word.

"She won," Mary Elizabeth said.

Michael smiled then, and Mary Elizabeth could not remember ever seeing such a soft light come into her cousin's eyes. Of course, he was older than she, and she saw him and his only once a year at the Gathering ever since Mother had dragged her out of the bracken and trained her up for a lady. But she knew him well enough to recognize sincerity when she saw it. The McElraeses might cut you where you stand, but they would be honest about it.

"She did not win, lass. I did."

Mary Elizabeth digested that bit of information, while the soft smile lingered on Michael's face. Bran made some commotion in the back then, and his father called to him to settle down before he spooked the mules or fell out of the wagon. Mary Elizabeth went to sit with the boy and help him shore up his defenses, but all the while she thought of Harry, and wondered who had won between them. As far as she could tell, they had both lost.

When Michael came to the gates of Glenderrin, Mary Elizabeth had him drop her and her bag at the old gatehouse. The walls had long since crumbled, brought down by some marauding English almost a century ago. Now the English kept their armies home and sent the taxmen in their place. There were no walls to build against the taxman, so the walls stayed down.

Her brother Ian said that was why the clan had turned wily and kept so much money out of the empire altogether. The Dutch were good bankers and kept clean accounts, but while the family was rebuilding, a great many of them had gone across the sea. The Waterses had found some of their lost cousins and had cobbled together a bit of a clan in Nova Scotia and elsewhere, but the damage the English had done to the Highlands still lingered. And Mary Elizabeth was thinking to marry one of them.

She stood at the gate to her father's lands and took

in the sweet smell of heather on the air. The cool, clean air of the mountains wafted down to her from a great distance, but she felt as if she were standing in heaven. She set aside her pain—the pain of today and the pain to come—and took in the scent of her home. She did not have long to contemplate it, for at her father's house, one was never alone for long.

Jamie, the gatekeeper's son, took her bag up to the castle. It held her most prized possessions: her fishing lures and her knives. She had left her sword tucked in Alex's room, as Fireheart was too unwieldy to carry on the road.

She had also left her tartan behind.

Mary Elizabeth lingered by the gate, dreading the time when she would have to see Davy and her da and tell them why she had come. She sat down by the stream that ran clean by the road, and listened to its music for a bit. She was not sitting long before Connie, her little cousin, came and sat beside her.

"Ye've been gone too long," Connie said.

Mary Elizabeth took the little one in her arms and kissed her. "Aye. I have."

Connie did not belabor the point but whistled, and in a trice, a little terrier came bounding out of the bracken. His little, white face and button eyes made Mary Elizabeth squeal with delight, though she was far too old to be squealing over anything.

"That's what I said when I saw him," Connie said. "Uncle Seamus gave him to me. I've named him William Wallace."

Mary Elizabeth petted the little bundle and then set him down, as he seemed intent on exploring the world, starting with the edge of her gown. "And a fine name it is," she said.

"You don't want to come up to the keep, but you must," Connie said. "Uncle Seamus is waiting for you. If you take too long, he'll only come down and fetch you."

"Aye, that he will."

Mary Elizabeth did not like the thought of greeting her father, but there was no way around it. She had come home, and she would see him and take whatever chastisement he chose to dish out. She had earned it, she supposed.

"Will he thrash you?" Connie asked as she and Mary Elizabeth began the mile-long walk to the old castle.

"I hope not," Mary Elizabeth said.

"If he does, I'll bring you ginger biscuits and tea. In case you're sent to your room without supper."

"You're a fine girl, Connie. I should never have left you."

The little girl was solemn, her maple eyes as clear as the burn behind the house. "No. You should not have."

Connie did not chastise her any further, but led Mary Elizabeth by the hand to the house, through the lands she would have to sacrifice the love of her life for. Mary Elizabeth looked at the beauty of that land and drank it in, for it filled her soul as it always had, as it always would. But there was still a spot, just above her heart, that stayed empty.

❧

Mary Elizabeth stepped inside the walls of her father's house and felt as if she had stepped into a warm embrace. Her mother was still South, and three of her brothers had not yet returned for the Gathering, which would fall in two weeks' time. So the house was as quiet as it ever was as Connie toted her in by the hand and took her straight to her father's study.

A smaller room than Davy's library, it had a cheerful blaze burning in the hearth. The smell of peat brought tears to her eyes, so her father found her crying when he rose from his wingback chair.

"You're home, then," he said.

Mary Elizabeth did not repeat the obvious but went to him, letting his arms enfold her as she cried. She did not come up for air, but wept out her misery on her father's twill shoulder. The wool of his coat scratched her cheek, but she welcomed it.

When she stopped weeping, she was not sure how to go on or what to say. She had never been a girl for crying, not until she was sent to London, and she had done her best not to cry there, either. Her time with Harry had almost made her forget how miserable she'd been, alone and friendless in the great city, save for her two brothers, who would no doubt have been better off minding their own business at home instead of squiring her about among the English *ton*.

She drew back at last and accepted her father's handkerchief. It was large, and blunt, and smelled of bergamot and honey. It smelled like him. She almost fell to weeping again, but rallied and dried her eyes. In the end, she did not have to speak, for he knew her well and knew that her pain was not worth speaking of.

"So are you ruined, lass?"

His voice held no censure. If Da had read a fevered

missive from her mother, sent by carrier pigeon into
the Highlands, he had not drawn his conclusion from
it. He would wait until he had heard both sides of the
story. And then, as like as not, he would point out a
third side, a middle ground that all might live with. He
had that way about him. Though Mary Elizabeth was
not sure what such a middle ground might look like,
she trusted her father to find it.

"I am, Da."

He patted her arm and drew her close to the fire.
It was midsummer, and the sun was high, but it was
cool in that stone house, in spite of the wood paneling
that had gone up sometime around the reign of Jamie
the Sixth. "Well, that's settled then. Come and have
a cuppa."

He rang a bell, and Brenna the kitchen maid
brought tea and scones on a tray. Mary Elizabeth
hugged her, and as she settled down to drink her tea,
she found that whatever might happen between her
and her man, she was glad to be home.

Davy stumbled in from his library, as he always
seemed to do whenever there was tea and food about.
Her brother did not ask her foolish questions, but
drank half the pot, talking to her of some book he was
reading about the making of sailing ships in the New
World, and how their clan might improve its fleet—or
at least the Waterses' five ships—when they next came
into port.

"The men of Boston are as clever a bunch as you'll
ever find," Davy was saying. "It comes from throwing
off the yoke of English oppression, no doubt."

Mary Elizabeth smiled to hear his fiery talk and

caught her father's eye. Da hid his smile in his teacup. "No doubt," she answered.

Her da and Davy talked of the Gathering to come and of how Ian would be home soon, once his ship had come to port in Aberdeen. Their mother was on her way as well from the Lowlands, with Robbie and Alex and their new brides in tow.

Mary Elizabeth wanted to ask if perhaps they had an English duke with them, but she held her tongue. She had made her bed, and now she had to lie in it. She kept saying she wanted her family out of her affairs. To ask about Harry would only draw her da and Davy into it. There were too many Waterses with a dog in that fight already, so she held her tongue.

Only that night, after dinner, after she had tucked little Connie in and her terrier with her, did her da speak. Mary Elizabeth meant to say good night before going up to her own room, with its view of the burn behind the house and the mountains far beyond that. She was looking forward to her soft bed with its heather-scented sheets. Her journey had been long and uncomfortable, and she was tired to her bones.

Before she took her lamp and lit it, her father took her hand. "Don't fret, Mary. It will all come out right."

"Will it?" She felt bleak of a sudden, as well as tired.

"I married among the English myself," he said. "They are a difficult race, and no mistake. Not for the faint of heart. But you are a Waters of Glenderrin. You have courage in abundance."

Mary Elizabeth did not answer, for her eyes had filled with tears again and her throat had sealed up.

She pressed a quick kiss to her da's cheek and took herself to her room, where she could watch the last of the sunset and the moonrise, and have a bit of a cry in peace.

Thirty

HARRY RODE HARD AND FAST, WITH SAMPSON AS HIS
stalwart ally. But a mail coach was driven by six fast
horses, and as valiant as his stallion was, even Sampson
had to stop for sleep. So Harry spent three less-than-
peaceful nights on the North Road, in the best accom-
modations that money could buy. As he traveled
North, he found fewer and fewer people impressed
with his station, but more than one man impressed by
the strength of his handshake.

On the fourth morning, he finally passed through
Aberdeen only to discover that, in the Highlands, to an
outsider at least, one glen looked much like another.

There were no highway robbers as in days of old,
for it seemed the King's Peace held this far north after
so many years of hard-fought war. That was just as
well, for in the mood he was in, Harry might just
dispatch a bandit and have to stand trial in the Lords
for murder.

Along those lines, he spent the last morning of his
ride contemplating getting his hands around a pretty
Scottish neck. But the fantasy soon turned to thoughts

of pulling his woman beneath him in some soft, heather-flowered spot, where there were magically no thistles to prick his skin and no family to pry into the debauchery he was perpetrating on their only girl.

He had better get his ring on her finger first.

Harry had decided on the second day as he rode through rain and thunder that he was putting his ring on her finger, will she or nill she. Mary Elizabeth was a woman who knew her own mind and who loved her homeland. He did not object to any of that and would even support her in it. But he would not let her run away from him again.

As he entered the Highlands proper, he began to see why she had run away at all. The land's majesty and grandeur surpassed anything he had ever seen, and the clean, crisp air carried the scent of her skin on it, which, for the first time, he realized was the scent of heather.

When he found a gatehouse with no gate and no wall, with a little girl in honey-blonde curls standing beside it, he slowed Sampson's paces. He waited to see if his horse would balk to see such a pretty, tiny thing in his path, but Sampson acted the true gentleman that Mary Elizabeth had always claimed him to be.

The great stallion stopped when Harry asked him to and did not flinch when the little girl—who could not have been older than nine—stepped forward and whistled.

Sampson's resolve was tested almost at once, for a tiny, white dog bounded out of the heather along the roadside and ran at them as if they were a marauding army come to claim his mistress. Sampson stood his ground and watched the dog warily. Harry patted his neck and promised him a bite of sugar.

"Sugar will rot your teeth," the little girl said.

"Too much certainly will," Harry agreed. "I only give him a touch of sugar, now and again, to keep him sweet."

Sampson snorted at this blatant falsehood, but settled down at once when Harry stroked his neck.

The little girl stared up at him with maple eyes very like the ones he had fallen in love with. She was a good deal shrewder than any English child he had ever met, it seemed, for all her slight age. She took him in with one long look, and his horse with him.

"You've come for Mary, then," she said.

"I have," he answered. Harry felt unaccountably rude, staring down at the little miss from so far above her head, so he swung down, keeping Sampson's bridle in his hand. For once, the horse did not seem interested in the greenery all around, but had become focused on the girl at his feet.

Unafraid, the child reached up and patted Sampson's nose, a liberty which the stallion immediately allowed. When the beast did not look to bite her, she stepped closer and rubbed his neck, finding his favorite spot quickly.

"You've a fine mount," she said. "And you must love Mary if you've come all this way alone."

"I do," Harry answered. He stood and let her inspect him a bit longer. Henry Charles Percy, Duke of Northumberland, had never submitted to anyone's inspection in his life, but he did so now, waiting almost with bated breath to see if he would pass muster.

"Well then," the girl said, her decision made, "I'll show you where she is. You'll never find her otherwise. Davy can never find her, even when she's in plain sight, on account of he always has his head in a book."

"I see."

Harry felt his heart sink a little and wondered if this Davy was a beau she had left back home, some swain he had never heard of before. He shored himself up and told himself that it didn't matter. Mary Elizabeth was his, and no backwater Scot was going to keep her from him.

Before she took him any farther, the girl made a little curtsy, one that would have done his mother proud. "I am Connie," she said.

He bowed. "I am Harry."

She smiled for the first time then, and whistled once. Her little, white dog stopped circling Sampson and came and sat beside her. "This is William Wallace. He is a fierce warrior, though he is small."

Harry had never been introduced to a dog before. He was not certain of the proper mode of address, but he soldiered on. "Hello, Mr. Wallace."

Connie's smile widened, though she did not laugh in his face. Harry supposed that she was being polite. She said, "You may call him William Wallace. He likes both of his names together."

"All right, then." Harry offered the dog his hand, wondering if he was like to lose a finger, but after a cursory sniff, the little dog licked his fingers once, then trundled off into the thicket.

"Where is he headed?" Harry asked.

"The same place we are. Off to see Mary Elizabeth. He knows she's fretting, and he likes to keep an eye on her."

"Is she fretting?" Harry fell into step beside the girl, leading Sampson as he went. To his eternal gratitude, they did not follow the dog into the bracken, but strolled along a path beside a small stream.

Connie gave him a measured look. "She is pining. Most likely for you. Guard her heart, or I'll gut you, guest or no."

Harry placed one hand over his own heart. "I give you my word of honor, her heart is safe with me."

Connie sniffed. "All right, then. I'll take your word, even though you're English."

They walked companionably in silence then, for Harry had no answer for that.

He found his girl sitting by the river, fishing with a well-worn line and pole. She was not looking into the water or watching her hook, but was staring into the distance, where he could see a line of mountains far off.

"Mary Elizabeth," Connie said. "Your beau is here."

Mary dropped her line and pole into the water, where they swirled away, whatever trout she had been hoping to catch gone with them. She did not heed them, but jumped to her feet and looked at him where he stood over ten feet away. His girl did not hesitate, but ran for him, leaping into his arms like a monkey, clinging to him as if she would never let go.

"Harry," she said. "You're here."

He did not take notice of her little cousin or her

dog, but kissed the woman of his life, his heart pounding in his ears. Sampson nudged him then, to remind him of his manners, and tried to separate the two lovers in order to get Mary Elizabeth all to himself. Harry set Mary Elizabeth down before Sampson knocked them both into the river, and Mary reached out and patted the horse's neck. She did not keep her hand on the stallion long, but wrapped her arms around Harry again.

"I'm sorry I left you," she said. "I love you."

"I love you. Thank you for the poem. Was that supposed to tell me that you were coming back?"

"It was. I was. I needed to come here first, to think. But I should have brought you with me."

Harry felt his heart lighten a little more, and he kissed her temple. "That would have been a bigger scandal."

"I'm a walking scandal, or haven't you heard?"

"Now that you mention it, I think I did hear something about you and the Earl of Grathton and a duel in Hyde Park."

"It was no duel. I drew on him. Grathton would never draw a weapon on a lady."

Harry tried his best not to laugh. "His lordship is too well-bred for that, I suppose."

Connie cleared her throat then, and Mary Elizabeth turned to her, not leaving Harry's arms. He pulled her closer just for good measure and breathed in the scent of her honeyed hair.

"You've lost Uncle Seamus's favorite fishing pole," the little girl said.

Mary Elizabeth moved to go after it, for the line had caught on a rock and stopped the pole's stately progress down the stream. Harry tightened his grip, and his girl subsided, content to stay in his arms, at least for the moment.

"I'll buy Seamus a hundred poles," Harry boasted. "Never fear, Connie."

The little one looked at him askance. "He doesn't need a hundred. And that one is his favorite."

William Wallace followed her as she plucked the pole from the drink. The line was good and snarled, so she cut it free with a wicked blade she had hidden somewhere about her person. The knife was sheathed and tucked away again just as quickly as it had appeared, and Harry blanched.

"Do all Scottish ladies carry knives?" he asked.

It was Connie who answered him. "Nay," she said. "Just the ladies of Glenderrin."

Pole in hand, the girl nodded to him and to Mary. "Don't keep her out too long," she said. "Uncle Seamus will come and fetch you himself if you tarry."

"But he doesn't know I'm here," Harry answered.

Connie scoffed. "Don't be daft. Of course he does." And with that, she whistled to her dog, and the pair disappeared into the bracken.

"I already love that little girl," Harry said.

"She's my favorite cousin. She's been a great comfort to me over the last two days."

"And Uncle Seamus?"

"Da was a blessing. But he always is."

Harry felt his throat tighten with envy. Where it came from, along with sudden jealousy, he could not say. Before he had first laid eyes on Mary Elizabeth Waters, he had always considered himself a reasonable man. Apparently, those days were behind him.

"And Davy?" he asked, unable to keep the annoyance from his voice.

Mary Elizabeth frowned up at him. "Davy keeps to himself most days. Why?"

"He's not offered you comfort in my absence?"

"Not really. He's not much of a comforting man. But then, none of my brothers are."

The word *brother* made Harry release his breath in one long sigh. He settled his arms around Mary Elizabeth and drew her close again. Harry felt the tension in his shoulders ease, and he called himself three kinds of fool.

Mary looked up at him slantwise. "Jealous of my brothers now, are you?"

Harry felt chagrined until she kissed him, and all thoughts of anything but the woman in his arms slipped away. He lost himself for a moment or two in the sweetness of her mouth, but then Sampson nudged him, reminding him of reality and of all that needed to be dealt with.

"Mary Elizabeth, we need to talk."

"You've had enough of me, then? And you've come all the way to Glenderrin to say so."

Harry took a moment to digest her words. He stood staring down at her, not sure whether to throttle her or kiss her again.

She made the decision for him.

Thirty-one

MARY ELIZABETH KISSED HIM ONCE MORE, HARD, THEN pulled away. "I can't think straight if you're touching me, so you just stay over there."

She was surprised to see the predatory light she had first witnessed in his bedroom rise in Harry's eyes there in the middle of the heath, in the middle of the afternoon, but she could not say she was sorry. If he still wanted her as she wanted him, maybe he was of a mind to forgive her.

"I've a few things to say myself," she told him, straightening her pink gown. It was an old one, for she had left all of her new things behind in Northumberland, along with her sword. It was more than a little tight across the bust, as her mother had it made for her over a year before. It fit otherwise, but Mary Elizabeth found herself squirming in it at the oddest moments, trying to make room for herself, and failing. Harry caught her at it now, and the gleam in his eyes turned from cobalt to indigo as he looked at her.

She cleared her throat. "You've ridden all the way from Northumberland," she said, stating the obvious.

She fell back on a semblance of good manners in an effort to calm the racing of her pulse. "Perhaps you would like to speak before I do."

Harry reached up and patted Sampson's neck. The great beast had stopped trying to get away from him, now that she had stepped away, and had gone to cropping the bits of green he could reach there by the water's edge. Harry leaned against him, no doubt tired from his long ride, as Sampson must be. Mary Elizabeth knew she should take them up to the castle and have Sampson seen to and Harry fed, but for some reason, she just could not bring herself to introduce him to the rest of her family, and to face all that would come after that. Not until she had made herself clear to him first, here and now.

"Ladies first," Harry said, as if bowing her through a doorway ahead of him.

She cleared her throat again, and summoned her courage. "I am sorry I left you."

"You said that."

"But you have not yet accepted my apology."

The predatory look on his face softened a little, and he straightened. For a moment, she thought he might reach for her, but he checked himself.

"I accept your apology, Mary Elizabeth, if you will accept mine."

She frowned. "What do you have to apologize for?"

"For not locking you in with me and saving us both the bother and annoyance of this time apart."

Mary Elizabeth felt irritation creep into her heart, but along with it came a lifting of the burden she had been carrying since she left him. She had been burdened with the knowledge that she had made a mistake, a mistake she might not be able to undo. Perhaps all was not lost. Perhaps he meant to keep her, in spite of her wild ways.

She smiled a little. "I accept your apology, too."

Harry laughed at that and would have closed the distance between them, but she took one step back, careful not to fall into the burn, and held up one hand to stop him.

"Harry, let me speak my mind before you touch me, or all that is important will be lost."

The predatory gleam was in his eyes again. "You'll remember it all eventually," he said. "After I let you up for air."

"We'll talk first, and then we'll go to the house. No canoodling in broad daylight in front of God and Sampson." Mary Elizabeth forced herself to sound stern, but Harry only laughed.

He sobered up almost at once, but she could still see the light of joy in his eyes. She was glad to see it. "All right," he said.

"I have been thinking hard ever since I got home. I know I left you because I love it here, and I had to come to my home, to my favorite places, so that I could make up my mind in the only place where I am truly myself."

She took a deep breath. She saw from the tightening of his jaw and the shadow coming over his face that Harry feared whatever she might say next, but he was a man, and he would hold his tongue and listen.

"I have been fishing by the burn, as you see. I have gone walking through the bracken. I even went hunting with one of the lads, though Robbie and Ian aren't here to go with me. I could not shoot the buck we stalked, however, nor have I caught one trout. I've been too busy thinking."

Mary Elizabeth took one step toward him, but stopped herself before she went any farther. "I am happy here, happier than I am anywhere else on earth. My thinking is clear here, and so is the voice of my heart. I've found that I love you here even more than when I was in England. I think that I will love you always, no matter where I go or who I'm with. If I turn from you now, as I once thought I might, I would lose a part of myself, a larger part than lives here in the Highlands. My heart is yours, Harry. I will be yours, if you'll still have me. I'll be your wife."

Harry did not move or speak, and for a long moment, she felt a creeping nauseous fear that she was too late. But then he smiled, and it was if the sun had come out after a long winter of ice and falling snow. He did not move to her, however, nor did he touch her.

"I'll ask for your word of honor," Harry said. "I'll ask that you promise never to run from me again."

He waited, and she nodded. "I give you my word."

He still had not fallen at her feet, nor declared his undying love, so she felt a bit faint, and more than a little frightened. But this was the mess she had made, so she knew that whatever came, she must wait on him.

Finally, he spoke. "I love you, Mary Elizabeth. But you know that already. You also know that by marrying me, you will be taking on a larger burden, that of being a duchess. It means that our son will be duke after me. It means that our daughter may well marry in the South, among the English, for better or for worse. Essentially, our children will be English, and not Scot. Can you live with that?"

Mary Elizabeth breathed deep and spoke clear, for she had thought of this as well. "Yes," she said. "I can live with that."

"I will bring you back here, every year, as many times as you like. But it will not be the same for you as living here. You will not be able to change your mind in five years, or in ten. If you come back to me now, if you marry me and become my wife, I will never let you go. There will be no haring off to parts unknown without me, not even to the Highlands. Do you understand?"

"I do."

She looked into his eyes, and though his face was softer, he was still in shadow. She knew that he needed more from her than what she had already offered. She would give him all, and not count the cost.

"I love you, Harry. I will leave behind my clan, my kith and kin, for months at a time. I will come South and be your lady. I will not be English, for I am myself, always, but I will stand by you and love you, wherever you go and whatever you do, for the rest of my life."

"And beyond," he said. And this time, as his face softened, his eyes were full of tears.

"And beyond," she echoed.

He kissed her then, and she came into his arms without reservation, without remorse. She knew what she was doing. She knew what she was giving up. She would visit her home in Glenderrin off and on for the rest of her life. She would see to her clan, what was left of it. She would watch it grow and help her family with money and time, in any way she could. But she would not live among them always. She was giving that up, for him. The price was high, but Harry was worth it.

He did not canoodle with her, for the moment was too solemn for that. Harry drew back and took a velvet bag out of his coat pocket. Sampson, almost forgotten behind him, raised his head from his snack of grass and leaves to look and see what Harry had, hoping it might be a treat for him.

It was not.

Harry opened the bag, and into his other palm slid a ring with a thin gold band and a line of rubies set into it. The rubies gleamed in the light of the summer sun, a deep, fiery red that matched the fire in her heart. She wanted to reach out and touch those stone. She wanted to take that ring and put it on her hand. But for once in her life, Mary Elizabeth held still. It was not her place to do it. It was his.

"Mary Elizabeth Waters of Glenderrin, will you marry me and become my duchess? Will you be my wife?"

A foolish part of her wanted to tell him that she had answered him already. But the love in her heart rose over that bit of nonsense and swept it away, like a wave sweeping a bit of driftwood into the sea.

"Yes," she said. "Harry Percy, I will be your wife. I'll be your duchess, too, but wife is the title I am most proud of."

He kissed her again then, a glancing touch, but it

had his heart in it. He slid the ring onto her finger, and she looked at the rubies against her pale skin, glad that she had not worn gloves.

"It was my mother's ring. She got it from her mother. I thought rubies suited you better than any other stone."

"I love it, Harry. I'll give it to our daughter, one day."

Harry drew her close. "No," he said. "It's yours. You'll give it to no one else."

Mary Elizabeth leaned comfortably against him and listened to the slow and steady beat of his heart. Had he been anyone else, she would have reminded him that he was not the boss of her, and that she would do as she pleased with her own jewelry in future. But she did not need to say it, for she knew that she would never part with his ring, not a year from now, not in a hundred years. In whatever English cairn where the Dukes of Northumberland tucked away their dead, she would have it on her hand the day her children laid her in the ground. She would wear it into Heaven, when she stood with Harry there.

They stood together for a long while, drinking in the sound of the river running by, simply taking in the moment, the beginning of the rest of their lives together. It was Sampson, in the end, who urged them on. The great beast nudged Harry once, then turned toward the castle as if he knew the way, as if he had been there a hundred times before. Mary Elizabeth laughed and took Harry's hand. They ran together so that Harry might catch Sampson's bridle. Then they walked into her father's keep, only to find her oldest brother Ian standing in the doorway to the house, waiting for them.

Ian's look was amicable, as it always was, but he was fingering his throwing knife. "So you're the English bastard who ruined my sister," Ian said.

Thirty-two

HARRY HAD JUST BEEN CONGRATULATING HIMSELF ON his restraint, as he had not pulled Mary Elizabeth beneath him on the hard ground by the river and tossed up her skirts to seal their engagement.

Instead, he had kissed her and breathed in the sweet scent of her hair, feeling the special license burning a hole in his pocket. He would have her signature on it, as soon as they reached the house. Surely there was a vicar up here, even in the back of beyond, who might officiate a quick wedding and drink a glass of the fine Glenderrin whisky with them to celebrate. For Harry knew that he would not wait another night to make her his, once and for all.

He felt as pleased with himself as he ever had, but he needed to get Mary Elizabeth married to him, and quickly. He had forgotten about her family. He supposed he would be able to find more than one witness among them to tie the knot that bound her to him for good.

Harry wondered if the man blocking the doorway, holding a wicked-looking blade, would stand as the first witness.

Mary Elizabeth tried to put herself between him and the man in question, but Harry held her firm against his side. Some kind lad had taken a tired and docile Sampson to the stables, so Harry did not have to worry about his favorite horse getting stabbed if this man missed his mark. He did worry for Mary, however, so he pushed her behind him.

"Good afternoon," Harry said, calling on all his ducal splendor. "Allow me to present myself. I am Harold Charles Percy, Duke of Northumberland. I am also your sister's betrothed. And you are?"

The huge man standing at the top of the stairs looked slightly less threatening upon hearing that, but only because the dog William Wallace had come running and danced between the giant's feet. The big man clucked to the dog, but he did not take his eyes off Harry. Nor did he sheathe the large knife in his hand.

"I am fresh home from the sea," the giant said, "only to find that my sister is run of with an English. Ruined, she is, or so I hear tell. And I don't like it."

"I'm not ruined, Ian, you daft bugger. I'm engaged." Mary Elizabeth no doubt would have torn a strip out of her huge brother's hide, knife or no, but Harry gave her one look, and she fell silent. He turned to the man before him.

"Might I have the pleasure of your name?" Harry inquired as politely as he could with eight inches of serrated steal staring him in the face. Though there was ten feet between them, Harry had no doubt that, if Ian wished, he would be skewered in a trice.

"Ye might, before I kill you," the giant said. "I am

Ian Blythe Waters of Glenderrin. And I am the man who will see you dead."

"Ian, for the love of God," Mary Elizabeth said from behind Harry. "Where is Alex?"

"Yon wee Alex won't save your man from me. Mind yourself, Mary. It's this man here I'm speaking with."

Harry was shocked for the second time in as many minutes as Mary Elizabeth did, indeed, fall silent.

"So you're a fancy English duke from the South, are you?"

Harry was not certain how fancy he was, especially after days of hard riding, but he did nod. "I am," he said.

"And you've offered for my sister?" Ian asked.

"And she has accepted."

"Ye've not asked me, nor her father."

Mary Elizabeth snorted at that, but held her peace behind him still. Harry reached back and patted her arm in silent thanks.

"Neither you nor her father were present at the time. I asked both Alexander Waters and Robert Waters, her brothers who were guests in my home, and they both gave their consent and the consent of the family."

Mary Elizabeth went as still as a rabbit behind him, he supposed in surprise. She had not known that, for she had flown the coop before all that had transpired.

There was a long, tense silence. It might have gone on for three minutes or more, but William Wallace had other ideas. The tiny dog got tired of waiting for Ian to acknowledge him and give him his due, so he leaped down the stairs and made straight for Harry.

Harry leaned down and offered the white terrier his hand. William Wallace slipped beneath his palm, showing Harry just where he wanted to be scratched. Harry obliged.

"Well," Ian said, "I suppose if William Wallace vouches for you, as well as Alex and Robbie, ye might do. But I dinna take my blade out without blooding it. So there will still be a need for blood between us."

The giant was as calm as if discussing the weather, and Harry felt his stomach flip. He had thought to talk his way out of this, but it seemed he was in for serious trouble, one way or another. He was unarmed, as he always was, and even had he worn a weapon, he would never have drawn against Mary Elizabeth's kin, no matter how mad that kin might be.

Harry stood to his full height and waited. He felt her tiny hand grip the back of his coat like grim death. The only member of their party who did not seem alarmed was William Wallace, who made himself comfortable and sat right down on the toe of Harry's boot.

Ian crossed the yard to him, and Harry felt Mary Elizabeth's hand twisting the fine wool of his coat. He paid her no heed, however, for her brother soon loomed over him, blocking out the sun.

Ian raised the knife and, with the sharp tip, cut into his own palm. He held the blade out then, and Harry took it, uncertain what bizarre ritual was going on now, but waiting to find out.

"You cut yourself, now, English, if ye can stand to mar your pretty skin. Then we shake hands and swear an oath together never to raise arms against each other, here or anywhere else. This oath will make you my brother, and after you take it, I can let you in the house."

Ian the Giant spoke as if this bizarre pagan ritual was some kind of normal proceeding. Harry did not blanch, even when he cut himself a bit too deep. Mary Elizabeth clucked but did not speak. Ian paid her no mind, but took Harry's hand, pressing their bloody palms together.

"Blood of my blood, bone of my bone, you are my kin till Judgment Day. May God ever be my witness."

Ian waited, not letting go of Harry's hand until he repeated the oath. He felt Mary Elizabeth go limp against his back and knew he had done the right thing.

Ian took the knife from him, wiped their blood off the tip, and sheathed it. Only then did the giant smile.

"Welcome to the family," he said, clapping Harry on the back.

Harry heard his Mary murmur from behind him, "God help you."

❧

Mary Elizabeth was sorely tempted to leap onto Ian's back and throttle him as she had once seen Robbie do when the two of them were fighting. But then she looked down at the ring on her finger, and her mood instantly improved.

"Leave my man alone after this," she hissed at her eldest brother as she passed him going into the house.

Ian raised his hands as if in surrender, looking suddenly as if butter would not melt in his mouth. "Now, lass, don't get your dander up. If your family won't test him, who will?"

"I will, I thank you. I have, and he passed. Now leave him be."

"He's one of us now, so I'll not kill him. But he'll have to hold his own among us, especially with him being English and the Gathering almost upon us."

Mary Elizabeth turned to Ian and stood on the tips of her toes, putting her finger in his face. "You'll leave him alone, or I'll know the reason why."

"I am the reason why," Harry said, wrapping his hand around her finger.

Harry was actually laughing, though God alone knew why. Ian was the largest of the boys in her family, but they were all fierce. Mary Elizabeth was still frowning at her brother's retreating back when Harry took her finger to his lips and kissed it.

"Thank you for defending me, love, but there is no need."

Mary Elizabeth was about to open her mouth to tell him that he had not met them all yet when his lips came down on hers and silenced her. When he let her up for air, she checked his palm, so that she would not be tempted to kiss him again, or drag him off with her into the small antechamber behind the first spiral staircase. In lieu of debauchery only one oak door away from whatever family had gathered in the great hall—the family that were even now waiting for them—Mary Elizabeth cut her handkerchief into three strips and used it to bind his wound up.

"It's a scratch, Mary. Leave it be," Harry said, his voice a soft warmth in her ear. She did not look up at him, but finished her task before taking one step back for safety.

"Aye," she said. "It's a scratch that needs soap and water on it, but that will do for now."

"Soap?" Harry asked, bemused.

"It's a folk remedy my mother's fond of. Clean a wound with water and whatever is to hand, honey or soap, then bind it to keep it cleaner still."

"I always put something on a wound to keep it from bleeding on my clothes."

Mary Elizabeth smiled at him and took his good hand. "That's not enough. Not anymore. You're in my mother's house now."

"I'm glad you finally came up to the castle, Mary Elizabeth. I was just sending Ian after you when he met you both at the door."

Her mother's voice was as calm and still as it always was. Mary Elizabeth could not tell if she was putting on calmness for their guest's sake, or because she was saving up a tongue lashing for later. She supposed she would find out soon enough. "Mother, how did you get up to the house without me seeing you?"

"The duchess's sloop brought us to Aberdeen, and a hired coach-and-six brought us home. Davy tells me you were down by the burn, watching the water go by, hoping to catch a trout for your father."

"I didn't catch anything."

"Well," her mother said, without a note of censure in her voice, "there is always tomorrow."

Mary Elizabeth did not have long to puzzle out this new and odd acceptance of her unladylike habit of fishing because her mother turned to Harry and smiled.

"Duke, if you might give us a moment alone, I would like a short word with my daughter."

Mary Elizabeth clung to his good hand tighter, but when she saw what she was doing, she eased her grip. Harry looked down at her and tilted her chin up so that she might meet his eyes. "I think you will want to hear what she has to say, Mary."

Mary Elizabeth disagreed, for she had heard it all before, since childhood, but she did not tell him that. She smiled at him, and kissed his cheek, and let him go.

"Don't turn your back on Ian," she said as Harry strolled calmly toward the great hall, where a great racket had begun, as if one of her brothers had let the hounds in the house and they had taken to chasing William Wallace. Mary Elizabeth had not known the little dog long, but she knew that he would make short work of the bigger ones, much to their chagrin, as Robbie often made short work of men twice as large as himself.

In that moment, she heard a triumphant terrier bark, followed by a wolfhound's whine for mercy. Connie said, "Good job, William Wallace. That'll teach the brute some manners."

So Mary Elizabeth was laughing as she stepped into the small sitting room, to hear whatever her mother had to say.

Thirty-three

MARY ELIZABETH WAS NOT LAUGHING LONG, HOWEVER, for her mother was frowning. For once, her ma looked not angry but sad. As far as she and her mother were apart in how they thought she should live her life, she did not want her mother to be sad because of her.

"I'm sorry I ran off, Ma," Mary Elizabeth said. "It was wrong and foolhardy. I should have stayed and held my ground and fought it out with you, and then told Harry where I was going so that he could decide for himself whether to follow me or not."

"Follow you he did." Her mother did not censure her all at once, as Mary Elizabeth had thought she might. Lady Anna did not even sit down, but stood as still as a statue in the middle of the room. Mary Elizabeth wondered if this meant that it was to be a short dressing down, and hoped so, for she knew there was tea in the great hall, and dinner soon after that. She felt her stomach rumble. Making up with her man, and kissing him senseless, was hungry work.

"I see his ring on your finger," Lady Anna said.

Mary Elizabeth raised her hand to the light that

was coming in through the room's only window. The rubies and gold gleamed like a promise of joy to come, and Mary Elizabeth smiled to see it.

"Yes, Ma. I did as you wished. But only because I wanted to. I came home and found that I love him enough to leave here and live with him in the South. I'll raise my children as English and only come North for the summers. But in spite of Harry being a duke, he's worth it."

"You are in love with him, then?" her mother asked, though Mary Elizabeth was sure she had already said so, more than once.

"I am."

Her mother sank into a chair and wept then, not even drawing out a fine linen handkerchief, but crying into her hands like a peasant woman, or like Mary Elizabeth herself.

Mary Elizabeth was not comfortable with another's tears, so she was not certain what to do. She thought to call for her da, but instead went and sat beside her and patted her mother's arm gently.

"I am glad you love him," her mother said. "I am sorry that you will be going away, but I am glad you found the love of your life. I could not leave you here to molder and discover only too late that your youth had fled, and you had no husband and no children to show for it."

Mary Elizabeth thought that notion daft, but then she reflected on her values and on what she loved. Left alone, she may well have stayed in the heather for years on end. And unless one of her brothers had brought a man like Harry to the North, she would never have laid eyes on a soul she had not been raised with. The thought of never seeing Harry, of never knowing that he was even alive, pained her. She felt her heart contract and she took her mother's hand in hers.

"You did not send me away to be rid of me, then?"

"No, Mary. I would never do that."

Her mother's tear-streaked face was lovely still, in spite of the weeping. Mary Elizabeth wiped her eyes for her and offered her own handkerchief, that her mother might blow her nose. Lady Anna did so with a very tiny noise, almost like a bird tossing grass about. Mary Elizabeth swallowed the laughter that rose into her throat at the sound. Her mother was delicate and no mistake. Perhaps once they were both married women, they might deal along together a bit better. Mary Elizabeth certainly hoped so.

"I love you, Ma," Mary Elizabeth said.

"And I love you. And I'm glad you know it."

"And I love you both!" Her da came in from the entryway then and stood in the center of the room, his hands on his hips. "Now get you both into the great hall before Ian eats all the tea cakes and jam."

Mary Elizabeth hugged her mother fiercely and then her da, then slipped out to leave them alone for a moment. From the doorway, she watched as her father folded her mother into his arms, and she realized for the first time that her own mother had left her people for love, and it had turned out well. Mary Elizabeth could only hope that she and her children would fare as well among the English.

When she stepped into the great hall, it was Harry

who greeted her with a fresh cup of tea just as she liked it and a plate piled high with cakes, two scones, and cream. She kissed him, lingering over his lips as she might linger when twisting together a good fly for her fishing reel, taking time with it, until the kiss spun out almost like a song between them.

"That's enough," Ian bellowed. "You're making Davy blush."

Her studious brother smacked Ian on the arm, which caused a ruckus, especially among the hounds and William Wallace, who joined in the fray. But Mary Elizabeth did not join in. She was content for once to sit and eat her cakes, with the man of her life beside her.

Harry took tea with his girl, listening to and watching the rollicking madness that was her family. By comparison, Mary Elizabeth seemed suddenly tame and demure, until she smiled at him.

He knew now why it was inappropriate for gentlemen to sample their ladies' charms before the wedding. Not knowing what it was like to bed Mary Elizabeth was bad enough. Knowing how she tasted, what she sounded like, how she looked as she came apart beneath him was enough to drive a man truly mad.

The rest of the family, even his own mother, seemed to think the matter settled, and to everyone's satisfaction. They seemed to have forgotten that less than a week before, his girl had bolted off into the night after giving him her sworn word that she would marry him. It was not that he disbelieved her now, for he did not. Harry knew that he would feel safe, and somewhat comfortable, only when they had both signed the special license and pledged their troth in front of witnesses and a vicar, making their alliance legal in the eyes of king and country.

He supposed that they must also have a priest. He cared little for religion himself, but his mother set great store by it, and the House of Northumberland had been Catholic even through the tides and wilds of King Henry VIII's reign, when to be Catholic actually cost a man something. They had ridden the storms of history, however, and come out the stronger. Harry remained Catholic for that reason, if for no other. That and for the fact that his mother would take his liver herself and fry it over a fire in front of him if he ever deserted for the Church of England or, God forbid, the Methodists.

Harry was ruminating over this and over how to bring up the subject of his hasty marriage to the company at large when Mary Elizabeth's brother Robbie strode up to him.

"Come with me, Your Worship. Ma's ordered a room ready for you."

"My thanks. And please call me Harry."

"Of course, Your Worship. Harry it is. Mary, ye'd best get on with changing before Ma catches you in that old gown."

Mary Elizabeth flared at her brother, but only half-heartedly it seemed to Harry, for she seemed for the most part as content as a well-fed cat to simply sit beside him and lean against his arm. Her breast was a delightful weight against him, reminding him of the delights in store for both of them if he might only get the bloody paper in his pocket signed and witnessed.

"Ye'll keep a civil tongue in your head about ladies' clothes, Robbie, or I'll tell Lady Prudence on you."

Robbie had the good grace to look chagrined at that and cast a guilty look at his wife, who was sitting with the duchess and Lady Anna, talking about God alone knew what. Harry prayed they were not colluding in some mad scheme that would keep him unmarried for six months or more while his mother planned the wedding breakfast of the year.

Mary Elizabeth did not seem concerned about their wedding breakfast or their wedding itself. She simply kissed Harry on the cheek, and when Ian glared at them from across the room, she kissed Robbie, too.

"I'll see you at dinner," she whispered, and promptly disappeared.

Robbie and Harry started for the guest wing, and Ian fell almost at once into step beside them. "So, wee Bantam, you like our man Harry here."

"I do," Robbie answered.

Harry did not try to puzzle out why Ian called his brother by the name of a chicken. He supposed it best not to inquire. As to referring to the hulking man beside him as wee, Harry assumed that any man next to Ian's bulk might seem small. Harry was musing on the oddities of his soon-to-be relatives when the three of them stopped at the foot of a spiral staircase.

Harry looked around for the first time, wondering if he would be able to find his way back to the main hall. He had a sinking suspicion that Ian had taken him, not to the guest wing after all, but to the door of a dungeon.

Ian smiled pleasantly enough, and Robbie looked

on, but somehow neither man's looks gave Harry any comfort.

"So, Harry, me lad," Ian said without preamble. "You'll be sleeping in the tower this night, and every night ye bide here."

"I will?" Harry asked, looking up the steep staircase behind him, lit only by torches.

"Aye," Ian answered, still smiling, but his hand had transferred to the hilt of his large blade. "And I will be sleeping here, in this room, at the foot of these stairs."

Harry began to see which way the wind was blowing.

"In case I might need anything in the night," Harry said.

"Of course." Ian's smile most definitely had an edge to it now.

Even if Harry had hoped to find his lady in the dead of night—or she, him—and anticipate their vows once more, he saw that he would not be able to do so without getting blooded by her brother again, and this time in earnest. Harry would not be able to get a sandwich from the larder, much less time alone with his girl. He sighed and acknowledged defeat.

"I thank you for your hospitality," he said, falling back on the manners he was raised with.

Ian smiled and so did Robbie, this time with warmth. "Welcome to the Highlands."

Thirty-four

MARY ELIZABETH WAS CONTENT TO EAT THE DUCK HER cousin Gregory had shot, and listen to the sound of her family fuss and talk over dinner. She could not remember the last time all four of her brothers had been under the same roof, for Davy went on book-buying trips often, and Ian was almost always at sea.

So she sat and drank in the gathering of her small family, even as she anticipated the larger Gathering that would happen in a little less than two weeks' time. She had no doubt she could persuade Harry to stay with her in the Highlands that long at least.

Harry, for a man who had finally won the prize he had been hunting for, seemed more than a little out of sorts. Instead of eating a bit of the duck, or even the fine mutton that was on offer, Harry fiddled with his fork and fidgeted in his chair.

"Do you not like the meat?" Mary Elizabeth whispered, careful to keep her voice low enough that none of her kin could make out her words over their own cacophony.

"The mutton is quite good," Harry said.

"Is it the sauce, then?" Mary Elizabeth asked. "Cook McCrery makes a fine mustard sauce that goes well with this. I might ring for it, if you like."

"No, thank you," Harry answered, forcing down a bite with a bit of soft bread. "This is delightful."

Mary Elizabeth did not try to soothe him again, but applied herself to her own dinner. She would ferret out what the matter was with him when they were alone later that night. She knew that Ian had hidden him in the top of the tower, like a prince in some fairy story, but Mary Elizabeth had never let a brother of hers nor a small thing like a tower stand in the way of her desires. She certainly had no plans to start now.

Only after the cheese was served, along with the last of the wine, did Harry finally speak his mind. And he did not speak low to her, but addressed the whole table. Clearly his duke-ish-ness was going to be a problem among her kin. Luckily, it was a problem she could overlook.

Harry stood before the ladies rose to leave the men to their whisky. He cleared his throat, and then spoke, his voice as beautiful and melodious as any song she had ever heard, in spite of his accent. She could not think of him as English even when he sounded priggish and bossy. He was her Harry, first, foremost, and always. The priggish and bossy bits were simply something she would have to live with. God willing, those bits of him did not drive her mad by May Day.

"Good people, I find myself at a loss," Harry said.

The chatting among her family fell silent as even her da and Ian attended him. Da looked vaguely amused and pressed her mother's hand. Ian picked his teeth with his dinner knife until Ma shot him a look, and he set it down.

"I am in possession of a special license, arranged by the Bishop of London, and given to me by Robert here."

Robbie waved to the whole table as if he had done something grand. Davy glowered at him, and Robbie made to toss a bit of cheese in his direction, but Lady Prudence stayed his hand.

Harry drew the license from his coat pocket and laid it on the table with a flourish next to Lady Anna's Brie.

"I would like your permission to have Mary Elizabeth sign this with me, and for us to say our vows this night, that we might be man and wife."

There was a long silence as the family looked at him as if he had run mad. Mary Elizabeth was grateful Ian did not speak, but her da did.

"Your Grace," her father said, "we're in Scotland here. There is no need for your fancy license, all due respect to yourself and his lairdship the bishop." He nodded to Mary's mother, as the bishop was her brother. Da spoke on. "In the Highlands, ye might marry when and where ye please."

Harry smiled, and Mary Elizabeth sighed to see it, for it lit the whole room for her. "Excellent," her man said.

"We have sent for Father Murphy, but he will not be here until tomorrow afternoon before tea. So settle yourself, Your Grace. You and your mother are family now. Relax and be welcome among us, and forget your English ways, if only for a night."

Harry stood mute and Mary Elizabeth saw clearly

that he knew not what to say. She tugged his hand until he sat down again, and the voices of her family resumed as the ladies began to rise to go to their crumpets in the great hall. Ian reached across the table and plucked up the expensive marriage license. Her eldest brother did not hesitate or even read it, but cast it whole and entire into the fire. Mary Elizabeth was not certain, but she thought she heard her man grind his teeth.

She took pity on Harry, leaning close to whisper in his ear.

"Bide awhile, lad," she said as she rose to go into the hall for a cup of tea and a cake. "I have all in hand."

Harry looked bemused, as if he did not believe her, but he also looked at her with love, and that was enough for her. He would learn, if he had not already, that when she said a thing, she did it, and did not hesitate. If he did not know it yet, he soon would. God help him.

❦

Harry did not even get to kiss his girl good night, as she was whisked off in one direction by Alex and Robbie and their wives, and he was marched off in another by her brother Ian, back into the guest wing, to the very foot of the tower staircase itself. So he found himself trapped in his tower room, with Ian ensconced at the foot of the stairs. The huge Highlander had all but locked him in.

"You have a good night, now," Ian said with a wink.

Harry found himself pacing the round room above the stairs, feeling very much like the bear in the Prince

Regent's menagerie. He hoped that the priest arrived on the morrow, for if he did not have his girl with him soon, and every night for the rest of his life, he feared for his sanity.

He made himself look around this tower room and saw that it was a room that could only comfortably be used in summer, as there was no fireplace. Old-fashioned braziers were scattered here and there along the walls, and some were even lit, giving off a cheerful but feeble glow. Harry found himself staring out of the room's only window, an arrow slit that had been enlarged to hold double panes of glass. He could not open it, for it was not made to be opened, but he could see the last of the summer sunlight fading beyond the mountains and the sky turning a shade of indigo.

He wondered at himself that he had followed a woman to the back of beyond only to be trapped in a tower. He wondered how one might escape if there were a fire, and assumed that, in such an occurrence, Ian would let him pass down the only staircase. He was thinking of these things, with his back to the door, when he heard an odd scratching along the wainscoting a few feet from the window. He thought perhaps a mouse had come to inspect him, but then the wall moved, and he leaped backward, reaching for a weapon that was not there.

"Dinna fash yourself, Harry. 'Tis only me."

Mary Elizabeth stepped out from the hidden door in the thick wall and closed it again behind her.

"Ian will hear you," Harry said inanely, trying to rally his mind into some semblance of order and failing.

She looked lovely in the failing light. Still dressed

in the too-tight pink gown, her golden hair had come loose from its pins and now fell around her shoulders and down her back, where she paid it little heed. She kissed him once on the cheek, and he thought to take her in his arms then, but she slipped away, sitting on a low footstool close to one of the braziers, using its light as she unfastened the hooks of her ankle boots.

Mary Elizabeth kicked first one boot off, and then the other, and then began to reach for the hooks of her bodice beneath one arm. Harry crossed the room and stopped her then, his hand on hers.

"What are you doing?" he asked, again inanely. His mind still had not rallied.

"I'm tired," Mary Elizabeth said. "I'm going to bed, and you're coming with me."

Harry's body caught fire then, as he watched the line of her calf move beneath the thin wool of her gown. Her petticoat dropped from beneath the skirt, and she stepped out of it, leaving it where it lay.

He did not ask another foolish question, but went to help her unfasten the skirt of her gown. Mary Elizabeth was not yet in a canoodling mood, it seemed, for she batted his hands away.

"Harry, see to your own clothes, for the love of God. That cravat alone will take ten minutes to untie. It looks fit to strangle you where you stand."

He would have laughed, but her bodice fell away then, leaving the creamy expanse of her breasts revealed, tucked high by the lace and linen of her stays. He almost swallowed his tongue, and found that his fingers had forgotten what they were about in the midst of unknotting his neck cloth.

"Mary Elizabeth," he said, striving hard for reason and failing, as she bent down and began to untie her garters. Her beautiful, well-rounded derriere presented itself for his inspection, and he knew that he needed to ask his question now, or it would soon be too late.

"What was that door you came through?" he asked. "Can I expect anyone else to come through it while I sleep, and throttle me where I lay?"

She laughed at that good-naturedly. "You're a guest, Harry, and family. No one will throttle you. Ian makes a good deal of noise, and some of the cousins might test you now and again, but the boys like you, Da likes you, and most importantly, Ma likes you, so all is right with the world."

"And you?" Harry asked, shrugging out of his coat and tossing it over a convenient chair. "You like me."

Mary Elizabeth stopped what she was doing and stood in only her shift and stays, one stocking on her leg while the other hung from her hand, its pink garter tight in her fingertips. She smiled at him, looking a little bemused, as if he were daft to state the obvious. "You are the man of my heart, Harry. I like you fine indeed."

Harry crossed the room to her, stalking slowly, taking in the color of her eyes as they shifted from maple to hazel, the green flecks clear in the candlelight. "And the door?" he asked again.

"This is an old keep, Harry. We've got a few secrets here. Ian doesn't know about that door, nor any of the boys. It's likely why Da let them put you here in the first place."

Harry stopped, his hand inches away from her cheek. "You mean to say your father knows you're here?"

"I mean to say that Da knows we are engaged, which makes this, and anything else we do, none of his business."

"Your brothers would not agree."

"Bugger my brothers. Now kiss me, Harry."

He did not chastise her for her vulgar reference, but drew her against him at last and kissed her, his hands drifting down her sides and around to cup her buttocks. The swell of her behind filled his hands and he drew her close against him. She gasped a little when she felt the hard heat of him, and he laughed a little, trailing his lips along her throat.

"Harry," she said, sounding more than a bit bemused by now, her voice softening as her body was with her desire for him. "You're still dressed."

"So I am," Harry answered. His lips found her earlobe and bit down gently. She shook in his arms when he did that, so he did it again, and she moaned.

"Perhaps you'll help me undress," Harry said, his fingers caressing her breasts, his thumbs running over her nipples so that they stood up proud against his palm. She shuddered then, and whimpered a little.

Only a moment passed, and then he heard her soft voice say, "All right."

He pulled back enough that she might get her hands on him, not in his hair, where they had been, but on his person. The heat of her small palms burned like suns on his chest as she ran her hands down his waistcoat and started to unfasten the buttons.

"I think I might retire Philips," Harry said. "I think I might have you dress and undress me each morning and night."

"And noon," Mary Elizabeth said, the last button coming free so that she could run her hands over the starched linen of his shirt. "I'll want you most noons, too."

He had bathed and dressed for dinner, so the shirt was clean and white, only a little wrinkled from his saddlebag. Mary Elizabeth did not seem to care about his shirt at all, but drew it from his trousers in one surprisingly deft motion. Harry took it off then and tossed it toward the chair where his coat already lay. His waistcoat ended up on the floor at his feet, and he kicked it aside.

"Don't muss it too badly, Harry," Mary Elizabeth said. "You won't really put him out to pasture, and Mr. Philips will be cross with me."

He kissed her then, and pulled her with him toward the great tester bed. The four posters were carved with mythical dragons and thistle, and held aloft a canopy of dark-green velvet. "This is a lovely room," he said to her. "But I would have been lonely if you had not joined me in it."

Mary Elizabeth smiled at him as she knelt to tug at his boots. "You will never be lonely again," she said.

He stooped down and picked her up, kissing her before he tossed her onto the bed. She landed in the center of the mattress and laughed out loud, bouncing a little more while she watched him strip off his boots and pants. She seemed to remember that she had a few clothes left herself, for she was out of her stays in a trice.

She reached for her last garter and hose, but Harry stopped her. "No," he said. "Let me."

He pushed her back on the bed so that she was staring up at him as he lifted her leg, setting one tiny foot on his shoulder. Her reached down to just above her knee and untied the pink garter very slowly, laying it gently on the bedclothes.

"I am keeping this," he said, "as a prize of war."

"You can't," Mary Elizabeth said, trying to sound bossy but clearly having trouble, as they were both breathless with desire. "I need that garter."

"I'll buy you a dozen more," Harry said, beginning slowly to roll her stocking down her leg one tantalizing inch at a time. "But this one is mine."

He kissed her instep then, tossing her stocking aside. She lay back, staring up at him in only her chemise. He leaned down and gripped it at the neck, where the little pink ribbon was woven through some eyelet lacing. "I'll buy you a dozen more of these as well," he said. He ripped her chemise down the middle, and pushed both halves back so that he might feast his eyes on her naked flesh.

Mary Elizabeth blinked at him, and he thought for a moment he had gone too far with his marauding ways. Then she said, "Get down here to me, Harry, or I shall surely die."

He smiled, pressing his naked body against hers in one long stroke, his manhood seeking her for all the strokes that were to come. "I cannot have you die. You are my wife, and I love you. I want you to live a long and healthy life in my bed."

Mary Elizabeth wriggled against him. She knew more than when he had first met her, but she had only made love once, and clearly she was not sure how to go about getting what she wanted. So she simply asked. "Harry, I need you. Now."

Henry Charles Percy, Duke of Northumberland, obliged.

Thirty-five

HARRY WAS ON TOP OF HER, HIS BODY HOT OVER HERS, his lips over hers in a maddening kiss. But still, she could not find what she sought. Until he lifted her hips and slid inside her, as he had the week before, on the night she had snuck into his room alone and changed both their lives.

She had snuck into his room again tonight, but found that here, nothing had changed. They were simply sealing a bargain between them, as if the marriage they both wanted was not happening on the morrow, but now.

"I love you, Harry," she said, her breath almost completely gone.

He stopped in midmotion, only to look down into her face and to kiss her again, this time more gently. "And I love you, Mary Elizabeth Waters. Now and for the rest of my life."

"And beyond," she said, as if reminding him.

"And beyond."

When Harry moved again, the lust still rose between them like a flash fire, but it seemed only to grow by what it fed on. Mary Elizabeth for once in her blessed life stopped being the one to act, and allowed herself to be acted upon, as Harry's body moved against her and inside her, lighting a fire that would never go out.

When the pleasure took her, it was like standing in the midst of a star or a sun that did not burn. It was not as overwhelming as the other pleasure he had given her had been, but it seemed to bring something out of her heart, some measure of love that she had not felt before, for anyone, not even for herself.

She found that she was crying when it was over, and Harry was laid out on top of her as still as one dead. He did not stay still long, but turned so that she was cradled in his arms, his arms warm around her, a haven within the cocoon of her family home, the haven that she knew now would eclipse every place of safety she had ever known. When she felt his cheek press against her shoulder, she found that he was weeping, too.

"The love is overwhelming," she said, clutching him harder.

"I would not change it, not for anything in this world," Harry said.

Mary Elizabeth turned to him and kissed him gently, so as not to bruise him. Over the last six months of her exile, Mary Elizabeth had come to know herself and her emotions a little better, but she was almost certain that when she had come into his life, Harry had walled himself off from his own heart as he had from everything else. A heart made the world a better place to live in, but also a more painful one. She was grateful that she would stand by his side and give him solace, both in joy and in sorrow, for the rest of their lives.

"You are mine, and I am yours, forever, Harry."

He smiled and kissed her. He did not speak until she finished her thought.

"God help you," she said.

And then the man of her life did not speak. He pulled her closer, and laughed.

❧

Harry fell asleep soon after he kissed her last, and so he didn't realize that midnight had passed, and now it was their wedding day. The sun had finished sinking behind the far mountains, and the last of the light had fled the night sky, leaving only the braziers and a few candles to light the room they lay in.

Mary blew the candles out when she was up for the necessary, then slipped back into bed with her husband, who was a warm furnace. Harry clutched her like a child's toy he had lost long ago and only now just found. She did not object, but lay happy in his arms until dawn began to creep in at the window, turning the indigo of the sky to pink.

It was then she kissed him and woke him.

"Harry, love." He snuffled against her, clutching her harder, his hair a halo of red-gold beauty around his head. She kissed his ear and he rolled over on top of her.

She found herself trapped in earnest then, with a large, aroused man pressed close. Mary Elizabeth found she did not object.

He woke completely and began to slide his hands along her naked body. He did not woo her as he had the night before, but played at the small button that was the fountain of so much bliss. He did not linger long, but slid inside her, moving without pause until she was gasping against him, holding on for dear life, Harry a rock in a stormy sea of desire. Mary Elizabeth had learned by now to simply follow him over the edge, and let the pleasure find her and carry her where it would.

Mary Elizabeth shuddered beneath him, the pleasure far keener than it had been the night before. He groaned as he fell against her, his own pleasure spent, and she pressed a kiss to his temple, the only part of him she could reach. She forgot how large a man her husband was until he lay on top of her.

"Harry," she whispered, trying not to break his spell. "You must scooch over, for I must be gone."

He did not answer her at all, and she wriggled a little beneath him. He had her trapped but good.

"I must be in my room before the sun begins to rise, Harry," she said, knowing even as she said so that she had missed that deadline.

He heard her then, and looked down at her, squinting at her with one eye. "Good morning, Wife."

"Good morning, Husband."

"I will see you at breakfast, then," he said. It was not a question.

Mary Elizabeth repressed a smile, for she could tell that his caveman instincts had come to the fore. Perhaps because it was early. Or perhaps because of their lovemaking. Nothing made him as interested in dominance as lovemaking. Thank God.

"I will see you there," she said.

She gathered her clothes and he watched her dress.

She blew him a kiss from the secret door that led back to the corridor downstairs, for she knew that if she got too close, he would only drag her beneath him again, and scandalize her relations. She did not mind, but the thought of her mother's displeasure made her get a move on.

"I love you, Harry Percy," she said from the door.

"I know," he answered. "And I love you. I'll see you at breakfast," he repeated. "No running off."

"Who? Me? Run off?"

Mary Elizabeth winked at him and listened to the bedclothes rustle as he lunged for her, but she slipped away down the dark, hidden stairs, and he did not follow.

Mary Elizabeth washed herself and combed out her curls in her own room, humming to herself. She wandered downstairs feeling as fit as if she had slept the night through like a babe in arms, but her stomach rumbled more than usual, and she found that lack of sleep and joy and love combined made for a hearty appetite. When she arrived in her mother's breakfast room, which looked just like the duchess's breakfast room at Claremont, there was a great deal of hot bacon on offer. And finally, some decent porridge.

Mary Elizabeth had seated herself at table with a heaping of both, and two bannocks besides, when the duchess came downstairs and sat beside her.

"Slept well, did you?" the duchess asked, looking at her from beneath slanted eyes.

"I did, Your Worship. I thank you."

"We may dispense with the *worships* between us,

Mary. You will be my social equal as soon as the priest says his words over you."

Father Murphy, the man himself, had arrived early and was seated alone at the end of the great table, eating kippers and scones with one hand while reading his Bible with the other. After nodding to the women, he pretended that they were not there.

"If I might make one other suggestion before the rest of your family comes down?"

"Yes, Your Worship? I mean, Duchess?"

The old lady gleamed with mirth and more than a little joy as she drew one of Mary's curls down and patted it over her neck, where her throat met her ear. "It might do to invest in a decent looking glass while you are at Glenderrin. We have plenty of them at Claremont, as you know, so you need not fear anything there."

"I don't fear anything here," Mary Elizabeth said, eating another slice of bacon.

"You might," the duchess mused, "if your eldest brother saw that love bite."

Mary Elizabeth touched her skin beneath the concealing curl, and found the bite she spoke of, and almost choked on a bit of bannock.

"We'll cover it with lace for the wedding," the duchess said, blithely sipping her tea. "After that, no one will give a fig."

"For we'll be married, right and proper," Mary said.

"No. Because everyone will be too busy dancing and drinking and eating to care."

Mary Elizabeth smiled. Clearly, the duchess had met her share of Highlanders before.

The wedding was as early as Harry could make it, for the kitchen was filled with food and baked goods for the Gathering the next week, and Cook McCrery simply kept on cooking. Mary Elizabeth thanked her, and gave her a bit of extra gold for helping her and taking on so much extra work.

Mary was content to marry at home, where no fancy licenses and no Church of England vicar were required. She would be able to stand with her man before witnesses and God, and be married in the eyes of the law. More than one thing was simple in the Highlands.

They married in the castle chapel at high noon, with the sun blazing down overhead, coming in the chapel's high windows. Mary Elizabeth wore the gown that her mother chose with Lady Prudence's and Catherine's help, as she did not care what she wore, and Harry loved her in anything.

Her gown was blue, then, to match Harry's eyes and to set off the bouquet of heather and irises her mother had bound with a ribbon. All of her brothers stood up with Harry, as did his friend Clive who had managed to make his way there from Claremont on his own, chasing Harry off into the wilds of Scotland. Clive brought his bride, Clarice, with him, who was also Harry's cousin, in order to get Harry's blessing on their hasty marriage after the fact. Mary Elizabeth thought perhaps they should have asked the duchess for hers, but as she was not Harry's wife yet, she said nothing, but welcomed them.

For her own ceremony, Ian and Davy watched her come down the church aisle with Da in tow, and Alex and Robbie watched their wives, who had stood up as witnesses for her. It amused Mary Elizabeth for the briefest moment that, among the three of them, she was the only one of her friends to have a decent wedding.

She loved having Catherine and Lady Prudence stand with her, though both women were fairly useless with emotion. Catherine wept quietly and prettily into her embroidered handkerchief, while Lady Pru tried to hold her tears back with a smile.

As they were not among the English here, Mary Elizabeth could stand up with whom she pleased and not worry about having children underfoot on the occasion. Only Connie stood with her as well, to cast fertility in the form of heather and thyme on the stone steps of the church and up the aisle. Mary Elizabeth was eager for children, though perhaps not for a year or two. Of course, such things, as all things, were in the hands of God.

Her mother watched her as well and waved to her a little from her place at the front. Mary stopped her da before they reached Harry, and gave her mother a kiss.

"God bless you, Ma, for helping me find him."

Her mother did not speak, but cried. Mary pressed her hand and walked on to meet her future.

Harry was resplendent in blue superfine and dark breeches. His riding boots gleamed, newly polished, in the light of the high windows, and his red-gold hair, no longer looking like a hedgehog, was combed neatly, waiting for her fingers to muss it.

"I love you, Harry," she said before the priest could speak, before there was time for anything else.

"And I love you," Harry answered.

All that followed, as solemn and holy as it was, seemed small compared to the look of love in Harry's eyes. They spoke their vows, and accepted the blessing of the priest and the joyful wishes of the people they loved. But from the moment she walked into the church and met his eyes, she knew that they were married already.

How to Tame a Willful Wife

One

Montague Estates, Yorkshire
September 1816

EVERYTHING DEPENDED ON THIS ONE SHOT.

Caroline Montague pulled back on her bow, the bite of the string sharp against her fingers. She closed one eye, sighted down the slender shaft of myrtle, and let her arrow fly.

There was a moment of stunned silence, followed by polite applause led by the man beside her. She had scored a perfect hit in the center of the target, besting every man present. Her parents would be furious.

"A lucky shot, though impressive, Miss Montague," remarked Victor Winthrop, Viscount Carlyle. Since she was not an official competitor, he had still won the day, but Caroline was pleased to wipe the smug look off his face.

"Luck had nothing to do with it, my lord." She

curtsied to the company gathered on her father's lawn and tried to smile demurely—a feat more challenging than any archery contest.

These men were here with one purpose: to win her hand in marriage. She was on sale to the highest bidder to cover her father's mounting debts. But damn them all if they thought she would be an easy prize.

Caroline handed her bow to a nearby footman and took up the trophy Carlyle had won, a golden bowl inscribed with the image of Venus rising from the waves, an object of art her father had liberated during the Italian campaign against Napoleon.

"Forgive my impudence, gentlemen. I can never resist a target when it presents itself." The men around her chuckled.

"To the man of the hour, Lord Carlyle. May his arrow always fly swift and far, and may his aim improve," Caroline said.

She grinned, meeting the earl's blue eyes as she handed him the golden bowl. His gaze shifted from the curve of her breasts to her face, and he gave her a rueful smile. All the men had spent that morning eyeing her curves. Carlyle was the first man to stare so openly, and to laugh at himself afterward. She laughed with him, not knowing that the eyes of her husband-to-be lingered on her even then, and on the man who stood beside her.

❧

Anthony Carrington, the Earl of Ravensbrook, his face as forbidding as stone, stared at the man who would become his father-in-law. Only his great respect for Baron Montague on the field of battle kept him in the room at all. "I have never seen such blatant disregard for a woman's place in the world. To take up arms among men, to best a suitor with a bow, even a man like Carlyle, is unseemly."

Even his own mistress, Angelique, an experienced woman of the world, would never be so brazen.

"Ravensbrook, consider," Lord Montague said. "My daughter is very young."

"All the more reason she should smile and obey, not humiliate the men around her."

Lord Montague sighed. "I am the first to admit she is spoiled. And headstrong. After my last son died, she has been the light of my life."

Anthony heard the sorrow in his old friend's voice and left the rest of his protest unspoken. He fingered the marriage contract that lay on the mahogany table in front of him. He had ridden for four days straight with a special license from London, so the banns would not have to be read. He could marry Caroline within the week and return to Shropshire to beget an heir, and his old friend's debts would be paid with honor. Every detail of his marriage to Montague's daughter was in order. Everything but the girl.

"Her mother warned me of this, time and time again, but I did not listen," Montague said. "I have been so long on the Continent that Caroline has grown up beyond my reach, without a father's hand to guide her. You must teach her, my lord. I have seen you take a battlefield in less than an hour. Surely you can tame one woman in less than a fortnight."

Anthony did not soften. His sister had paid the price of a family's indulgence and would continue to pay it for the rest of her life.

"She must be pure," Anthony said. "I cannot present a woman to society as my wife without a guarantee of virtue, both in the past and in the future."

Frederick Montague rose slowly to his feet. "I have been your friend as well as your commander. I love you, Anthony, as if you were my own son. But if such words pass your lips again, I will not be able to answer for myself."

Anthony swallowed his ire and tried not to dwell on the mistakes his sister, Anne, had made. Frederick's daughter had to be more sensible than his sister had been. He was allowing his fears and his pain from the past to color his view of the present. And now, in his fear, he had begun to insult his host and his friend. Frederick needed a way out of the mire of his finances. He needed to see his daughter married and settled before the year was out. Anthony would do a great deal more than marry a beautiful, penniless girl to help the man who had twice saved his life.

"Forgive me, Frederick, if I spoke harshly. But she has too much freedom, and you have been away for so many years. How can you be sure?"

"She would never betray me by tossing aside her virtue under a country haystack. Caroline has known her duty all of her life. She has always known that her marriage would be arranged as soon as I came home from the war. The war is over, and I am here. It is time."

Anthony bowed once. His friend was an honorable

man, but like all honorable men, he could not conceive of dishonor in those he loved. If Anne could fall victim to a seducer's lures, then any woman could.

"Of course, any daughter of yours would be virtuous, Frederick. I never should have said otherwise. But I would speak with her alone."

Montague met Anthony's eyes, and for a moment, it was as if the baron could read his thoughts. Anthony wondered if even the protection of the Prince Regent had not been enough to squelch all rumors. Perhaps his sister's seduction was common knowledge, in spite of all that had been sacrificed to conceal it. Anthony stared into the face of his friend but could see no evidence of pity or contempt. Frederick knew nothing of Anne, then. Anthony wished he could be certain of it.

"You may speak with Caroline," Frederick said. "If you find that she is not virtuous, you may cast the marriage contract into the fire."

Caroline strode into her sitting room, slamming the door behind her. The sound gave her a small measure of satisfaction. The long evening, with its endless dinner and its games of charades felt interminable. Her suitors had not come alone but had brought their sisters and mothers with them. All London women wanted to talk about was fashion and one another. She hoped her father chose a match for her soon so she could get a moment's peace.

After years of living in a society of fewer than twenty families, the influx of London nobility into her world was more exhausting than she would have believed possible. Southerners, with their superior ways and nasal accents, grated on her nerves. How could they talk so much without really saying anything? And yet she was honor bound to marry one of them. Why her father could not find her a decent man from Yorkshire, she could not imagine.

She stopped fuming then, for in the shadows of her bedroom, she found a man sitting in her favorite armchair.

"Good evening, Caroline."

She opened her mouth to scream, but reminded herself she was not a fool, nor was she a swooning female like those in the novels she read. She closed her mouth again, the voice of her mother rising from her memory, telling her that open mouths catch only flies.

"Who are you?" she asked, working to keep her voice even and calm.

"A friend of your father's."

"I've never met you before. If you were Papa's friend, he would have presented you along with the rest of my suitors."

The man laughed, his chestnut eyes running over her body. His black hair brushed his collar and was tossed back from his face to reveal a strong jaw. Dressed in a linen shirt and dark trousers, he had cast off his coat, and it lay beside him on the arm of the chair. His green-and-gold waistcoat gleamed in the candlelight, his cravat loosely tied.

His large body was too big for her delicate Louis XVI furniture, but he sat with one ankle casually crossed over the other knee, as comfortable as he might have been in his own drawing room.

"I am your friend, too, Caroline."

"You are no friend of mine."

He was the most beautiful man she had ever seen. She thought it foolish to call a man beautiful, but she could not deny it. And clearly, he agreed with her.

In spite of his arrogance, this man was worth ten of every fool she had spoken to that day. There was no doubt in her mind that if he had entered the archery contest that morning, she would not have beaten him.

There was a latent power in his gaze, in the stillness of his posture that made her think of a lion set to devour her. Instead of frightening her, the thought gave her a moment's pleasure. She had never before met a man who seemed to be as strong-willed as she was. She wondered for the first time in her life if this dark-eyed man might be her equal.

She dismissed that thought as folly. No matter how beautiful, whether he was her equal or not, a man alone in her room could be there for no good reason. The heat in his eyes warmed her skin, but she forced herself to ignore that, too. She would be ruined if anyone even suspected she had spoken with a man alone in her room. He might be there to kidnap her for the ransom her father would pay... or worse.

As if to echo her thoughts, the stranger spoke. His words were like cold water on her skin, waking her from the madness of her attraction for him.

"I've come to claim you, Caroline."

She did not look at him again but reached into her reticule. No man would claim her. She would be damned if her father's work, and her own, would come to nothing. Not this man, or any other, would touch her that night.

She took a deep, calming breath. Her father's men had trained her for just such a moment, when she would be alone and threatened. Now that the moment had come, she was ready.

"You'll 'claim' me only when you pull the last weapon from my cold, dead hand."

She drew her knife from her reticule and threw it at him.

Her aim was ill-timed, for the man moved with sudden grace and speed, slipping like an eel out of the way of her missile. Her dagger was sharp, and its tip embedded deep in the cushion of her favorite chair. Caroline swore and turned to flee.

She did not get far, for he caught her arm before she reached the door. She moved to strike him, but he dodged her blow with ease. He caught her wrist in one hand, wrapping his other arm around her waist. "Settle, Caroline, settle. I mean you no harm."

"Then let me go."

"I will release you if you promise to stay and speak with me."

His scent surrounded her, spicy and sweet together. She took in the smell of leather, the scent that made her think of freedom, and of her stallion, Hercules. The stranger held her but not too close, his hands gentle now that she had stopped trying to kill him.

"I have nothing to say to you," she said.

"I have something to say to you. Give me just five minutes, and then I will go."

She nodded once. He released her, stepping away carefully as if she were a wild mare he hoped to tame. She stood suspended in the center of his gaze, his unswerving regard surrounding her like a soft trap. There was something in the way he moved, in the heat of his hand on her arm that was distracting.

She forced herself to forget his touch and the sweet scent of him. She kept a careful distance between them, moving with unstudied grace to light the lamp on the table by the door. As her match caught, the lamp cast a buttery light, bringing the room out of shadow. She infused her voice with a confidence she did not feel.

"Speak your piece, then go."

"You are used to giving orders, it seems, Miss Montague. You will find I am not accustomed to taking them."

She drew her breath up from the depths of her stomach and used all the power her father had taught her, giving added strength to her voice. This man claimed he wanted to talk, though he did nothing but plague her. Caroline stared him down, as she had been taught to stare down unruly servants until they bent to her will.

"Give me your name or get out."

The man laughed. He stepped back toward her favorite chair, drawing her blade from the cushion, leaving a few downy feathers to trail the air in its wake. Those bits of down settled on the carpet, and Caroline cursed again. Her mother was always telling her not to throw daggers in the house, that they ruined the furniture.

"My name is for my friends," he said.

His fingers caressed the edge of the blade as he contemplated her, a half smile on his face. Her eyes narrowed. She could not begin to guess why he was so familiar with her. She had met many men that day, but he was not one of them. She would have remembered him.

She kept her voice even, in spite of her rising temper, in spite of her nerves. She did not move to the bellpull to ring for assistance. She could not allow word of his presence in her room to get out to the guests at large. Her reputation would be lost, along with her father's plans to pay his debts from the profit of her marriage.

"My friendship must be earned," she said.

"And yet, I seem to have your enmity, though I have not earned it."

"You're here, aren't you? After I have asked you repeatedly to go? I say again, leave this room, or next time my blade will not miss you."

Caroline kept her eyes on the man who stood holding the weapon he had claimed. His dark gaze drifted from her face to her breasts nestled against the soft silk of her gown. Her breath quickened. She had been ogled a great deal in the past twenty-four hours, but her body responded as if it knew him already.

"I would not attack again, if I were you," he said. His eyes moved over her breasts where they swelled above the high waist of her gown, and over her hips where they curved beneath her skirts, returning once more to her face. "Whatever you choose to do, I am going nowhere yet."

There was a promise in the way he looked at her. Though he was half a room away, she fancied she could feel the heat rising off his body through the thin silk of her gown. Unable to look away from him, like a snake with its charmer, Caroline wondered what it would cost her to stand in that man's heat even for a moment.

"If you will not go, then I will."

"And leave me in possession of the field? I am surprised to find you such a coward."

The fury in her belly rose like a flash fire, lodging itself in her throat so she choked on it. Her anxiety was burned away as she sputtered with ire.

"I would never be afraid of the likes of you."

"No?" He raised her knife to the light before laying it down gently on the mahogany table. "You seemed quite frightened when you first saw me, frightened enough to cast this dagger." He sat in her favorite chair once more and smiled at her. "It seems you missed. Perhaps you need more practice."

"It is dark in here," she said, the excuse paltry in her own ears.

He laughed. "Myself, I prefer a more biddable woman who does not carry knives."

"Then by all means, you have my permission to go to her."

"You will find, Miss Montague, that I do not need your permission for anything."

He did not move to leave but stared at her, taking in the contours of her face as if he were trying to read her soul. She forced her body to relax as she always did before a fight. She thought of the second knife hidden beneath the mahogany table beside him. If she could not get her dagger back, she could always take up the second knife and kill him with it.

The thought was not as comforting as it would have been five minutes before. He watched her, still smiling, as if he knew all her secrets, as if he wished to teach her one or two more.

She shook off the stupor she had fallen into. She dismissed the thought of the hidden knife and turned her mind to escape. Whether or not she lost her reputation, whether or not he thought her a coward, she had to get out of that room.

The man rose to his feet and closed the distance between them so swiftly she did not see him move. She felt only the warm pressure of his hand as he drew her against him. His body was hot on hers where his chest pressed into the softness of her breasts. He breathed in her scent, as if she were a loaf of newly baked bread or some morsel he meant to devour in one bite. He did not keep her standing but sank down once more in her favorite chair, bringing her onto his lap in one smooth motion.

After a day of men ogling her, all eager to paw her if they could, Caroline had had enough. She struggled to free herself from his grip and managed to get at the knife on the table. Her father's training came back to her without thought, without fear. She drew the blade up to his throat but found she could not drive it home. "I could run you through right now, sir. But first, tell me who you are."

"I am impressed, Caroline. You have defended your honor well. But you do not need to defend yourself against me."

"Who are you?" she asked.

"I am Anthony Carrington, the Earl of Ravensbrook. The man you are going marry," he said.

Caroline barely registered the stranger pushing her arm away from his throat as he claimed her dagger. She blinked at the shock of the news that she was betrothed to this man, and then wondered if he might be lying.

Caroline found herself distracted once more by his touch. He kept one of her arms pinned between his weight and the arm of the chair. He held her other wrist so she could not move against him again. His free arm wrapped around her waist, drawing her close, keeping her safe from falling. They sat together, her skirts foaming around them as she perched on his lap. His thighs were hard beneath her, unyielding. His chest was warm against her breasts.

Their breaths mingled as they looked at each other, his dark eyes holding her prisoner just as his hands did. Caroline forgot about decorum, reveling in the scent of him and in the new-discovered flame he stoked deep in her belly, one that burned even as she touched him. She was still pressed against him, her breath coming short, her mind lost to all but what she felt, when his hand touched her breast.

She leaped like a scalded cat, moving so quickly he lost his grip on her. Freed from his embrace, Caroline was on her feet in an instant. She raised her hand to him, intent on causing him what harm she could.

The man stood and caught her wrist before she struck his face. Her aim was true, and he had to move fast to stop her. They were both breathing hard, as if they had been engaged in mortal combat. They faced each other like enemies, measuring each other with their eyes.

"Never touch me again. Get out of my room," she said. "Get out of my father's house."

His chestnut eyes lost their intensity. The fire in them was banked slowly as he breathed. She watched the effort he made and what it cost him to let her go. She snatched her hand away, rubbing her wrist where his grip had bruised her.

"I had to know if you'd ever been touched before, Caroline."

"I was not, until you sullied me. Now get out."

He straightened, donning his coat with the air of a man pleased with himself and with what he had discovered in her room. Caroline felt the overwhelming need to curse him, but she swallowed the words. She would not give him the satisfaction.

"Good evening, Miss Montague. Until tomorrow."

"If I never see you again, it will be too soon."

Anthony smiled, his dark eyes gleaming as he walked away. "I think you'll change your mind."

"You are wrong, my lord."

"I am never wrong."

Her fingers closed on the dagger he had left on her mahogany table. She threw the knife without thinking, embedding it in the frame of the servants' door, just inches from his head. She heard his mocking laughter as he closed the door behind him.

Two

CAROLINE STOOD STARING AT THE CLOSED DOOR. SHE strode across the room and drew her dagger from the door frame. A flake of white paint fell from the wound in the wood, and she cursed under her breath.

Marriage to a stranger was bad enough. Marriage to Lord Ravensbrook would be a nightmare.

Her interminable day had gotten even longer. She sank onto her favorite chair, still warm from Anthony Carrington's body. She could not stand to be reminded of his touch. She stood up and tossed the cushions on the floor. Another feather escaped from the tear her dagger had made.

She sighed, placing the knife on the table beside her. Her mother was going to kill her.

She stared with longing at her bed covered with dark green velvet brought from France before the Terror. The softness of that haven beckoned her. She wanted to bury her head under those pillows and forget the man she had just had the misfortune to meet.

Lady Montague walked into the sitting room beyond, the door thrown open before her as if by a great wind. Caroline plastered on a smile and went to meet her. Lady Montague's dark blond hair was streaked with silver, tucked away beneath a cap of lace.

Caroline forced herself to meet her mother's eyes. She knew the baroness saw everything, even things Caroline so often wanted to hide. She could not bear the thought that her mother would look at her and somehow know Lord Ravensbrook had just been there. As long as no one knew of his visit, she could pretend she had never met the insufferable man. Desperate to distract her mother, Caroline curtsied.

No doubt it was the spectacle of her daughter showing obedience that made Lady Montague stop in her tracks, the sound of her lightly tapping feet suddenly silenced on the hard mahogany floor. Caroline realized then she had gone too far with her curtsy, but she braved it out, summoning a sweet smile.

"I have news, Caroline. News that would not wait."

"Will you sit, *Maman*? Shall I call for tea?"

"No, Daughter, I have just drunk pots of tea with the ladies downstairs. Southerners do not know when to go to bed. I am exhausted from all this to-do."

"I am sorry, *Maman*. It is all because of me."

"No, *ma petite*, it is all because you must marry. And marry you will. Your father has made his decision."

She wanted to ask her mother if her betrothed was a tall, beautiful man with black hair, chestnut eyes, and insufferable arrogance but for once in her life, she held her tongue.

Lady Montague was French by birth, and very tiny,

the top of her head coming only to Caroline's sternum. She put her hands on her daughter's arms, drawing her down to kiss her cheek.

"In two days you will have the honor of becoming the wife of Anthony Carrington, the Earl of Ravensbrook.

Two days. The words rang like a death knell over her head. It was bad enough that she would have to spend the rest of her life with that arrogant man. But the thought that her new life would commence in two days was absurd. She would speak with her father. Surely they could extend what was left of her freedom into weeks, not days.

Her mother continued, never acknowledging that her daughter could barely stand upright. "You will live in his country house in Shropshire most of the year. You will be an obedient wife to him, and you will bear him fine sons."

The word *obedient* filled her ears like poison. "But I don't even know him."

"He is rich and titled. You will be a countess. That is what you know of him, and all you need to know."

Caroline swallowed hard. She knew her duty, though it chafed her like an ill-fitting harness on her best horse.

"We could not afford to give you a Season in London," her mother reminded her. "This marriage is the best path for you, for all of us. Your father has chosen the best man he knows."

Lady Montague did not speak of her husband's mounting debts. Protecting and feeding the veterans of his regiment, giving even the wounded men a place in the world, was the honorable thing to do. And as her mother was fond of saying: honor cost money. Caroline would marry an earl, and the earl would pay her father's debts.

Her parents had not bred a coward. It was one thing to learn knife play from trusted men who had served under her father in war, or to ride to hunt on an unruly stallion. Now it was time for her to show true courage. Women were married off to strangers to make advantageous matches for their families every day. Caroline knew this truth. She had been raised on it. She would prove her courage now, by facing her future unafraid. She straightened her back and raised her gaze from the floor.

"I will do my duty, *Maman*."

Lady Montague gave a Gallic shrug, as if the matter had never been open for discussion, but her eyes softened. "Of course you will. When all is said and done, you are your father's daughter."

Caroline was startled when her mother raised herself on the tips of her toes and kissed her lips in blessing. As she took in the scent of her mother's light perfume, she realized she would miss her deeply when she was gone to live in her husband's house.

Lady Montague's voice did not waver. The warmth in her eyes was not betrayed in her tone as she gave her daughter the last instructions of the day. "His lordship will send a dressmaker to attend you tomorrow, to fit you for the wedding gown of his family."

Caroline held her tongue. She could not believe her fiancé had already chosen her wedding dress. It boded ill for their future that his need for control extended to her wardrobe. She did not voice these concerns to her mother, who she knew did not want to hear them. "I will be ready."

Lady Montague's pride shone in her eyes, along with moisture that might have been tears. "Daughter, I have no doubt of that."

Her mother closed and locked the outer door to her rooms behind her. By now, the men downstairs would have heard of her father's choice. No doubt, her husband-to-be sat among them. Numb from the sudden onslaught of her future, she turned back to her bedroom, reaching for the bell to ring for Tabby, her lady's maid.

Caroline would marry Lord Ravensbrook, the most insufferable man she had ever met. What kind of future was that?